MW00834319

THE GIRL FROM PARADISE HILL

A MCCLINTOCK-CARTER CRIME THRILLER

SUSAN LUND

Copyright © 2018 by Susan Lund

All rights reserved.

No part of this book may be reproduced in any form or by any electronic or
mechanical means, including information storage and retrieval systems,
without written permission from the author, except for the use of brief
quotations in a book review. This is a work of fiction. Any resemblance to
persons living or dead is entirely coincidental.

❀ Created with Vellum

PREFACE

"Three may keep a secret if two of them are dead."

Benjamin Franklin

BEFORE

Stirring the pot...

The posters flapped in the cold winds of October, the ink faded, the photo blurred. People in town still talked about her, *Melissa*, the pretty little girl from Paradise Hill, but their voices were hushed, their expressions resigned.

That was going to change, if he had his way and he most often did.

He drove to the cabin along the narrow dirt road bordering the lake, past the cemetery at the edge of town. A cathedral of tall pines sheltered the historic graveyard, with its row upon row of headstones and crosses, some of them so old they were covered in moss. The girl should have been laid to rest there but the body wasn't buried with the other dead of Paradise Hill.

It was hidden. Maybe too well.

The girl with the sad brown eyes and long wavy hair had been missing five months. The case was still warm enough to have a detective assigned but with no leads, no suspects and no crime scene, it was rapidly growing cold.

Stupid pigs.

They thought they were so smart. The killer was right under their nose. Hell, some of them even drank with him on the weekends, but they were just stupid local cops without enough sense to call in the feds. People didn't go missing in Paradise Hill. Or at least, they went missing so rarely that people didn't make the right connections. The last one had been a decade earlier. Before that, it had been eight years. The gaps were too large for a serial killer, or so they thought. Besides, children went missing every year for legitimate reasons. They left abusive homes. They ran away to the other custodial parent.

Only the rarest of rare cases were murders.

Without a body, a crime scene or suspects, the cases were as cold as the grave.

He needed a few items for his mission that night, but thankfully, a well-stocked storage shed at a cabin north of the lake contained everything he required. He'd have no problem carrying out his plan. No one took note of what he did and that was just the way he wanted to keep it.

Being unimportant and forgettable was key in his line of work.

Why stir the pot? Why call attention to that which was hidden?

Frankly, he was bored. There were no more news stories about the latest missing girl to keep his interest. He needed a diversion to keep him from going completely insane. He could take another girl, relieve the need that felt like an itch all over his body, or he could nudge the police along the right path in Melissa's case and enjoy the resulting spectacle.

He'd dropped little clues around town, but so far nothing had been found so he'd obviously hidden them too well. When the original case was opened, no one had even thought to ask him about his whereabouts because he wasn't one of the usual suspects.

It helped to have family in high places…

Melissa had been a shock to the town, which had been in a continuing state of decline for the past decade. Usually, his targets were in different towns and were forgotten girls no one cared about except maybe a mother or sister. Girls a little older, but not old enough to be considered consenting. Melissa was just ten and her disappearance was an affront to the community. They cared about girls her age but for some reason forgot about them when they went through puberty.

Like they were guilty of being desirable.

A ten-year-old girl from a poor family got everyone's sympathy. Everyone in the town was momentarily united, joining search parties and going door to door with pictures of her, stapling posters to telephone poles and fences, sticking posters up in storefronts.

Have you seen Melissa? Please call…

As soon as a girl turned thirteen, though, they'd forget about her, which made his job a lot easier over the years.

What was she doing out so late at night? She used drugs? What was wrong with her family that they let her go wild like that?

He'd heard the gossip whenever one of the girls who walked the dark streets behind the strip malls at the outskirts of Seattle went missing.

Working girls, tsk tsk tsk. What can they expect in this world? Getting in cars with strange men…

They practically justified what he'd done by blaming the victim. They didn't look quite as hard for Jennifer or Carly as they did for little Melissa. Innocent little Melissa with the wide brown eyes.

Whatever. They were all hypocrites anyway. Men who went to church every Sunday and then surfed barely legal and not-even-legal porn late at night while their wives were sleeping, fantasizing about what they'd like to do if there was no God and if they could get away with it.

Well, there was no God and he was living proof. He'd got away with it.

For twenty years and counting.

The cabin at the base of the mountain had been closed because it needed a new roof. In May, it came in handy when he needed a place to hide his take. No one would be renting this cabin anytime soon — not until the economy turned around and Old Man Gilroy could justify renovating the roof and no one knew when that would be.

Back in May, he'd brought a shovel and sacks of cement and an old plastic barrel. Then he buried her underneath the floorboards.

That was it.

Five months had passed and he'd waited long enough for some action. He didn't think the cops had done nearly a good enough job trying to find the girl. He'd covered his tracks so well that they'd found no evidence. None.

She just went missing out of the blue. Walked off into the dark night alone and hadn't been seen since.

Just like Lisa and Zoe and the others.

A fire should get things moving again.

Everything he needed was inside the locked shed behind the rental office, including a stock of lighter fluid for the barbecues at each of the cabins. He used his master keys to get inside. He'd cleaned the cabins for his uncle when he was a teen and had access to them all, which turned out to be a blessing. Back in the day, he reported that his keys were missing but he'd secretly kept them so that he could gain entry whenever he liked. Luckily, his uncle was lax enough about security that he didn't care, and since he had a second set of duplicates, he just went ahead without getting the locks changed.

Then his uncle sold the cabins to Old Man Gilroy who never bothered to change the locks.

It was too expensive a venture, Gilroy said, given the state of the economy at the time. It would cost hundreds of dollars to change all the locks on the dozen cabins he had around the lake, not including labor. So, Gilroy did nothing, just took over and left things as they were.

All the better for him because it meant he kept his free reign over the cabins. He'd used that access to hunt. He didn't take anyone from the cabins – but he still hunted. That was almost as much fun as the actual kill.

Almost.

But every now and then, hunting no longer cut it for him, and he had to cull the herd.

He sprayed the floor and furniture with lighter fluid, not caring whether the firefighters knew right away that it was deliberately set. He wanted them to think it was arson.

He *wanted* them to find her.

He could already imagine the consternation and horror people of the small town would feel when they realized what they'd found.

The girl from Paradise Hill.

Missing for five months, poor little Melissa. Another one of their latchkey kids, out alone too late at night given her age. Why, she was practically asking to be picked off.

It sent shivers down his spine to imagine the news coverage, to listen to the gossip in the coffee shops and at work.

People wouldn't be able to get enough of it.

He'd sit there and nod, listen to them bleat on and on about how horrible it was, poor child. He'd offer a word or two of commiseration. Make a sad face.

Terrible. Just terrible.

What's this world coming to?

All the while delighting in secret about the uproar he'd caused.

He lit a match and threw it on the floor. The lighter fluid erupted in a ball of flame when the match hit the liquid with an audible and very satisfying *fooom!* He watched for a moment until the heat of the fire pushed him back a step and he had to shield his eyes from the intense brightness. The flames licked the walls and furniture until they ignited, adding to the conflagration. He stepped farther back, mesmerized by the blaze, the crack and *whoosh* as one window shattered from the heat.

The heat had reached an intolerable level. He had to get out, and fast.

For a brief moment, a small part of him considered letting the flames encircle him, consume him, burn him up until he was no more. Part of him would welcome an end to things, if he were honest, for he had not lived a happy life, despite the superficial perfection of it. He'd suffered almost every waking moment and, truth be told, he'd be relieved when it was finally over, when they drove up to his building and knocked on his door, holding out their badges and telling him they had a warrant to search his apartment. Then, once they'd found enough evidence, they would tell him he was under arrest for the murder of so many of their precious little girls.

He'd laugh in their faces for taking so damn long.

He had imagined it many nights when sleep would not come, lying in bed and playing the final act over in his mind. He didn't feel guilty. Not at all. He felt *justified*. His kills were all in service of bigger truths – the truth that he could kill whomever he wanted and get away with it. The truth that their ability to control him was a fantasy. The truth that none of them were safe.

No, his momentary fantasy about immolation was because he felt tired, not guilty. It took a lot of brainpower to plan, execute, and cover up a kill, and then maintain his cover as the perfect ex-husband, father and adopted son. It took a lot of mental energy to keep up the façade of going to work every day and fitting in with the rest of them. It took stamina to laugh at their jokes and keep up the camouflage. In time, he would be ready for the day of revelation, almost welcoming it, but not yet.

Not yet.

He had things to do and humans to kill. There was good hunting left and he always loved the hunt.

Until there wasn't and until he stopped loving it, he'd keep hunting.

He drove off, taking a circuitous route back to Paradise Hill. If anyone saw him coming into town, it would be from the opposite direction. By the time he heard the first sirens, fifteen minutes had passed. He checked his watch. It had taken them that long to notice the fire and send the trucks. The cabin would have been completely engulfed and burnt to the ground by then.

There was barely any traffic at that time of night and so he didn't pass a single car on his way back to the house. Anyone who was out at that time was on their way to or from the bar, or to the fire to gawk at the aftermath.

He parked his car around back, quietly closed the door and entered the building, making as little noise as possible so no one would note the time of his arrival. He managed to make it back without running into anyone, and sat down with a beer from his fridge. He flicked on his flat screen television, scanning the channels looking for something to watch, but there was nothing worth it.

He itched to go and watch the fire, to see what was happening. He could take his mountain bike and ride the back roads in total darkness to check things out. He was an avid cyclist and often took his bike out late at night when he couldn't sleep. No one would question if they saw him out so late. They knew he would be training for a race and would understand.

He dressed in his night gear, put on a pair of night-vision goggles from his collection and drove off with his GoPro camera so he could record what he saw for posterity. A moth to the flame, he thought to himself as he debated at the last minute whether to go. Would this be the one decision that would put an end to his career as a wolf in sheep's clothing? He knew he shouldn't return to the scene of the crime because that's what stupid serial killers did and it was often how they got caught. Police videotaped crime scenes, funerals and any press conferences held to update the public about the case's progress. He wasn't stupid – twenty years had proven that.

But no, he couldn't help it. He loved to see his handiwork, especially when it was surrounded by cops and firefighters.

He wasn't disappointed.

When he drew close to the cabin, he hid his bike in some underbrush and crept closer to the location. In total darkness, he blended in with the brush, and managed to get within a hundred feet of the cabin, off to the north of where the fire trucks were parked.

The cabin itself was a write-off. The roof had caved in and all that remained was the stone fireplace and some pipes sticking out of the ground. He'd done a good job with the fire, but whether it accomplished his real purpose he wasn't sure. Would they find the barrel and its contents?

He had been fastidious about everything – using gloves and wearing a knitted hat to keep his hair from falling and leaving behind trace evidence. He had a record – a petty crime – a youthful transgression that he served no time for, but still, his prints were in the system. He didn't want to leave any trace of his presence at the crime scene so he had to be extra careful.

Now, he could wait with excitement to see if they found anything that would tie the crime to him, but he doubted it. If they found the clues he'd left, those clues would tie the disappearances together. And implicate others.

They'd pulled a big blank on his kills all these years. There was no reason to think they'd be any better at it now. But it would be fun to watch them flounder around, looking for the killer.

Looking for *him*.

CHAPTER ONE

Four girls had gone missing from Paradise Hill over the past forty years. One girl had gone missing in the last five months and a half-dozen or more other girls were missing in the neighboring counties over the past two decades. Police had no idea who was responsible but one thing was clear: a serial child killer was loose in Washington State.

As the crime reporter for the *Seattle Sentinel*, Tess McClintock was on the case, compelled by a history with one of the missing girls and an undying need to see justice done. While most people heard about child abductions and felt bad for a while, Tess had been haunted for the past eighteen years. Not a day went by that she didn't think about Lisa Tate, one of her best friends in elementary school, who vanished after leaving their tent during a sleepover eighteen years earlier.

Ten years old and small for her age with long wavy brown hair and amber eyes, Lisa Tate walked away into the darkness and was never seen again. Tess's guilt over her role in Lisa's fate was a constant in her life from that day forward.

The town's missing girls hadn't brought Tess back to Paradise Hill. Her father died the previous day after a short and secret battle with pancreatic cancer. Now Tess was returning to bury him and sell the family house. Her parents divorced and Tess's mother was too sick to do the work herself. Tess's brother, Thad was away at work in the logging industry in Alaska, so it was up to Tess to take care of business.

Summer was over and the forests on either side of the highway were painted in vibrant shades of red, yellow, and orange. As beautiful as the scenery was, Tess hated autumn. Autumn meant that soon, the trees would lose their leaves.

It always reminded her of the year Lisa went missing. That year marked the dividing line in Tess's life – before and after Lisa's disappearance. The day before the abduction, Tess and her friends had been innocent school children, playing outside without a care in the world. Over the next few days, Tess would sit in the police station with her mother and answered questions about the night before, poring through books of suspects in case she recognized anyone who might have been hanging around the neighborhood. Two weeks later, Tess's parents had separated, and Tess moved with her mother and brother to Seattle.

Even now, Lisa's abduction and the resulting search and missing person case was what motivated Tess. She'd gone to school in Seattle to complete a bachelor's degree with a double major in criminology and journalism and had been working the crime beat for the *Seattle Sentinel* since graduation.

Tess drove along the secondary highway south and west of Seattle that led to Paradise Hill, through the pass between the hills and deeper into Washington State. The landscape was lush, filled with pine forests and dotted with small lakes.

For a kid, living in the mountains was fantastic. Before Lisa's disappearance, Tess had loved living in Paradise Hill so close to nature. Dad had taken her and Thad to his friend's cabin for vacations where they fished and hiked. The air outside the city was clear and crisp. Being so close to nature was the one thing she missed living in Seattle, surrounded by cement and glass. The scent of pine reminded Tess of a happier time when she was unaware of the evil around them all.

When she arrived on the outskirts of Paradise Hill, a sense of dread filled her. She'd have to go back to the old neighborhood – to her father's house, and the area where Lisa went missing. While Tess had many good memories of living there, the ones that dominated now were bad, especially given her most recent assignment conducting research for an investigative piece on missing and murdered women in Washington State for the *Sentinel*. Her memories of Paradise Hill now were of the days following Lisa's disappearance and the week they packed up and left for good, leaving her father behind.

A tumultuous year for an eleven-year-old on the brink of puberty.

One day, after the searches for Lisa had been called off, Tess's mother had packed up a few items of clothing and personal effects and left Tess's father. Mom had never explained why, but Tess knew it was because of Lisa. Her parents rarely talked about it, but Tess heard their whispers.

Her mom didn't feel safe after Lisa went missing. Whoever the killer was, he was too close to home. Despite the idyllic setting, Paradise Hill was not a safe place for children. Mom said living in Seattle would be safer than out in the boondocks, as she called Paradise Hill.

What Tess saw of the town while she drove through told

3

her not much had changed. The main street was still wide, with dozens of angle parking spaces in front of old storefronts. A few cars traveled along the streets, going slower than she was used to back in Seattle. No one was rushed in Paradise Hill, as if a kind of paralysis had set into the town. Even the smell was the same – pine.

She'd missed that after she moved away.

Neither Thad or Tess wanted to leave. It meant saying goodbye to their father and their schools. For Tess, it meant saying goodbye to Kirsten and to everything she'd known all her life. Tess cried when her mother took them away in their beat-up old station wagon, but there was nothing the two children could do. Thad was old enough to stay with their dad, but he didn't want to. Their dad was a long-distance trucker and was always away on the road.

So, the three of them left Paradise Hill for good, and went to live in a sublet in downtown Seattle until Tess's mother could find a better job and move to a nicer house. Once the divorce was settled, she promised they'd be able to move from the basement apartment and buy a house in Seattle.

The old house in Paradise Hill never sold and they'd stayed in that basement apartment for a decade.

Now, Tess was returning to bury her father and sell the house. Tess's mom would finally get the money she had expected to get when she'd left their dad. She didn't relish returning to Paradise Hill. She had grown distant from her father, and he'd never made the effort to connect. He'd become a stranger to Tess. All she'd had from him during that time were a few cards on her birthdays or Christmas cards with a few dollars tucked inside. Occasionally, he'd send her a trinket he'd picked up on his travels across the state to flea markets and garage sales.

He never remarried, living a bachelor's life in the house he never sold. Her mother told Tess that he once had dreams of being a writer and had tried his hand at writing novels, but that never amounted to anything. Instead, he dropped out of high school in his senior year and ended up driving a truck for a living.

A sad death for a man whose life seemed to end when Tess's mother left him and took their kids with her.

TESS DROVE along the familiar streets, past the playground where she and Kirsten and Lisa used to play after school and then she saw it – her old street. The last row of houses before the forest at the base of the mountain. She parked her rental car in the driveway behind her father's old Ford pickup and turned off the engine. Down the street a few houses, a police car was parked on the street beside Lisa's old house. The truck from a work crew trimming trees around the power lines was parked nearby. She recognized the woman talking to the police officer immediately, despite the years that had passed.

Mrs. Carter. Kirsten's mother.

Curious, Tess got out of the car and walked down the street to where they were gathered outside Lisa's old house. The scent of smoke was strong in the air and Tess wondered whether there had been a forest fire nearby.

Mrs. Carter had barely changed. Her hair, which had been jet black as a younger woman, was now salt-and-pepper grey, but everything else was the same. Her arms were folded, and when she turned to see Tess walking up the driveway, her mouth dropped open.

"My *God*," she said, coming over to cup Tess's face in her hands. "Tess. Tess McClintock. Look at you! How big you've grown. But that red hair and green eyes? I'd know you anywhere."

"Hi, Mrs. Carter," Tess replied and they embraced briefly.

Mrs. Carter made a face of sorrow and stood back, her head turned to one side. "I'm so sorry about your dad. What a shock, and such a terrible way to go."

"Thanks." Tess forced a smile. "None of us knew until yesterday."

"He was a hermit, that's for sure. Never went out. Never had visitors. Sad end for him. He never called to say he was sick?"

"No," Tess replied. "The hospice worker said he didn't want to trouble us." She glanced over to where the police sedan was parked. "What's up? Was there a fire? I can smell smoke in the air."

"No, that was last night. A cabin burnt down near the lake."

Tess nodded. "What happened here?"

Mrs. Carter made a face. "They found another dead cat behind the old Tate house and so Officer Blake is here to check it out."

Tess shivered at the thought.

"That's terrible. What kind of monster kills cats?"

Mrs. Carter frowned. "Sick ones, that's who. It's the third one this week. Some sick kids are torturing them, setting them on fire and then hanging them from tree branches. It's like what happened before. You know. When Lisa went missing. And little Melissa's still missing." She shook her head.

Tess nodded, thinking the same thing. That meant that four girls had gone missing from Paradise Hill over the past forty years. Tess had read up on all the missing children in Washington State for her article, and had taken an interest in this latest case because it was so much like Lisa's. A girl of ten walking off into the night, never to be seen again.

"It's terrible that there are no leads," Mrs. Carter asked. "What do you know about it? This is your area, right?"

"From what I read, they have no suspects. No crime scene. Just a missing girl."

They walked up to the police car where the maintenance workers and police officer were talking. A worker stood beside the police car dressed in white overalls and jacket, the logo of a local tree pruning service on his back: *Hammond and Son Services*. A middle-aged balding man dressed in white overalls joined them and slapped the younger man on the back. They looked over at Tess and Mrs. Carter as the two women approached.

"Do you know of any missing cats?" Officer Blake asked when Mrs. Carter arrived at his side.

"None around here that I know. Honestly, I don't know why people let their cats run wild," Mrs. Carter replied. "I called the Humane Society to come and take away the strays, but they don't seem to do that anymore."

The older worker standing beside the cop shrugged.

"Why would a kid want to hurt a cat? I don't understand the interest. I mean, if a kid wants to hunt, there's lots of game around here. Don't need to kill cats. Gotta be a really sick person to do that."

7

"You can't know what goes on in someone else's head," Officer Blake said.

"That's the truth," the man replied, shaking his head sadly. "Who knows what evil lurks, right?" He gave Tess a pointed look. "You Tess McClintock?" he asked, stepping closer, a long tree-pruning tool in his hand.

"I am."

"Sorry about your dad. I'm John Hammond," he said and extended his free hand. "I grew up with your father. Went to high school with him, played football with him. Known him all my life. He was a good friend."

"Hello," Tess said and shook his hand.

"This is my son, Garth."

Tess smiled at the younger man beside John Hammond, who was much thinner than his heavier-set father. Garth had a long face and a weak chin with a pronounced cleft. His dark hair fell over dark eyes.

She shook his hand awkwardly. "Thanks."

She remembered her father talking about John Hammond. The Hammond family practically owned the town. John Hammond Sr., the patriarch, started Hammond Cartage, a trucking firm that serviced the south-west part of the state and for whom Tess's father had worked for years. His middle son cornered the market on the building trade and real estate, such as it was in a town as small as Paradise Hill. One son served as mayor for two decades when he retired from business and turned it over to his eldest son. Joe Hammond, the third son, was Chief of Police. John Hammond, the youngest son, ran a smaller business doing yard work, snow removal and other personal services. There was a whole new generation of Hammonds, but they hadn't yet made their mark on the town.

Kirsten had even been married to one. The joke was that you couldn't go a yard in Paradise Hill without running into a Hammond or one of their kin.

Officer Blake eyed Tess. "My condolences as well. Your dad's last few years were hard and at the end, he was practically housebound. Then he got real sick and died fast."

"Thanks." She felt strange talking to people who had known her father better than she did.

Officer Blake took a plastic garbage bag out of the trunk of his patrol car and headed for the back lane behind Lisa's old house, John Hammond leading the way with his son in tow. Empty now, the doors and windows boarded up, Lisa's old house was ramshackle, with graffiti drawn across the walls in swaths of bright spray paint.

"The kids use it as a flop house," Mrs. Carter said, her face scrunched up as they walked past the side door, which had been cracked open, revealing an empty hallway. "They drink and do drugs inside. We call the cops and they come and chase them out but they keep returning. Deadbeat landlord just lets it sit there. Can't sell it, I guess. Not in these times." She glanced at Tess, her eyes narrowed. "You come back to sell your dad's place? Is your mom coming?"

"No, she's not well." Tess's mom had been sick with various ailments, most of which Tess suspected had to do more with depression than anything else. "We'll sell it if we can."

"Sorry to hear about your mom. I'd love to see her again. Good luck selling the place is all I can say. Your dad tried for years but had no luck. We tried to sell ours, but there's just no one interested in this neighborhood. Can't say I blame them. Worst neighborhood in the middle of nowhere."

They followed Officer Blake to the back of the house and

across the back lane to the trees. Tess stopped at the tree line, not wanting to see a dead cat. Not after what had happened when Lisa disappeared. Back then, there'd been a rash of cats killed and left around the neighborhood. They'd all been burned or otherwise tortured. Tess's mom hadn't wanted to leave their cat with Tess's father when they left Paradise Hill, so she'd packed Sprite up in a carrier and took her with them to Seattle.

"Aren't you coming?" Mrs. Carter asked, eyeing Tess up and down. "You're a crime reporter for the *Sentinel*, aren't you? I thought this would be right up your alley."

"I am," Tess said. "I don't like to see this kind of thing." She shivered, but she followed along anyway.

"Hope it's not Twinkie," Mrs. Carter said, following Officer Blake and workers into the trees. "He's always out roaming around the neighborhood at night. I tell Mrs. Carmichael to keep him in, but she believes in letting cats roam free. They're predators, she always says. Can't tell some people anything."

The small group went deeper into the trees to where the power line ended.

John Hammond spoke to Officer Blake.

"I saw it when I was up on the pole. Garth went in to check. Said it was a dead cat."

Hanging from a tree branch next to the power pole was a dead cat, its body limp.

Tess felt sick at the sight.

"Terrible," Mrs. Carter said, her arms folded. "I don't like cats as a rule, but the poor thing…"

Officer Blake quickly placed the cat in the plastic bag, thankfully. Tess would have a hard-enough time sleeping in her father's house as it was, even without the image of a dead, burned cat in her mind's eye.

"So, you don't recognize it?" Officer Blake asked when he got back to the patrol car.

"No," Mrs. Carter said. "I know all the cats around here, and it doesn't look like one from this neighborhood. Must be a stray."

Officer Blake nodded curtly and laid the plastic-wrapped cat beside the toolbox in the trunk. Then, he spoke with John Hammond.

"Thanks for calling this in," he said. "If you find any others, let us know."

"There's some sick people living around here," John Hammond said.

"Kids who do this?" Officer Blake said, shaking his head. "They go on to worse things."

"Serial killers," Garth offered. "Start off torturing and killing animals."

"That's right. If we catch the little sonsabitches who did this, we'll send them to juvie hall. Get their minds fixed."

"Can't fix a killer. Not ones that hunt humans," Garth offered. He glanced up and over to where Mrs. Carter and Tess stood.

"I always thought you should have been a cop, Garth," Officer Blake said. "You really should go to college and join up."

"Got a juvenile record," Garth said.

"You could get a pardon. You've been living an exemplary life ever since."

"Just might do that," he replied with a crooked smile.

They watched while Officer Blake got back into his vehicle. Tess squeezed Mrs. Carter's arm. "I'm going home."

"Is there going to be a funeral?" Mrs. Carter asked when Tess was a few feet away. "I know your dad wasn't the religious type, but still…"

Tess stopped and turned back to Mrs. Carter.

"According to the hospice worker I spoke with, he didn't want one. He said it would be hypocritical for him to step foot in a church after all those years being away from one."

"That's wrong," Mrs. Carter replied. "What is church for but to forgive us our sins?"

Tess took in a deep breath. "I'll ask the pastor of the local church we used to attend if he could say a few words at the graveside. My dad would think even that was too much. He was an atheist at the end."

Mrs. Carter nodded. "He was a lonely man, last few years. Might have had some comfort in his last days if he'd stayed in the church." Then she glanced over Tess. "Come by and have some coffee later, if you want. I'll call Kirsten and see if she can come, too."

"Thanks," Tess replied with a smile. "That would be nice. I'd love to see Kirsten. Is Michael in town?"

"Yes, as a matter of fact, he's on vacation and is staying with me. You knew he works in Seattle with the FBI. He's working the Violent Crimes Against Children task force up there."

"Yes," Tess replied. "Kirsten told me. He always wanted to be a police officer. Even after everything that happened."

"He did. I think all that business with Lisa made him want to be a cop or FBI Special Agent even more. He's really excited about another nephew. His own little football team, he likes to joke."

"Kirsten's pregnant?" Tess couldn't help but gasp, surprised that she was having another baby.

"More than pregnant. Ready to deliver any day now. That's why Michael's in town. He wants to be here when she pops."

"What about Phil? Isn't he in town?" Tess asked, wondering how Phil, Kirsten's new husband, would feel about Michael being present for the birth.

"Sure, but Michael had some time off and wants to be around for the birth."

"How is he? How's his family?"

"Not good," Mrs. Carter said with a frown. "Kirsten must have told you he's getting a divorce."

Tess frowned. "No, she didn't. We haven't talked in a while. That's too bad."

Tess had kept track of Michael over the years, in emails from Kirsten, but she hadn't known about the divorce. The last time she'd heard, he'd been living in Seattle and working for the FBI. She knew he was married with two boys, but that was it.

"Julia was unhappy and their split was nasty. It hit him hard. She said he was gone too much and his work was too consuming. So, what does she do? Takes the boys away to Tacoma."

"That's awful for him."

"Yes, he's still hurting. It was so hard on him. Anyway," Mrs. Carter said and patted Tess's arm. "Come by and have coffee later. You'll need it. Last I saw of your father's place, it was a junk house." She made a face of disgust and waved her hand.

"I haven't been inside yet. I'll see how much work I get done."

Mrs. Carter walked to her house across the street, and Tess turned back and watched as the tree pruning crew finished packing up their tools and drove off. The younger Hammond, Garth, had turned to watch Tess, and she felt his gaze on her as she walked to the front door. When she turned back after unlocking the front door, he was still watching her. He didn't turn away, like any ordinary polite person would when caught staring.

Tess glanced at the police car, which still sat on the street blocking the driveway to Lisa's old house. Officer Blake appeared to be typing something into a small laptop computer perched on his dashboard.

Finally, Garth turned away.

Tess tried to push the whole business out of her mind. She remembered the sight of the cat hanging from the tree and then its tail sticking out of the black plastic trash bag. Another cat – one of several that had been killed in the area over the past few weeks, apparently.

That wasn't a good omen. All the talk about serial killers made Tess shiver, remembering the day after police had discovered Lisa was missing. Her disappearance marked a divide in all their lives. It separated the old, naïve Tess from the new one – eleven years old and already conversant in matters relating to serial murder and animal mutilation.

Nothing in Tess's world had ever been the same.

CHAPTER TWO

Special Agent Michael Carter couldn't escape the feeling that something big was brewing in the small town of Paradise Hill.

He tried to tell himself it was just the impending birth of his newest nephew, and that was it. Paradise Hill was one of those small towns in rural Washington where nothing much ever happened.

Until it did and then it seemed that all hell broke loose.

He ran around the lake outside Paradise Hill, needing the exercise to keep his mind off his personal problems and focused on his health. A good sweat would help him sleep at night, and chase away the nightmares.

He'd been off work for the past two weeks on medical leave due to the stresses of his work as one of two Child Abduction Coordinators at the Seattle Field Office. In that role, he was often called to serve on the FBI's Child Abduction Rapid Deployment Teams, as part of the FBI's Violent Crimes Against Children Task Force. Truth was, without something to occupy his time, his mind found its way back to the most recent cases he'd worked and he became caught up once more in the dark underworld of child abductions, child murders and other crimes against children.

He'd recently been separated from his wife, Julia, and struggled to keep in contact with his two kids, Nathan and Craig. Julia complained that he'd been distant for the past couple of years, and claimed that she felt unloved but it was the work, not his feelings for her or the boys. He'd been obsessed with the cases he worked, haunted by the faces of the children he saw in videos or in print – or worse, the bodies they'd recovered afterward.

He tried to give Julia and his boys the attention they needed on weekends and vacations, taking them to the coast or deeper into the state on camping trips. But during the week, and especially when he was working a case, he was away long hours, working twelve- and fourteen-hour days.

He barely saw them during those periods. He'd believed that Julia accepted his heavy work schedule, especially when he was on a case that took him out of Seattle, but apparently not. She'd grown frustrated with him being away and of how tired he was when he did get time off, how he couldn't disconnect from the cases no matter what.

It was the nature of the job.

Being an FBI Special Agent wasn't nine-to-five. It was more than a job, really. It was a calling. He was called to the work, and had been ever since Lisa's disappearance. He was trying to atone for his lack of responsibility that night she went missing. He could never truly atone for it, but each case he closed absolved some of his lingering guilt.

He missed his boys so much his chest ached. He missed seeing them in their beds at night when he came home late, kissing their heads as he tucked the blankets around them. It wasn't much, and maybe they didn't realize he did it every night, but he needed to reconnect with them physically when he'd been gone for a long time or hadn't been able to spend time with them due to a particularly grueling schedule.

Now, with Julia and the boys in Tacoma, he couldn't even kiss them good-night the way he had almost every day of their lives when he was in Seattle. When he was out of town, he had Skyped with them to say good-night when he could take the time.

It wasn't enough for Julia.

She needed more from him than he could give.

He was angry with her for leaving Seattle, and for taking the boys without consulting him, although he knew he would never have agreed. But at the same time, she was only doing what she thought was right for herself and the boys. At least in Tacoma, she'd be close to family and her old friends.

Julia had never liked Seattle. It wasn't her home. Now, she was surrounded by her sisters and her parents, plus her best friend. There were kids Nate and Craig's ages that they could play with, and a good school near their rental house in her sister's neighborhood. They could have a good life there.

But he needed the boys in his life.

He'd move to Tacoma and commute if he had to, so he could be close to them. The past month had been a personal hell for him. When a case went sour, he wasn't sleeping and was hitting the bottle too hard. Plus, he was relying on sleeping pills to get any rest, and he knew that something had to change.

His supervisor said he should take a leave of absence. He'd been diagnosed with PTSD and would get full pay during his leave. That would give him time to recharge, get some therapy, and spend time in Tacoma visiting the boys.

But it also made him worry that the work he'd been doing was taking too much of a toll on him personally. He also worried that his superiors and his colleagues at the FBI would secretly think he couldn't take the stress.

It was the Murphy case that did it to him. Five-year-old Colin had been abducted, kept for several days in a dark basement with no food, then abused, tortured, and slowly hanged until he was dead. The serial child killer Blaine Lawson who had taken him, revived him once because he didn't want the boy to die so quickly.

That broke Michael.

Broke him. Finding the boy's body, seeing the ligature marks on his wrists, ankles and neck. Seeing his body sexually abused in such a violent way.

There had been three sightings of him reported, sending police on a wild goose chase to Tacoma and then to a small town outside of Spokane. It was Lawson taunting them. The entire time they'd been chasing down clues, the killer had been abusing the boy in Lawson's home, in a pit in the basement of his mother's old house.

Nate was that age. It was after Michael had found Colin in a dumpster in downtown Spokane that he developed insomnia. Night terrors woke him up even when he did sleep.

With everything going on in his life – the distance from Julia, the stress at work – his PTSD diagnosis was just icing on the frigging cake.

He'd been off for two weeks, and was starting to feel better. For the first week, he'd done nothing but sleep, eat, and run, trying to get healthy again. He'd stopped drinking completely, and started sessions with one of the staff psychiatrists, but the man was busy. Michael knew he'd be in Paradise Hill for a few weeks to spend time with Kirsten before and after she had her baby, so he only had two sessions.

They'd barely scratched the surface of his nightmares.

"What if I can't work in child abduction anymore?" Michael asked.

"You might not be able to. There are many worthwhile occupations in the Bureau for someone with your training."

"I'm going away for a couple of weeks to spend time with my family," Michael said when the psychiatrist wanted to book another appointment.

"Don't stay away too long," Dr. Fitzgerald said, patting him on the back. "You need to do some personal work, figure out how to deal with the stress of your job. If you don't, if you can't, you may have to transfer to some other classification. Whatever the case, we'll support you."

Michael thanked the man and then left the office. In that moment, he decided he would not let that bastard Lawson ruin his life.

Lawson had already taken three young boys from their families. He would not take Michael's boys from him or diminish his passion, which was rescuing kids from evil monsters like Lawson.

If Michael left his job, Lawson would have won and he would not let that happen.

HE REACHED the end of his run, a five-mile route he'd traced along the back roads bordering the lake, and stopped, leaning against the car to catch his breath. He stood up and glanced out across the still lake at the mountains rising behind. The scenery was spectacular. He missed that back in Seattle for as picturesque as the city was, nothing could compare to the verdant beauty of Paradise Hill. But there was a sense of decay in the town. A malaise that masked persistent poverty and benign neglect due to a recent downturn in the industries in the area.

Something gave him a sense of dread about the place. Maybe it was just his memories of the Murphy case. Maybe it was his memories of Lisa's disappearance eighteen years earlier. Whatever it was, he didn't feel the peace he hoped to feel when returning to Paradise Hill.

HE ARRIVED at the end of the road bordering the lake and the scene of the cabin fire from the previous night. He'd heard the sirens after midnight and wondered what was up, only to hear on the radio that morning that one of the Gilroy cabins had burned down. The Paradise Hill volunteer fire department did the best they could but by the time trucks arrived, the cabin was completely engulfed and had already started to collapse in on itself.

He walked up to the local cop who was standing on guard, keeping the scene clear of onlookers, of which there were a few, and introduced himself.

"Michael Carter," he said and held out his hand.

"I know you, Michael," the cop said and shook, giving him a smile. "Pete Martin. Your mother's my mother's second cousin."

Michael laughed, shaking his head. "I feel like I'm related to everyone in this town."

"Probably are," Pete said. "It's a very incestuous town. Everyone's up into everyone else's business." He shrugged.

"What's up?"

Pete made a face. "Found a body inside. Looks like little Melissa Foster. Chief Hammond's called in the Feds."

"Oh, God," Michael said, a sense of gloom descending over him. "That's too bad. I was holding out hope she was abducted by a family member and was still alive somewhere."

Pete turned to him. "That's your bailiwick, right? Child abductions? Chief Hammond said you're on the CARD team."

"That's right, but I'm on vacation."

CARD was the FBI's Child Abduction Rapid Deployment team and as one of two Crimes Against Children Coordinators, operating out of the FBI Field Office in Seattle. If there was a report of an abduction in the Washington area, he would be the point person and may even be part of the Team, depending.

"Well, FBI's on the road and will be here soon," Pete said.

Michael turned to watch the local police examining the burnt-out hulk of the cabin. What was the girl doing in the cabin? Had she been kept there all summer?

He had a lot of questions, but was officially on a medical leave and his doctor admonished him before he left not to become involved in any cases.

None.

He had to get his head back into the right space if he hoped to continue in his role as a CAC. Ever since Lisa Tate's disappearance and the ensuing investigation into her abduction, finding missing kids and bringing their abductors and murderers to justice had been pretty much his only aspiration.

He returned to Paradise Hill to take part in the most blessed and happiest times in a person's life – the birth of a child. The last thing he expected was to be drawn back into the murder of one.

He thought the cares of his job and personal life would lift when he returned, but instead, he felt an oppressive sense of dread threaten him, like the dark clouds of a fast-approaching storm.

CHAPTER THREE

Tess searched for her key to unlock the door to her father's house.

Her father had given her the key when she turned eighteen and had the right to visit if she wanted. She had come back and stayed with him a few times after they moved away, but he was so aloof that she stopped soon after. By the time he died, Tess hadn't seen him for five years.

He'd spent the last week of his life in a hospice. Tess got a call from one of the workers the day he died. She was the only person he'd asked them to call and he refused to let them call her sooner, not wanting her to see him so sick. According to the hospice worker, he was emaciated by the time he died, his organs shutting down one by one until he was nothing but yellowed skin and bones.

It was a lonely, painful death, and Tess's gut had been knotted for the past twenty-four hours at the thought of him dying all alone with no family beside him. She had been in the middle of an investigative report on missing and murdered children in Washington State, tracking down cold cases and joining up with a private organization of online amateur sleuths and retired law enforcement types to try to reopen cold cases. She had a few weeks' worth of vacation time saved, and asked her editor, Kate, for a week or two off to take care of matters in Paradise Hill.

Kate had been supportive. "Just find out as much as you can about the cold cases in the area while you're there."

"There are a few," Tess replied. "The one I knew – Lisa Tate. There were a few others too. An old case from the seventies, a couple from after Lisa went missing."

Tess promised to read up on the cold cases from the county, and so between burying her father, packing up the house, and getting it on the market, she'd interview a few people about the cases and see if she could track down any useful information for the article.

Tess opened the door and stood inside the dim entryway, listening to the quiet. She took in a deep breath, and then wished she hadn't. A horrible smell filled her nostrils and she had to cover her mouth.

"Oh, *God.*"

Was something dead in the house?

She flicked on the light switch but nothing happened. The power must have been out. With no one checking, whatever circuit breaker flipped was still out. That meant the fridge and freezer would have been without power for more a week.

He'd become a hoarder, the house filled with garbage, clothes, boxes of junk. A narrow path led from the front door through the living room heaped with piles of stuff – Tess couldn't even make it out as she passed by. It seemed to be mostly clothes and empty boxes – appliances, tools, cleaning supplies.

Too much junk.

The kitchen was a nightmare. The faucet was dripping into a basin filled with dishes covered in dried-up or festering food. The floor was filthy and every spare inch of space in the room had boxes on top of boxes. She didn't even want to imagine what kinds of bacteria covered every surface, or what bugs crawled around in the darkness.

A bag of groceries with a rotting chicken was the source of the stink. Her father must have done some shopping, had a bad spell, and called someone. Since he had no one in the town to look out for him, he'd probably been taken to the hospital and that was that – the food would have been left on the counter, where it had remained for the past week.

She didn't want to open the refrigerator, but needed to see what was causing the stench. Inside was a carton of milk that looked positively swollen. There were condiment bottles, ketchup, mustard, relish. A package of hot dogs looked grey in the cold cut tray. A box with week-old pizza sat on one shelf.

Had her father really been eating pizza in his condition? Maybe one of his work buddies had come to visit him his last week at home. He had been sick for weeks before the doctor diagnosed him with terminal cancer and told him he had only a few weeks, at most, to live.

Tess's father hadn't bothered to tell any of his actual family members.

It was just as well. They hadn't been part of his life for almost two decade years. It would have been very awkward to make them part of his death. If Tess had known how sick he was, she would have tried to come out and help, but he'd kept that from her, just like everything else about his life.

Except this. He'd left her this house and this huge mess.

Tess stood there and wept, covering her mouth both from disgust at the smell and horror that her father's life had come to this.

She had studied hoarding for an article once, and knew that hoarders had suffered some great trauma in their life that they just couldn't get over. Hoarding was the consequence. They weren't just lazy. They were paralyzed with sadness and loss.

What had Tess's father suffered that would lead to this? Was it really the divorce? Was it losing his wife and children, them moving away and abandoning him? People divorced and lost contact with their children all the time and didn't become hoarders.

Whatever the case, Tess's father had died alone surrounded by junk. It was a sad end to an even sadder life. Her heart ached for him and Tess wished things could have turned out differently.

She wiped her eyes and went back to the living room. There was no way she could live in this house with the way it was. She'd stay at a motel in town. After she got a room, the first thing she had to do was contact someone to get rid of all the junk.

Tess left the house and drove through the neighborhood to find a motel. Paradise Hill was too small for a nice hotel like the Best Western in the next town over, so there were only a few choices. She picked the Mountain Star, a motel a few miles away at the edge of town. It looked like the cleanest place, and they had a room. The website even touted a diner with room service available and, of course, the view of the mountain behind town.

Tess knew the woman at the front desk – Andrea, a girl from her school, who recognized Tess immediately.

"You're Tess! Tess McClintock, right? Oh, my God, I haven't seen you for years."

"You were in Mrs. Peacock's class with me, right?" Tess replied, remembering it like it was yesterday. "I'm living in Seattle."

"I know," Andrea said and raised her eyebrows. "Sorry to hear about your dad," she said and tilted her head to the side. "He used to come to the diner now and then with John Hammond and his son Garth. He stopped coming recently. I guess that's when he got sick."

"Thanks," Tess said and smiled softly. "He only found out a few weeks ago, but from what I understand, he was feeling sick for quite a while."

"How long has it been since you were here? You guys left after Lisa disappeared, right?"

"Yes, we left soon after."

"Your mom thought your dad did it."

Tess frowned. "What?"

"Yeah, my mom said your mom thought your dad did it, so she left him and took you and Thad away." Her face turned red. "I thought it was common knowledge."

"Not to me," Tess said, shocked at what Andrea said. "My mother said they'd been unhappy for a while." Tess finished signing in, her mind whirling at the suggestion that her dad could have been involved in Lisa's disappearance.

"Oh, right. Sure. Of course." Andrea smiled at Tess, one of those patronizing smiles when you feel sorry for someone who is obviously in denial. "Probably just town gossip. You know what small towns are like."

Tess glanced around the lobby of the motel. It was small, but they made a stab at mimicking the bigger chains. There was a small diner off to the side, with a bank of booths and a counter with old stools. There were even jukeboxes along the side. A worker dressed in a blue uniform cleaned off tables, so it appeared that the restaurant was popular. The woman glanced over at Tess, and seemed to recognize her. The woman didn't look familiar to Tess. She looked too young to be a former classmate.

"Who's that?" Tess asked, pointing her out to Andrea.

"Oh, that's Serena. Serena Hammond. Garth Hammond's daughter. She doesn't talk."

"She doesn't talk?" Tess said with a frown.

"No. She's got selective mutism. You can talk to her but she doesn't answer. Doesn't make much eye contact either, but she's a hard worker and does all the cleaning."

"What happened to her?"

Andrea shrugged. "Who knows? She just stopped talking as a kid. Anxiety disorder or something."

"Oh, that's too bad."

"Yeah. Quit school, too. Here you go," Andrea said and handed Tess the key.

Tess took it. "Thanks."

"If you need anything, just give me a jingle. I'm on every day till midnight."

"Will do."

Tess left the front desk and went back to her car, all the while wondering about Andrea's suggestion that her mother had left her father because of Lisa's disappearance. Had they left Paradise Hill because Tess's mom thought their dad was guilty?

If so, Tess's mom had never let on. She even allowed Tess return to Paradise Hill and stay with her father, so it couldn't be true.

He was quiet. He'd pretty much neglected them after they left town.

But he wasn't a killer…

WITH THAT BREWING in her mind, Tess parked her car in the slot outside her room and let herself in, carting her suitcase and bag inside. The room was what you would expect for a small-town motel, and Tess was thankful for how new it looked. While the building was older, it had been recently renovated. There were two double beds, a desk, a flat-screen TV with cable, a coffee maker, microwave, a modern bathroom and the motel provided Wi-Fi. Most of all, it was clean and bright, in direct contrast to her father's place.

She unpacked her laptop and then set to work, looking up business services, cleaners and dejunkers to come by and start working on the house. That part was easy. A company she contacted in nearby Yakima did industrial cleaning. When Tess told the man in charge of booking work about her father's house, he said they had handled a few hoarders before and knew what to do. A crew could come and start cleaning the next day if Tess wanted. It was the middle of the month so they were less busy than at the end of the month, when most people scheduled their moves and cleans.

Next, Tess called Pastor Greg at the local church and asked if he could conduct a graveside service. Pastor Greg was pleased to do the service. He'd spoken with her father and knew he had once been a church-going man, even though it was long ago. According to Pastor Greg, her father had spoken with him before he died and asked forgiveness.

"For what?" Tess asked, her mind going immediately to what Andrea had said.

"We've all sinned, Tess," Pastor Greg said softly. "Everyone needs to seek salvation."

Tess didn't reply. Instead, she thanked him and called the funeral home where her father's body was being kept. In the space of half an hour, she had worked out the cost of a plot in the local cemetery, the price of a headstone, and flowers to be ordered from the florist. The funeral manager said he'd make sure there were a few dozen chairs at the graveside, as well as anything else needed for the service.

The date was set for the following Monday, which meant Tess had four days to get herself together and be ready for the service.

Between now and then, she'd work on background for her father's eulogy and research for her assignment.

There were four missing girls – suspected murders – in the county, but no bodies had ever been found. Tess wanted to talk to the police about all of them, especially the most recent. She was glad to work on the cases while she had downtime from taking care of family business. Focusing on someone else's loss would take her mind off her own.

Of course, that meant researching Lisa's case – not that she hadn't already. Lisa's case had been her obsession for the past five years, although she'd learned nothing new.

The case was ice cold – almost twenty years cold. Still, it was her job and she wanted to keep in good with her editor. Maybe she'd be able to learn more about what the police had thought about potential suspects back in the day. Maybe Tess's dad *had* been a suspect. If so, nothing she'd read about the case in the internet archive ever suggested it.

After a few hours of research on the Missing Persons' Washington Database without finding one reference to her father, Tess's anxiety eased somewhat. From what she'd read, her father had been out of town on a long-distance trip. He wouldn't have been able to get back to Paradise Hill in time to take Lisa even if he wanted to.

Tess paused from her reading and remembered back to the night Lisa went missing. On weekends, Tess regularly spent the night at Kirsten's. That night, Lisa wanted to sleep over, too, and Kirsten agreed – reluctantly. At ten, Lisa was the youngest of the three girls and Kirsten didn't really like the fact that Tess had befriended her.

"Two's company, three's a crowd," Kirsten argued when Tess told her she invited Lisa to stay over. Tess didn't care. Lisa's mom worked late on weekends and she had to stay home with a babysitter otherwise since her brother was out of town.

Lisa had been scared to sleep out in the tent, afraid of bears in the woods behind the row of houses but Tess tried to calm her fears.

"The boys are just a few feet inside."

That night, Kirsten's brother Michael had been charged with babysitting them while Kirsten's parents were in Seattle overnight for a concert. After his parents left, Michael and a friend started drinking beer and smoking marijuana in the family room. The skunky scent wafted on the late autumn breeze to the tent where the girls were.

They weren't usually allowed to sleep out in the tent, just stay out until midnight, but Michael insisted they could. Tess knew he wanted to party and didn't want little girls hanging around.

That's what he said when he scooted the girls outside, despite Lisa's reluctance.

"We're inside just a few feet away. You got nothing to be afraid of. The back gate's locked. If the bogeyman comes, just scream. We'll be right there." He and Curt laughed, but it didn't make Lisa feel any better.

At first, the night was fun. Tess handed out temporary tattoos she got from the local grocery store and the girls applied them using water from the hose. Tess chose Mulan, Kirsten picked Supergirl, and Lisa chose a My Little Pony tattoo. Tess applied hers to her wrist, Kirsten put hers on her bicep like a man, and Lisa's went on her ankle. They helped each other apply the tattoos, admiring them when they were dry.

Then, Tess wanted to tell ghost stories. Michael had given them flashlights, which made things creepier. They sat in a circle, flashlights in hand and each on had to make up a story that was intended to scare them. When it was Lisa's turn, she could barely speak, her throat was so choked with fear.

Later, when they were ready to sleep, Lisa opened her backpack and pulled out her things for the night: her pajamas, her toothbrush. A worn and tattered Ted E. Bear fell out of the bag as well.

At thirteen, Kirsten was older than both Lisa and Tess, and rolled her eyes when she saw Ted.

"Why'd you bring *that?*" Kirsten's expression was withering. She laughed and elbowed Tess. "She actually brought her teddy bear?" She turned back to Lisa. "Aren't you big enough to sleep on your own?"

Lisa frowned. "It must have got caught up with my pajamas," she said and dropped the stuffed toy off to the side of the tent. "I don't need it."

"Then take it back home. What are you? Five?"

"You know I'm ten." Lisa unrolled her sleeping bag. "Mom's at work and Graham's in Seattle with my dad. I'm supposed to stay here."

"Take it back. Bring Graham's cassette player so we can listen to our own music."

Lisa shook her head. "He doesn't let me use it."

"You just said he's in Seattle. Bring it back."

"I can't," Lisa said and pulled the zipper down. "I'll get in trouble if I even go into Graham's room. Besides, Mom said I wasn't allowed to go back in the house."

"What a *bay-bee*. Do you do everything your mother says?" Kirsten shook her head. "What a suck." Kirsten turned to Lisa, a mean expression in her ice blue eyes, the flashlight she held up casting her lean face into all kinds of scary shadows. "Do you have a pacifier, too, or did you give that up?"

Tess felt torn, wanting both Kirsten and Lisa to be friends. Now, Kirsten was mad and Lisa's eyes were wet with tears.

"Don't be so mean," Tess said and elbowed Kirsten, then she smiled at Lisa. "I still have a Barney doll in my room."

"But you didn't *bring* it," Kirsten said acidly. She turned back to Lisa. "This is the big girl tent. Take your toy back home or stay there."

"Mom won't be home until really late," Lisa protested. "Besides, my dad gave this to me."

"That's not our problem. Our problem," Kirsten said and folded her arms, "is having little babies in our tent."

Tess elbowed Kirsten again, but Kirsten was insistent. She was the most popular girl in school and Tess was her best friend, but Tess was always nice to Lisa, who tagged along like a little sister.

The tears that had been biting in the corners of Lisa's eyes finally welled up enough to fill them. She stuffed her sleeping bag back in her backpack, grabbed Ted and left the tent.

"Come back," Tess said, peering out the tent opening. "She didn't really mean it."

But Lisa didn't reply. Instead, she clutched her bear tighter and walked to the front yard, into the darkness and whatever fate awaited her.

When the police first questioned Tess, she hid the fact that they'd been teasing Lisa, until Tess's mother gave her a stern look.

"Tell them why she left," her mother insisted.

"Kirsten was teasing her because she had her teddy bear."

The two older girls couldn't have known at the time that Lisa was being stalked – that they all were – but that didn't matter to Tess's eleven-year-old mind. She should have insisted that Lisa stay.

Even now, eighteen years later, Tess still felt guilty about her role in Lisa's disappearance.

TESS GLANCED around the motel room, feeling at a loss. Then she remembered Mrs. Carter's invitation to come over for coffee. She packed away her laptop and drove back to the neighborhood, parking at her dad's place and walking over to Mrs. Carter's. Tess noticed a different car in the driveway and wondered if it was Kirsten.

Tess had made a few friends in Seattle when she'd moved there, and no one had ever truly replaced Kirsten in Tess's heart. Kirsten had come to Seattle a few times to visit in the first two years after they moved away, but then Kirsten got pregnant at age fifteen and married the father, Eugene

Hammond, who had been at least six years older than Kirsten at the time. Kirsten often joked about her shotgun wedding, but she seemed happy to be married and a mother, missing out on graduating high school or going to college. After that, their lives diverged so much that they never seemed to have the chance to meet and see each other as grown women. Kirsten became a stay-at-home mom and Tess worked long hours at college and then after, her entire focus on writing and research.

Despite these differences, and even after so long apart, the last time Tess and Kirsten saw each other, the years melted away and they were best friends once more.

She hoped it would be the same again this time.

CHAPTER FOUR

Paradise Hill was a small enough town – population 2,245 on a good day – that everyone pretty much knew everyone else. Someone new showed up and people soon learned their name, where they were staying, and why they were in town. People watched the streets and noticed when something looked different. New car or truck? People would talk.

Cars didn't drive through Paradise Hill on their way to somewhere else. You had to take an exit off the highway to get there, so only its residents or people with business in the tiny town entered its streets.

Not many people stopped in Paradise Hill, not even for gas, because there were bigger towns with better facilities nearby. Paradise Hill was one of those small towns in America with just enough population to have a school or two, a few businesses, and a lot of run-down real estate. The main street had a couple of buildings from the Gold Rush era, when people had flooded out west to search for gold, and the old storefront façades were among the town's only tourist draws. Incorporated in the late nineteenth century, the town had seen better days, but those days were gone.

The woman arrived in Paradise Hill in her Honda and he remembered her right away, especially when he saw her drive up into Ron McClintock's driveway and park behind his pickup.

He remembered the red hair.

Tess. Tess McClintock.

Ron McClintock's only daughter, Tess was a reporter for the *Sentinel* up in Seattle. Left town with her mother and brother after Lisa. Kirsten's best friend.

He rubbed his chin and watched her walking up to the front door. He expected Mrs. McClintock or Thad to come to town and take care of business, but he wasn't unhappy to see Tess.

Not at all.

That night way back when, he would have been happy to have taken Tess, that's for sure. She was a pretty thing with that hair and those green eyes. She was all grown up now, and that didn't appeal to him, but back then? Prime real estate. He could have had a lot of fun with her back then if she'd been more vulnerable.

She wasn't.

She had a mother who watched over her like a hawk and a brother who was always there lurking in the background, making it damn near impossible to pick her off. Then Lisa had left the tent. Had a fight with the older girls, or so they told the police. Made fun of her bringing her teddy. Lisa was vulnerable and the boys inside were stoned. She was one of those girls with absent parents, too drunk or stoned or busy to care much, trying to juggle several jobs just to be able to buy food and pay the bills.

Lisa was ripe for the picking and he had been in a picking mood.

He'd had lots of fun with Lisa, once he had her.

He wasn't interested in Tess that way anymore now that she was all grown up, but at one time, he'd imagined it. He'd imagined what he'd do and how, using her for his own special purposes.

Then, her mother had taken her away and he'd had slim pickings.

He sat in the truck and remembered. Twenty years earlier on a day not too different from today.

HE'D BEEN WATCHING the girls for a while.

That night, the Carter's back yard was pitch black despite the light from the kitchen window. Tall hedges grew on either side of the yard and at the back stood a grove of tall poplars. Behind the yard, the forest stretched for at least a mile up the side of the mountain.

He'd watched from a tree-covered spot just back of the house, his scope trained on the tent filled with the three girls. He'd glanced inside the house through the sliding glass door to see the older boys were laughing and drinking beer, shirking their duty as guardians of the younger girls. Michael and his best friend Curt were both preppie types who played on the football team. All-American, red-blooded, all that B.S. They were also smoking pot, so neither of them was lily-white after all.

He watched Michael rolling a joint, then lighting it and passing it to Curt. They were supposed to be babysitting, but it was Friday night and boys their age wanted to party, not watch over prepubescent girls.

Shirking their responsibility made his job that much easier.

Loud music drifted through the screen door up to where he watched. Something metal. He recognized it. "Bleed," by Soulfly. He hated metal, but the guys at work always played it. It made his heart pound and brought out his anger. He wanted to punch the boys for playing it so loud and disrupting his thoughts, but he just smiled and continued working.

Smile and they won't know what's going on in your head.

He'd gotten away with so much for so long, no one could touch him.

A smile lets you hide in plain sight.

That night, the ground was soft beneath his elbows as he lay on the peak of the hill and pretended he was a soldier stationed somewhere exotic, watching targets on a military mission to take out bad guys. He imagined having a real scoped rifle like soldiers had and picking them off, one by one, watching them fall like so many dominoes.

All of them, the boys included. He hated them all.

The girls in the tent giggled together like stupid girls their age did. He'd like to see the smiles wiped off their faces when the bullets slammed into their chests, the look of surprise in their eyes at the pain and the first gush of blood out of the wound.

He hated the girls especially.

Hated how he wanted what they had between their legs, but none of them would offer. He'd like to point his rifle at their smiling faces and let one off, watch their heads explode.

Not so happy now, right, bitch?

He could have brought his father's rifle with him, but it was locked up and his dad kept the key. Besides, for what he wanted to do, he needed stealth and quiet while he watched his targets. He knew he couldn't shoot them, as much as he wanted to. No. He had to be smarter than that.

Shooters were always found. Eventually. He'd read books on serial killers, and the ones who got away with it varied their routines, didn't show a pattern of behavior, and only picked targets that were unknown to them.

He may have been a pervert, as his mother called him when she found him beating off to porn. He may have been unlovable – another one of her disappointed-mother words when he'd fought her attempts to smother him.

But he wasn't stupid.

It was stupid of the girls to sleep out in the tent this close to the forest. There was no way of knowing what kind of person with malice on their minds might lurk there.

Like him. He had malice aforethought and malice aplenty. That much was certain.

Once upon a time, he'd thought maybe he could exorcise the hatred from his heart if he attended church enough, if he worked hard enough at his job, if he biked far enough and shed enough sweat, but it never went away. It was always there, biting at the edges of his consciousness. The hatred. The searing anger. His pain was enormous, and nothing stopped it. The only thing that helped was imagining the kind of revenge he'd like to take on the world. Pay it back for all the crap he'd put up with in his life.

Like he was imagining catching the cat he saw roaming through the darkened yard. He could grab it and squeeze its neck until it stopped fighting. Hang it up in the trees bordering the backyard, so the owners could see what happened when they let their cats run free.

Killing cats helped somewhat, but the hatred inside him always returned. It never left him completely.

Even his dreams were filled with mayhem.

When one of the girls left the tent and walked to the front yard, her backpack in hand, he realized she was going home.

Lisa.

Lisa Tate. Nine or ten years old with pretty dark hair. She lived with her mom and brother, Graham, a few houses down next to the park. He'd already scoped her house and seen that it was empty, Mrs. Tate – Darlene – was working late at the bar. Graham was out of town at his dad's place in Seattle.

He'd been watching the little family for a while, and Lisa was often alone, but usually locked away in the house while her brother went out or when her mother was at work.

Opportunity knocked only occasionally. He knew what he had to do.

The neighborhood was quiet so late at night. It was autumn and the trees behind the line of houses had already lost most of their leaves. He stole along the back easement behind the houses to Lisa's house at the end of the block.

The last one on the lane next to the park, Lisa's house was the smallest. An older bungalow, it needed lots of work, but Darlene couldn't afford it on her paycheck as a waitress in downtown Paradise Hill. Lisa's dad didn't live with them, and didn't contribute anything either.

Everyone knew everyone else's business in Paradise Hill, good and bad.

He lived across town in a better neighborhood, but he'd always hunted in the poorer neighborhoods. He'd seen Lisa a few times at the football field while her brother played for the Spartans, his high school football team. He'd watched her when she went to get an ice cream from the cart, picking her out from the others.

The house was completely dark and, as he watched, Lisa lifted the mat at the back door and picked up a key. She clutched her teddy bear to her side as she fumbled with the key in the lock before finally getting the door open and entering the house.

As he watched, the cat scooted out between Lisa's legs before Lisa could stop her.

"Maisie!"

Lisa ran after her. In the darkness, she would have a hard time finding the cat, but he had his night vision glasses, thanks to a birthday gift from his uncle.

"Maisie?" Lisa called out in a small voice.

Lisa went back and turned on the outside light. When she returned, he stepped out of the darkness, the night vision glasses removed and attached to a clip on his belt so she wouldn't see them.

She stopped abruptly when she saw him standing there, a small gasp escaping her lips.

They stared at each other for a moment.

"Looking for the cat?" he said finally.

"Yes," Lisa said in a startled voice. "Who are you?"

"I'm Graham's friend, Ted," he said, making up a name on the fly, picking one of his favorite killers. "I'll help you."

"What are you doing here?" Lisa said and stepped back hesitantly.

"I was watching the stars. Where I live, the stars aren't nearly as bright. I brought my telescope." He held out his scope, turning it around in his hand, hoping to distract her.

She glanced up into the darkness and he did as well. Out here the stars were bright. You could see thousands of them on a clear night. But that night, the light of the full moon outshone most of the stars.

"I have to go."

She turned and went back to the door, probably worried that he was a peeping Tom. In the meantime, he saw the cat and grabbed it by the scruff of the neck. Before she could get the door locked, he took hold of the knob.

"I got it," he said and held up the cat for her to see. "Open the door so I can let it in. You don't want it to run off again."

Lisa hesitated, clearly not wanting to open the door, but wanting the cat to be safe.

She cracked the door just wide enough to let the cat through, but he had other plans. He barged in, pushing the door hard and throwing the cat to the floor.

The cat rowled in pain and ran off down the dark hallway.

When Lisa glanced back, he closed the door and turned the deadbolt. Then he faced her and leaned against the door, excitement growing in his gut.

The look on Lisa's face said she knew she was in real trouble.

HE CAME BACK to the present, and watched Tess enter her father's house.

No one was quite as pretty as Tess...

He drove his truck past the house and stared in through front picture window, hoping to catch a glimpse of her to see what she was doing, but he only saw the truck reflected, his own face staring back at him.

He'd return to watch, more out of curiosity than having

any firm plans. No, he was curious. Of course, it still made him breathless to hunt, and let's face it, it made him hard when he watched them without their knowing. Just the act of watching gave him a thrill – seeing people going about their days, doing their mindless pastimes, all the while unaware that he could see them, could watch them, and if he really wanted, he could take them. He'd taken many over the years, and no one had ever suspected.

She probably wouldn't be staying at the house, if she did stay in town. The place was a dump. You could barely find a clear spot to stand, there was so much junk. He'd been inside many times over the last few years, and it was disgusting. It was an affront to his fastidiousness to be surrounded by so much junk and filth. He didn't know how McClintock could stand to live in the place. But Ron had been a broken man, and didn't seem to care how he'd lived at the end.

HE DROVE BACK to the garage and parked the truck, then went for lunch, sitting with the other guys while they all ate their food out of their metal lunch boxes or brown paper bags. While he ate, he planned to drive by Ron McClintock's later to see where Tess was staying, if she was staying in town. He figured she was there to bury her father, and would be around for a while.

Seeing her and thinking about Lisa made him feel that old itch again. The excitement of an ongoing mission and the following investigation. His breathlessness when the police came by and asked their stupid questions. He knew how to answer them. He knew how to dupe them. They thought their fancy educations and training made them better than him, but they were all wrong.

He knew more because he did the work. He studied it and he had perfected it so that now, all these years later, they still suspected nothing. He knew what they would look for and he made sure not to give it to them. So far, he'd succeeded.

Close to twenty years and nothing.

Oh, they'd talked to him. He was the right age and all. Local cops, murder cops from Seattle, FBI special agents with their blue windbreakers and yellow lettering. Flashing their badges in his face, trying to judge him, watching him to see if he acted guilty.

He was guilty as hell, but they could never pin anything on him because he was too fastidious. He had the very best mentor and had studied murder, made a vocation of it. It was his passion, he liked to think, and he took it very seriously. He'd even considered studying criminology in college, but school learning wasn't his idea of fun. Besides, they taught a lot of theory, whereas he was more interested in methods and tactics. He could study the methods of killers online or in books. Learn from those who'd lasted a long time without getting caught.

So far, he hadn't been caught. He'd been extra careful, taken all precautions, and had managed to avoid detection.

The killer among you.

He wouldn't get caught for any penny-ante shit. No, if he was going to go down, he'd make sure it was for something big. Something monumental. Memorable.

They'd talk about him in their precinct houses and in their FBI ivory towers for years. Washington State had a moratorium on the death penalty, but he'd probably get the death penalty for the case in Idaho. Hell, he deserved it, considering everything. But before he did get the big needle, he'd take as many of their pretty little girls with him as he could.

They had no idea how many.

He had them catalogued and indexed. He knew each one by name, age, location, and specific details. He remembered reading about one serial killer – the BTK killer, Dennis Rader – who couldn't remember all his kills, he'd done so many, and most of them so quickly that they weren't memorable.

That wasn't his MO. He did it slowly enough to remember each detail.

Most of the time, he only took the ones people didn't care about. It was a risk to take too young a girl because no matter what their background, a prepubescent girl elicited sympathy from everyone. People were motivated by sympathy for a young girl under the age of twelve, even if the family was poor and the mother was a drunk or the father a drug addict. In fact, they often felt even worse for the girl if that was the case.

But if it was an older girl from the wrong side of the tracks? If she had something seedy in her background, slept around, did drugs, was a dropout? They didn't care nearly as much. The public didn't come out for the searches and they didn't donate money for the families.

Mostly, he took the ones who had no one watching over them. It was so easy to take those girls. He picked them off one by one, from back streets and dark alleys, in the small towns and big cities, where they did things that no one wanted to really talk about. It made them vulnerable. Good hunting.

Hell, for them, it was open season.

CHAPTER FIVE

S ure enough, when Tess knocked at the front door, Kirsten answered and immediately grabbed Tess into a bear hug, made awkward by Kirsten's very pregnant belly. The two women laughed when they finally pulled back and got a good look at each other. Kirsten was the same, with the same long dark hair and blue eyes. She was taller than Tess, and at present, heavier due to her impending delivery.

"Oh, my *God*," Kirsten said, holding Tess at arm's length and eyeing her up and down. "You look amazing. Look at you. So tall and slim." She glanced down at her own body, which was noticeably more rounded.

"Baby number three, right? Your mom said it's due any day," Tess said, envious that Kirsten had the perfect life – married to the son of a wealthy landowner, a real estate agent, someone she met after she and her first husband split. They lived in a home across town in a better neighborhood.

"He's already overdue, but I swear, this is the last. I can't do this again. My ligaments are all so stretched, I can barely walk, but Phil and I wanted a child of our own. This is probably my last chance, so..."

Tess didn't say anything in reply because of the implication that she was too old. Instead, she overlooked the inadvertent judgment and forced a smile.

"Oh, I'm sorry. I didn't mean that. I mean, for me. You can still have babies into your forties, but I've already had two so this is my last."

"That's okay," Tess said and squeezed Kirsten's arm.

She followed Kirsten inside and the two of them sat in the living room – just like old times. Over the next hour, they caught up with local news and news of their families and of course, Kirsten's and Tess's lives.

"So, you're the career woman and I'm the stay-at-home mom," Kirsten said. "I would have thought it would be the opposite. You were always so maternal and I was such a competitive bitch."

They laughed, because it was the truth. Something had changed over the years to take them on entirely different routes. Kirsten got pregnant at fifteen and married the father, had a family right away, while Tess finished high school, then went to college, got a degree, and started to work right away covering crime in Seattle. It was the opposite of what Tess would have expected for each of them.

"Life has its way of surprising you," Tess said.

"Tell me about it. I met Gene when I was still in high school. He romanced me so hard I couldn't resist. You know – an older guy. A man, not a boy. Then I got pregnant and Dad said we had to get married. Gene's dad agreed and pretty much shamed him into it. There was no college for me. Didn't even finish high school."

"What happened with you and Gene?" Tess asked, curious about the end to Kirsten's first marriage.

Kirsten shrugged. "I was happy for a while, but in the end, he was too old for me and I guess we grew apart." Kirsten smiled, but it appeared forced. "Anyway, I met Phil last year and things are so much better now."

"Life has different plans for us than what we had as girls, I guess," Tess said and drank her coffee. She wasn't sure which of them was happier with this turn of events, but Kirsten at least looked happy now, with her new husband and baby on the way. "Is Gene still in Paradise Hill?"

"Yes, he works for his uncle, of course. The bastard," Kirsten said.

"Bad split?" Tess asked, watching Kirsten carefully.

She made a face. "He's a control freak. The kids don't spend much time with him."

"That's too bad. I know what it feels like to never see your father after parents split."

"Sometimes, kids are better off not spending time with their dads," Kirsten said dismissively. "That's all I have to say."

"That bad?" Tess asked, trying not to show any emotion in response but she was curious. The split seemed bad if Kirsten thought that.

Kirsten sighed. "Forget about Gene. He's not really all that bad. He's just distant."

They talked a while longer about Kirsten's pregnancy and Tess's life in Seattle.

"I'd say we should go out for dinner but there's no way I'd be much company. Maybe you and Michael could meet up. You work the crime beat, and he fights crime. I think the two of you would have a lot in common."

"I'd like to talk to him," Tess said, and she meant it. When she was ten, she'd had a crush on him. Even at fourteen, he'd been classically handsome with a square jaw, blue eyes, and the Carter dark hair. And, of course, he was a star on the football team and anyone who was a star on the team was a star in town. Tess had seen pictures of him with the family over the years and if anything, he'd grown more attractive.

"I'll give him your cell number. He'll call you if he has time."

Kirsten was right. He would be someone Tess could tap for information on missing persons. He worked out of Seattle, but she was sure he'd know a lot about cases in Washington as a whole.

Tess had seen his name on a roster of FBI contacts in the online group of internet sleuths she belonged to. Known as The Missing, the group tracked cold cases and tried to crack them, interviewing old witnesses, checking out evidence, and advocating that more resources be devoted to solving them on behalf of families who contracted them. They even had a podcast that highlighted recent cases and updated followers on the progress of ongoing investigations.

It had become Tess's obsession.

The members of The Missing were a mix of interested laypersons, retired detectives, FBI agents, and crime geeks who spent their off time or retirement working cold cases. Tess had made some friends among them, and used them as sources for her investigative pieces.

Michael would be a good source for ongoing cases, and might be able to help direct Tess's research on old cold cases in the area.

"Hey, Mrs. Carter, can I ask you something?"

Tess had been itching to ask Mrs. Carter about the rumor that her mom had left her dad because of Lisa's disappearance, but had been embarrassed to even bring it up.

"Sure, sweetie. Ask away."

Tess took in a deep breath. "I spoke with Andrea over at the motel and she said something that confused me. It's kind of embarrassing, but I figured you'd know."

Mrs. Carter nodded, folding her hands in anticipation.

"She said Mom took Thad and me away because she thought my dad was involved in Lisa's disappearance."

Mrs. Carter's face changed expression briefly, but then she appeared to catch herself.

"Aw, honey. That was just a rumor," she said and reached out to brush a lock of Tess's hair off her face. "Your dad was away at the time and was never a suspect. People gossiped because of the timing, that's all. It was just because your mom thought Paradise Hill wasn't safe that she left. She and your dad had been having problems for a while – probably because he was away so much on the road. He didn't want to leave town and she did, so they decided to separate. We all thought he'd come to his senses and follow her to Seattle, but he didn't."

Tess nodded, feeling a little better after Mrs. Carter's assurance.

"I knew he wasn't involved," Mrs. Carter added. "You know how people are, especially in small towns. They have to talk about everyone's business."

Tess smiled to herself. Of all the town gossips, Mrs. Carter was one of the biggest. She had her finger on the pulse of every scandal and crime, large or small, committed in the city. If anyone knew the news, it was her.

They spent another half hour talking about old times,

and Kirsten showed Tess pictures of her kids, two boys aged fifteen and thirteen. Her new husband Phil Hammond was a real estate agent working in Yakima and had recently been promoted to manager of one of the regional office. They had a nice quiet small-town life.

"Phil can help sell the house, once you get it cleaned up. The market's really depressed, but he knows the area. If anyone can sell your dad's house, Phil can."

Tess was glad that was settled. Selling the house was not something she looked forward to. It sounded like a real pain and she wanted to put that part of her life on autopilot. She'd leave the house clean and empty, and it would sell – or not – when she returned to Seattle once the funeral was over and everything was in place.

LATER, when they'd finished rehashing all the news, Tess said goodbye to Mrs. Carter and Kirsten and went back to her father's place to get started looking for a suit for him to wear in the casket. There would be no memorial service, but Tess wanted him to go into the ground wearing something nice. She went to his bedroom, which was just one more room filled with junk, piles and piles of old clothes that looked like they'd been collected from Salvation Army drop-offs, and boxes of recyclables.

Where did he get all this junk? Tess couldn't imagine where it had all come from. He collected bottles and old clocks, bar signs and old dishes. What a strange pastime for a man like him. He must have spent all his money on this junk, which now had to be thrown out or sold.

Tess climbed over piles of stuff to get to his closet, and searched through the shirts and jackets hanging there. She saw an old box from her childhood – a tackle box her father kept all his treasures in: flies for fly fishing, her and Thad's first baby teeth in tiny envelopes marked with their names, locks of their hair tied with pink and blue ribbons, special medals he had received when he was a volunteer ambulance driver. He used to take it out and add things to it, showing her all his treasures, and now she pulled it down and set it on top of a nearby box to look at the contents.

As she expected, there were many small items inside related to fly fishing, and all the other items she remembered from her childhood – photos from when Tess was a child, pictures of Thad and Tess out at the lake fishing with him.

Underneath the top shelf, Tess found a larger box. Inside were several spiral notebooks that looked ancient, the pages yellowing. She opened one and read the first few lines. Her kept a journal as a young boy, the pages filled with notes and musings as well as snippets of stories, both science fiction and horror. Her father had aspired to being a novelist one day, but he'd given up on the dream after dropping out of high school and getting a job.

Besides the dozen or so journals, there was a scrapbook, as well as a small ring with a large oval stone. She covered her mouth when she opened the scrapbook and saw read first news clipping carefully glued into place. The news article was about a girl who had gone missing back when Tess's father was a teenager. Janine Marshall, thirteen years old, missing for a week at the time the article was published on November 17, 1978.

Tess remembered the case from her research on Lisa's disappearance. Janine had been a runaway and had been living on the streets the year she disappeared. With makeup and her well-developed figure, she had looked older than thirteen, but she was still only a child.

Hers was the oldest cold case in the area, which was technically a missing person case since the body had never been found. There had been the occasional report that she was seen in a nearby town, or in Seattle, but they were just stories and eventually, the case had gone cold. No one in town had seen her after the Friday night she went missing. The police did a cursory investigation, concluding that Janine had left town, but there were whispers that she may have been taken into the sex slave trade and moved to one of the bigger cities in Washington State.

That was a common event in the sex trafficking black market operating across the country. A girl might have run away from home, and get mixed up in the sex trade. Then, her pimp would likely move her to one of the larger cities, such as Tacoma, Spokane, or Seattle. Sometimes they moved across the country or, in the worst-case scenario, were taken out of the country to be bought and sold like slaves to service pedophiles and child molesters around the globe.

Tess thought the true worst-case scenario was that Lisa had never left town at all, had been abducted and murdered. It was understandable that some in Janine's family held out hope that she was in the sex trade and not dead. Every now and then, they'd make a public appeal to Janine or anyone who knew her whereabouts to contact them. There had been a small reward for information leading to her whereabouts or her fate.

Janine's extended family had even hired a clairvoyant to help on the case. The woman, Mistress Diane, said Janine was in a small dark place and couldn't see the light. Tess vividly remembered reading the news reports on the case, angry at the charlatan who was preying on the bereaved family members for notoriety.

At the same time, the aunt was angry at the local police department for shrugging off the girl's disappearance. The aunt was right – Janine had always called when she stayed with relatives, so the fact that she never contacted her family did not bode well for her fate. Even if Janine had wanted to cut off contact with her family, she had friends in town and none of them had ever heard from her again – not in forty years.

She was a few years younger than Tess's father, who had been sixteen at the time and a junior at Paradise Hill High School the year she went missing. They'd attended the same elementary school as young children, Pleasant Valley Middle School.

Usually, children three or four years apart in age didn't socialize together. So why had Tess's father kept a clipping of her obituary all these years?

CHAPTER SIX

Tess read over the article again and wondered if her father had saved the clippings because he'd mourned her loss. It would not be uncommon for a sixteen-year-old boy to date a thirteen- or fourteen-year-old girl, but while she looked older, Janine wasn't the kind of girl Tess's father would likely have known. While Tess had grown up in a poor area, Janine was from an even poorer area – the Mountain Side Mobile Home park on the other side of town.

The entire scrapbook was filled with news clippings about her disappearance and from various crimes committed in Paradise Hill. Janine's disappearance was just the first of those she found in the pages. There were others – a couple of outright murders that had been solved, several dozen cases of arson of local businesses and residences. There were articles about Lisa's disappearance. That case had the most news clippings taped to the pages. The news reports covered at least a dozen crimes, cut meticulously out of the newspapers and organized by date.

There was no handwriting in the scrapbook, nothing but

various news clippings taped or glued in place spanning decades. There were no other clippings after another girl went missing. Zoe Wallace. Eleven at the time of her disappearance.

Was her father just an interested citizen or had he been involved in some way? Worst of all, had he been the killer? Tess knew from her studies that killers often kept trophies of their kills, and liked to follow the cases in the news, even inserting themselves into the investigation by offering tips being part of the search team.

Tess pocketed the ring and closed the scrapbook, tucking it back into the box. She removed a couple of her father's journals, wanting to read them and learn more about her father as a person. She'd do some research on the cases included in the scrapbook; it would be directly related to her work for the *Sentinel*. But first, she wanted to talk to someone with more expertise than her.

She was beginning to think her father was just an amateur sleuth, like her, and had been interested in crime the way any other citizen might be, perhaps a bit more obsessed. Like her. Maybe she'd inherited it from him, although she never remembered him talking about such cases or being focused on them. She didn't remember much about her father as a person, though, so her knowledge of him was spotty at best.

She gathered the suit she'd chosen for her father, including a pair of shoes from deep in the closet, a tie from a tie hanger on the back of the closet door, and some socks and underwear from the chest of drawers. She had to wrestle with the boxes surrounding it to get the drawers open, but finally succeeded.

Her father would look decent when he went into the casket, even if no one would see him. Maybe in some distant future, if they ever exhumed his body, they'd see that at least someone had dressed him in the fashion of the day. Someone – some future archaeologist – would be glad Tess hadn't merely had him wrapped in a shroud.

At least, that's what she told herself. In truth, she didn't want to see her father's body. She'd seen what cancer did to people. It sucked the life out of them so that they looked like walking corpses.

Instead, she would remember her dad the way he was the last time she saw him – tall, with ginger hair like her own, freckles on his face and arms, and blue-green eyes.

She packed up the suit in a dry-cleaning suit bag she found tucked in the bottom of the closet and left the house. She wanted to get as far away from the stench of the fridge as possible.

The cleaners would be coming tomorrow and Tess would be glad to turn the work of sorting through the junk and trash over to them. They could decide what to save, what to sell and what to throw out. They'd know better than her what was of value. It wasn't like he'd have many items from her childhood that should be saved. Tess trusted that the organizer she had spoken to on the phone would have a good plan for how to sort through all the junk to find the valuables, if any still existed. Most of it looked like it had come from a flea market, and that was where it would go once the place was cleared out and all the contents sorted.

WHEN SHE ARRIVED BACK at her motel room, she spread her work out on the desktop and leaned back, examining the news clippings and scrapbook she'd found in her father's closet and tackle box.

Janine Marshall had the most extensive coverage in the pages of the scrapbook, including several articles from the *PH Express*, the local newspaper – if you could call it that. As Tess remembered it, the paper was mostly advertising, articles about local businesses masquerading as news and comics.

According to one news article, there had been several 'bad dates' reported among the streetwalkers who haunted the alleys in the downtown area and on the outskirts of town. Maybe one of the Johns had gone beyond the usual roughing-up that sex trade workers had to become inured to. Tess had read so many depressing cases of missing and murdered sex trade workers that she had little hope that Janine would be found alive – if indeed she had been a street prostitute.

Janine had a rough life, according to the archive of information on her in The Missing's database, which Tess had opened so she could search through the articles. Sent to live with her aunt at age eighteen months, she'd gone back and forth between her mother's and her aunt's, depending on how her mother was doing with substance abuse and run-ins for petty crimes. She ran away from her aunt's multiple times, and had been on and off the street.

How had Tess's father known her? Why had he kept such a complete set of clippings of her case? Was it simple curiosity or was it something else?

The notion that her father had known the missing girl worried Tess as she sat in her motel room and stared at the photo, taken from a school yearbook during the last full year she'd attended. Was that the year Tess's father met Janine?

She was a pretty girl with a big smile. Long dark hair parted in the middle, her picture didn't betray her sad story. She looked like any other student that year, fresh-faced and eager to face the grown-up world. Soon after that picture had been taken, she'd died, not even making it through her last year of middle school.

Tess searched the files archived at The Missing and read reports from police and family members about her disappearance. On a cold Friday night in winter, she didn't come home. When she still hadn't called three days later, the police took her disappearance seriously. There had been a door-to-door search in the area, and passed around a picture of Janine among the few homeless youths in town – not that she wasn't already known on the street. She'd been wearing a skimpy jean jacket, a black leather skirt, and a black T-shirt and leggings the night she went missing. Not warm enough for anyone planning on spending any time out on such a cold night.

Search parties had focused their efforts on the forests surrounding Paradise Hill, but no trace of Janine's body was ever found, and eventually the case went cold.

Tess couldn't ask her dad about it now. But she could ask her mother.

SHE GOT on the phone and dialed her mom.

When her mother answered, she sounded distracted.

"What's up, hun? How's Paradise Hill? Same old small town with nothing but bad news?"

"Dad's house is a junk heap. Did you know he was a hoarder?"

There was silence on the line for a few seconds. "I knew he became a bit of a hermit the last few years, but no. Was he a hoarder? Really?"

"Yes, really. You should see the house. It's as bad as anything on the TV shows. I hired a moving company to come and get rid of everything. They have a cleaning service so at least I don't have to deal with the worst of it, but it's going to cost some money to get it in shape to sell. Mrs. Carter said the market around here's really depressed, so even if we get it cleaned up, it probably won't sell. Dad could never sell it. I don't think anything's changed."

"It is what it is," her mother said with a sigh. "I gave up hoping for money from that house years ago. When's the memorial?"

"Just a graveside service, on Monday."

Tess told her about the pastor and what suit she'd chosen, and how she was doing research for her piece on missing girls and women.

"I'm sorry you have to do all this," Tess's mom said. Tess thought she really did sound sorry.

"No, it's okay. It's not like you could do it. And Thad can't do it, so it's me."

"At least you get to do some work on your article."

"There's that," Tess replied. "Hey, I want to ask you something."

"Ask away."

Tess hesitated. "I know it might be hard to talk about, but I met this woman I used to go to school with. She said something that seemed really strange."

"I'm all ears."

"Did you leave Dad because you thought he was involved in Lisa Tate's disappearance?"

There was a silence on the line for a beat.

"No, not really." She sighed audibly. "It wasn't that. It was, well, I felt like it wasn't safe anymore in Paradise Hill. There'd been some stuff happening in the neighborhood – cats being killed and hung in the trees. There were a few disappearances before Lisa, and I thought Paradise Hill was unsafe for you. I wanted to move to Seattle but your dad didn't. He hated the big city, so we agreed to separate."

"You didn't think he was involved?"

"No, of course not, dear. He was away on the road when it happened, so he was never a suspect. But it was creepy and it was far too close for comfort. Lisa lived just two doors down, and the police thought that someone must have been watching her. That meant he could have been watching you as well. There were dead cats hanging in the forest around the neighborhood, even one behind our house. I took that as a bad omen. I wanted to get you and Thad out of there and your dad – well, he hated the thought of living in Seattle. His entire life was spent in Paradise Hill when he wasn't on the road. His friends were all there. His mom. I wanted him to come but he didn't, and we couldn't find a compromise, so it was over."

A sense of relief washed through Tess. Then she remembered the news clippings and scrapbook.

"Do you remember a local girl who went missing back in 1978? Janine Marshall?"

There was a longer pause. "You mean the hooker?"

"She was only thirteen, mom. They're not hookers. They're child victims."

"Of course," her mother replied, sounding tired. "But rumor had it that she was doing it for drug money. What about her?"

"I found something in Dad's closet. It was her obituary and a scrapbook of news clippings about the case. There were other crimes around town in the scrapbook. Arson, robbery. Shootings. Then there was this ring. Some kind of weird gemstone. Kind of brownish-green, but changes to blue when I put it on."

"You mean a mood ring?"

"What's that?"

Tess's mother laughed softly. "Oh, it was a big fad back in the day. We all had them. They change color supposedly based on your mood, but it's really all just body temperature and blood flow."

"Why would Dad have clippings of her death and a scrapbook with all those news stories? Did he have it when you were with him?"

"Not that I know of. I don't think he was much of a news hound but he did want to be a writer at one time. He never had a scrapbook that I know of, but he was gone for long stretches. Who knows what he was doing while he was away?"

"Did he know her? The girl who went missing? Janine?"

"Who can say? She wasn't really our kind of people, if you understand my meaning. She was from the wrong side of the tracks. Your dad was a few years ahead of us back then and was on the football team. He had cheerleaders interested in him. He didn't need street kids, if you get my drift."

"Hmm," Tess said. "I guess he was just interested in the case."

"Must be. He never said anything about it to me – but he always was a quiet, introspective man."

Tess thought her mother sounded a bit breathless, as if the questions were upsetting her, so she decided to dial back. "I had a nice visit with Mrs. Carter and Kirsten. She sends her love."

"You send it right back to her. I haven't seen her for years."

They spoke a bit longer about Kirsten's pregnancy and family and then said goodbye.

Tess sat for a few moments in silence, thinking about her father and how sad it was that he had died sick and alone in a hospice with no family around him. What had happened to him that made him become a hoarder and hermit? Was it really just because of the divorce? Was it his injury?

More importantly, why had he saved the news clippings for all these years?

CHAPTER SEVEN

Tess spent another hour reading through old police reports from the year Janine disappeared, and at about four thirty, her cell rang. When she saw Michael's name in the call display, her heart did a little flip. After debating for a ring or two whether to answer, she picked up her cell. He was as close to a real expert on the issue of missing girls and women as she could get.

"Michael, hello. Thanks for calling."

"Tess, hello. How are you?" he said, his voice deep and warm. "Mom gave me your number and I thought that since we're both in town, we should get together and compare notes. Kirsten tells me you're writing an article for the *Sentinel* on the cold cases from this area."

"I am. You're just the man I'd love to talk to."

"Feel like dinner? We could get something to eat and talk."

"Sounds good. Is there anywhere in Paradise Hill that has decent food? I have no idea where to eat."

"The Tap and Grill has decent steak, if you haven't gone full Seattle and are still a meat eater."

She laughed. "I am. I still like a good steak if I can find it."

"They have decent ribs and, believe it or not, craft beer."

"When should we meet?"

"Six thirty, but if you want, you could come with me to one of the Gilroy cabins. Burned down last night. They found a body in the ruins that might end up being a missing girl from town."

"You mean Melissa Foster?"

"Yes. When the firefighters went in to check if anyone had been inside, they found that the floor had collapsed. There was a space beneath the floor that contained a plastic barrel filled with cement. I don't have to tell you that's a red flag."

"You don't normally fill a plastic barrel with cement."

"Exactly. The floor collapsed and the heat from the fire melted the plastic barrel and cracked the cement. The police were called in to check. They're waiting on the coroner to come by and do a more thorough identification, but they saw enough to do a tentative ID."

"And they think it was Melissa?"

"I've been talking with the chief. Something she was wearing – a t-shirt – suggests it's Melissa."

"I read a police report about the case," Tess said, her heart sinking at the news. "The t-shirt was a Hello Kitty, right?"

"Yes. A pink cat. I'm not familiar with girls' toys, but you're right. It was a Hello Kitty t-shirt."

Despite being familiar with child murders, a sense of horror filled Tess at the idea that someone could take a child, put them through unimaginable horrors before killing them, and then stuff their body into a barrel and fill it with cement.

"So, someone put her in the barrel and buried it in the cellar beneath the cabin?"

"Apparently. We won't have any idea how she died until the medical examiner can do an autopsy, but given that Melissa went missing earlier this year, it's pretty much certain it's her."

"Will they be able to tell when she died, given how long the body's been in the cement?"

"Usually with these cases, the child dies within three hours of being abducted. It's possible it was a family member who accidentally killed her and panicked, then hid the remains, but in my experience and given everything else we know about the case, she was abducted and killed. She didn't run away to stay with a family member, no matter what people say. The coroner will probably find that she was killed soon after she was last seen and has been buried there since the day after she went missing."

"Oh, God…" Tess covered her mouth. "She's been there for five months and no one knew?"

"Apparently, the cabin's been closed all year because of a leaking roof that the owner couldn't afford to get fixed. If the fire hadn't exposed the ground beneath the floor, it might have been missed entirely, but any time you find a large hunk of cement buried somewhere, it's suspicious. I can't tell you the number of bodies encased in cement the FBI has discovered over the years."

"It's common with serial killers," she said, for she'd read practically everything there was about them and had heard about it before. Still, it made her nauseated.

"Killers in general who are hoping to hide the body,"

Michael replied. "Usually, they're discovered because of the smell, but this was hidden until the floor collapsed. It's hard to know how the cabin would catch fire since the power had been turned off, according to the owner. But it gives us some new evidence to track down."

"Such as?"

"The kind of cement. Who had access to that cabin and when. They'll be interviewing people who were renting cabins back in April. New evidence and new suspects means a better chance of finding the killer and closing this case. I thought you might like to tag along with me in an unofficial way. I'm going to the cabin to talk to the detectives involved."

"I'd be allowed to come with you?"

"Off the record, of course, and just as a friend. But if you want to ask questions, I already cleared it with Hank Wallace, the local detective on the case. Just for background. You'll have to wait with the rest of the press to get the official briefing."

"I'd appreciate going with you."

"Okay. Meet me at the cabin. It's easy enough to find. There's an FBI evidence response team going there to do forensic work. They may already be there."

"I want to pick up a cup of coffee first. Do you want one?"

"Black, one sugar. Thanks. The coffee at police stations is notoriously terrible."

"I'll meet you there in fifteen."

Tess got in the car, driving off with the image of the poor little girl in her mind, dead and stuffed in an old plastic barrel encased in cement.

CHAPTER EIGHT

Michael stood a dozen feet away from the burnt-out hulk of the cabin and watched as the forensic team did their work. The cabin was one of the last on the road by the lake, tucked into a thick wood that ended a few feet from shore. The fire marshal's vehicle was parked on the street a few hundred feet away, and a white tent had been set up to cover the barrel of cement and remains from the public's view. Inside, an FBI forensic team was at work collecting evidence.

Michael kept his distance, intending to be as unobtrusive as possible. Neither the local police or the FBI team in charge needed him inserting himself into the case, especially since he was not there in any official capacity.

Tess arrived and parked behind one of the police cars. Michael watched as she walked up the hill to the cabin, thinking how she looked remarkably like the girl he remembered from the last time he saw her at one of Kirsten's baby showers. Tall, fair with long strawberry blonde hair and green eyes, she was pretty in a delicate way.

"Ah, Tess," he said and went right over, extending his hand. They shook and he leaned in close. "Good to see you. Sorry about your dad."

"Thanks," she said, smiling perfunctorily but he could see she was still shaken by the dark circles around her eyes.

"Sorry we're meeting at a crime scene, but I guess that's both our lives, right?" he said, trying to lighten the mood.

"Yes, it is," Tess said and glanced around. "Thanks for inviting me."

"No problem."

Two of the FBI Special Agents walked over to them, most likely interested in meeting Tess. Michael turned to them and gestured towards her.

"Gentlemen, this is Tess McClintock. She's an old friend from Paradise Hill who's currently working as a crime reporter for the *Seattle Sentinel*. I invited her to come by and ask a few questions — off the record of course." He shot Tess a smile. "She's working on a piece about missing and murdered girls in Washington State."

The other two men turned to Tess and one extended his hand.

"Mike told us about you," he said. "Special Agent Dan Barnes and this is my partner, Brent Parker. We're with the task force in Seattle."

Tess shook both men's hands.

"So, this case is hot again? You've taken over from local police?"

"Yes," Barnes replied. "It wasn't very cold anyway. We were still tracking down suspects, but given the nature of the case, it's pretty slow going. No body. No crime scene. Just a missing girl and a lot of statements about the last time anyone saw her. We interviewed all the main suspects in town, but so far, everyone had an alibi and no one really stood out in our minds."

"Shall we take a look?" Barnes pointed to the cabin, which reeked with the stench of charred, wet wood.

"Yes."

Barnes led the way up the steep incline to the cabin. Inside, beneath the floor and under burnt and charred rafters, stood a white tent to cover the forensic team from the elements. It was overcast but so far, there had been no rain.

Michael stopped beside the cabin and Tess joined him, standing by his side.

"What do they think caused the fire?" she asked, peering at the remains of the burned-out cabin.

Michael shrugged, his hands deep in his pockets. "Looks like arson. There's evidence that an accelerant was used."

"Someone deliberately set fire to the cabin?"

"Yes. Which opens up all kinds of interesting possibilities."

"Such as?"

Michael turned to her, his eyebrows raised. "Maybe someone wanted the barrel to be found."

"Who would want it to be found?"

"Someone who knows who did it and has been quiet so far but now wants to expose the killer. Maybe even the killer himself."

"Does that mean he might have an accomplice?"

"Possibly. Sometimes the killer wants to get caught," Michael replied said. "Sometimes they mess up by accident, but sometimes, they mess up on purpose, when they're tired of keeping up a front."

"Do you really think that's the case?" she asked. "Serial

killers go to a lot of trouble to cover up the murders. Why expose it?"

"You have to remember that most serial killers believe they're smarter than the cops. Smarter than the FBI. This killer may have wanted to get the case back in the news. They like the publicity and watching the police and FBI struggle to find them."

"They like the attention," she offered.

"Yes. Many collect the news reports of the case and some even insert themselves into the investigation, take part in searches, attend funerals and offer up tips. Anything to keep the case in the news. It's like they're taunting the police. They find it exciting to be talking to police and the officers having no clue."

Beside him, Tess sighed audibly. "Police must be suspicious of everyone who becomes involved in the case."

Michael nodded. "We film the funerals. We check out all tips. Anyone who comes in with evidence and theories. Who talks to officers at crime scenes."

Down in the cabin, several forensic team members dressed in white protective clothing worked away, collecting samples and inspecting the barrel of cement in which the body of young Melissa had been entombed.

At that moment, the coroner arrived, driving up in a new Volvo station wagon. An older man, he was balding with wire-rimmed round glasses, giving him a nerdy older Harry Potter vibe. Dr. Prosser worked for the local police on the side of his family medicine practice in Paradise Hill.

He walked over to the two FBI Special Agents and spoke to them, then turned to the cabin, walking over to where Michael and Tess stood.

"Dr. Prosser?" Michael said and held out his hand. They shook.

"That's right. And you are?"

"Special Agent Carter, FBI Violent Crimes Against Children task force operating out of Seattle. I'm on vacation but stopped by as I have an interest in this case."

"Good to meet you." He turned to Tess. "And who are you?"

"Tess McClintock. Investigative reporter with the *Seattle Sentinel*. I'm here on a personal matter."

"Your dad was Ron McClintock? I saw him at the hospice before he died. My condolences."

Tess nodded. "Thanks."

Dr. Prosser walked past them and went over to a table where he put on a white protective scene suit and rubber boots, then wrapped black duct tape around the tops of his boots. After that, he pulled up his hood and tightened the string around his face. Finally, he put on protective eyewear and slipped on rubber gloves. He wrapped more black duct tape around the wrists.

He climbed down a ladder into the pit holding the cement block which held Melissa's remains. He had his black kit with him, which contained the tools of his trade. Then, he disappeared behind a white sheet set up to prevent onlookers from seeing what was going on.

It was impossible to know how Melissa died until the coroner did his report and determined the cause of death. It would likely be either strangulation, blunt trauma to the head or blood loss due to being stabbed or shot. If the girl had been lucky, she would have been killed quickly. If any indignities had been done to the body, Michael hoped it would have been done after death, not before. With a child predator, that was the most one could pray for.

While they watched, one of the other forensic team members began snapping photos using a large camera as they opened the cement casing and more of the remains were exposed.

Special Agent Barnes walked over to where Michael and Tess stood.

"From what the local forensic team said, it looks like her body was almost perfectly preserved inside the cement block," he said when he arrived at their side. "Often, the killers don't know how to work with cement and there are air bubbles left that might create cracks and allow the scent of the decaying body to escape and alert people to its presence. If she was put in the barrel soon after death, the body went undetected for three months and it was only the fire that revealed its existence."

"Who do you think did this?" Tess asked. "Set fire to the cabin?"

He shrugged. "Someone might have accidentally or deliberately set the fire. It could have been kids playing with fire in an empty cabin. It may have been a local pyro in the making. Or, it might have been someone who wanted the body to be found."

Michael glanced down to the road below. Whatever the case, news was spreading and there were several cars parked on the street and a half-dozen people standing in a small group at the edge of the barricade tape, watching the police milling around the crime scene.

"Word spreads fast," Michael said, gesturing toward the crowd of people peering up at them. "I forget how it is in a small town like Paradise Hill."

A sudden gust of cold wind blew through the trees. Michael glanced up at the sky as the first drops of rain hit his face.

"Great," he said and pulled up the hood of his jacket. "Just what everyone needs."

Beside them, Barnes smiled. "Good old Washington weather."

The coroner appeared from behind the curtain, his hands covered in what looked like sludge.

"You should come and see this."

CHAPTER NINE

Tess peered closer, wondering what they'd found that would arouse such interest.

While she watched, Special Agent Barnes put on his own protective suit, fastidiously covering himself and taping everything shut. Then he climbed down and joined the coroner behind the curtain.

"Wonder what they found," Tess said, anticipation growing in her.

"Must be something of interest to the case. Something that may be tied to the killer."

Parker stood beside them and waited, apparently not interested in going down to see for himself.

"They got something," Parker said. "We could use a break." He left them and went to stand closer to the cabin. Tess heard him speaking to the coroner and Special Agent Barnes, but his voice was low enough that she couldn't make out exactly what it was.

Parker returned after a moment and nodded to them. "Something in the girl's hand. Looks like a bracelet of some kind. One of those charm bracelets. May be something she had on her person when she was abducted. But if so, the parents didn't report it. She may have picked it up after. Could have been planted. Won't know until we have a closer look at it, but it's something at least."

"Do you think the girl was murdered at the cabin?"

"It's hard to know," Parker said with a shrug. "Given the condition of the cabin, it will be difficult to tell if she was killed here or brought here after. They just found a shovel in the corner of the cellar and a melted plastic pail, which appears to have had cement in it. At a minimum, the body was brought to the cabin for disposal. Whether she was killed here or not will be harder to determine."

Tess drank her coffee but the liquid didn't sit well and she turned to Michael. "I need food."

He nodded. "Let's go."

SHE DROVE behind Michael's Jeep, past the cemetery where her father's family had been buried and where her father would soon be interred. It cast a pall over her and coupled with the house and the missing girl, Tess felt a sense of gloom fill her.

When she arrived at the Tap and Grill, which was a short car ride downtown, it was already dark, the sun having gone down just after six thirty. Michael snagged a booth by a picture window. He sat down and pulled out several files from his briefcase, one of which he opened, showing several photographs of a young girl. Tess recognized the face right away.

"That's Melissa Foster, right?" she said and sat down

across from him, slipping off her coat and turning the picture so that she could see better.

"Yep. I figured you'd be interested."

"Are you working the case? I thought you were on vacation."

"I'm officially on medical leave and vacation, but a coworker asked me to look at the case a few months ago and it's hard not to get involved, considering I'm here. I made a copy for my own personal files."

"I haven't really read much about Melissa. I just started work on this article and have been researching the Seattle area. I haven't expanded to the rest of the state yet, but Paradise Hill is a focus, of course, given Lisa."

Michael nodded and turned a page. "Melissa Foster, went missing three months ago. Family didn't report it for a full day, so the trail was already cold by the time the police were notified of her disappearance. Sketchy family, father recently out of prison for trafficking, mother an addict."

He flipped through the file. "Last she was seen was at the park near her house around nine at night. Was supposed to have been watched by an older sister, but she must have been busy with her own friends and lost track of her. Parents thought she might have gone to play with her best friend, but she hadn't seen her after the park. Local police have been handling it, but called us in."

"What was a ten-year-old doing playing in a park on Saturday night, and why wouldn't someone have checked to see if she was home – or somewhere?"

Michael shrugged. "We used to play outside when we were kids as a group, but we had to be home at nine sharp and our parents were waiting, watching the clock. In the summer, it's still light at nine so I guess the kids were just on their way home the last time she was seen. Reports say there were a lot of kids at the playground and she was one of the last to leave. Never showed up at home."

"That's terrible," Tess said. "The mother is a drug addict?"

"Yeah. Supposedly just out of rehab and relapsed badly. The girl went between the mom, the aunt, and her best friend on a regular basis when the mom was having problems. Dad was out of town for work. Mom had been on a bender. When she sobered up, she started looking around and couldn't remember if the daughter had gone to the aunt's or the friend's for the weekend."

"Would she have run away? Was there anyone in the family she would go to?"

"None found so far. No one saw her after nine on Saturday night. Not a trace. Reminds me of when Lisa went missing."

"Yeah, actually," Tess said, "I wanted to talk to you about that. I've been reading up on old case files that are archived on The Missing's website. You and Curt were questioned."

"We were. That's part of the reason I went into law enforcement."

"I would have thought it might turn you off. You were treated badly by today's standards. Interrogated without your parents present…"

"We were. Luckily, we were innocent and the cops finally turned to other less savory characters, but it didn't matter. The case went cold."

"Who were the main suspects?"

"We always look at family first. They're most likely to kill a child. Sometimes, it's accidental and the parent tries to cover it up, or a punishment that's gone too far. Sometimes, parents are depressed and plan on killing themselves and their kids but don't follow through. Lisa's brother and father were out of town. Her mother was working."

"God, I don't know how you can do it," Tess said, examining Michael closely. "Doesn't it bother you to read this stuff every day? I have nightmares and I just do research. I don't deal with ongoing cases. It must be really stressful."

"It's important work," Michael said and closed the file. "Someone's gotta do it. I studied this in college and I feel like it's my calling. I know that sounds corny, but…"

"It doesn't sound corny at all. It sounds like you're doing exactly what you always wanted. You're lucky."

He shrugged and took a sip of his beer. "Anyway, as far as suspects went, her dad couldn't have gotten back in town and killed her and then got back to where he was seen the night that she went missing. They checked a local known sex offender but he was at work as well, and had been all night until late. Then he went with his girlfriend to a party." Michael shook his head and opened the menu.

The waitress came over and Tess finally opened her own menu and searched the options. She ordered a steak, salad, and baked potato and watched while Michael ordered the same.

When the waitress left, Michael turned back to her.

"Someone was most likely watching her and when he saw her alone, he took her." He shrugged, almost helplessly. "Honestly, there were a few suspects the police liked for it but they could never get any evidence that a DA would take to prosecution, so they were never picked up."

"Who?"

"A long-haul trucker who was in and out of town, who had a few allegations of trying to pick up underage prostitutes. He's dead now, so even if he was the perp, there'd be no justice."

Tess frowned. "A long-haul trucker?" she said, an uneasy feeling in her gut. "My father was a long-haul trucker for a decade before he hurt his back. I wonder if my dad knew him."

"Name's Grant McDonald if you want to check."

Tess nodded. "I will."

"There was a construction crew in the area at the time that had a guy arrested for approaching children in playgrounds. Had an alibi. They checked the rest of the extended family members, but nothing. Detective who had the case said they talked to pretty much every adult male in town and came up with nothing but a few perverts who had alibis. Nothing to really follow up, and since they had no body, there was no evidence. The house was swept for prints, but nothing came up. Whoever took her was smart enough not to leave any evidence."

Tess sighed. "It sounds so much like Lisa. All my life I felt like it was my fault that Lisa died. If I had only shut Kirsten up." She looked up at Michael to see his expression. Was he disgusted with her and Kirsten for being so petty and teasing Lisa until she left and went home? His face was unreadable, so if he felt that, he didn't show it.

"If I had tried harder to make her come back, she might still be alive. We figured she'd be safe at home. She stayed alone sometimes, with the doors locked until her brother or her mom came home. We never thought she'd be abducted."

"Don't beat yourself up," Michael replied and placed his hand over hers briefly. "If we hadn't let you guys sleep out in the tent, we could have stepped in and stopped the catfight, and maybe she'd have stayed. But we were more interested in getting stoned than being responsible."

She smiled at him, thankful that he didn't blame her.

"Anyway, I'm sure you can interview George Martin, the detective who had the case. He still lives in Paradise Hill. If you want, I can introduce you, grease the wheels a bit."

"Thanks," Tess replied. "That would be helpful. I remember him. He talked to us the next day. I remember him asking us if we had gone anywhere else, maybe near one of the rivers, suggesting that maybe something bad happened to Lisa and we were afraid to tell anyone. He really tried to give us an opportunity to confess. My mom and Mrs. Carter were there with us. I don't know why they interviewed you two alone without your parents."

"We were more likely suspects than you girls. Two teenage boys babysitting three girls and one goes missing? That's the first place I'd look. There have been cases where a male babysitter has sexually assaulted a child, killed them by accident, and then covered it up, pretending that the child went missing. Several cases I've researched before, as a matter of fact."

"I had no idea the extent of child sexual abuse until I started researching this for the article. Frankly, I've had trouble sleeping ever since."

Michael nodded knowingly. "Welcome to my world."

At that, the waitress brought out their salads and placed them in front of them. When she left, Tess removed the paper napkin from her cutlery and began eating.

"It must have been hard to deal with the task force, considering you have young kids."

He exhaled audibly. "I think I got over the shocked-and-appalled phase a few years ago, and moved into the numb-to-it-all phase. Sometimes, I come across a case that's just so plainly evil I have problems sleeping. As a father, I can't," he said and shook his head, "Can't imagine – a parent, or anyone for that matter, harming a child. But it happens all too frequently. There are thousands and thousands of men actively looking for children to have sex with. It's like a disease."

They ate in silence for a moment, and Tess imagined they were both recalling the particularly horrible cases they'd read about. Tess had been shocked by what she'd read when she had started her research for the article.

It wasn't that Tess didn't know about the problem. She'd studied social science along with journalism and knew about child abuse in a general sense, but she had often thought that sexual abuse was what sociologists called a "moral panic." Moral panics occurred when an issue got blown out of proportion compared to its reality by people fearing for the moral fabric of their social world. It was usually due to some other factor such as bad economic times or rapidly changing social mores.

But child sexual abuse and child trafficking for prostitution were not moral panics by any means. If anything, their incidences were under-reported. Both were far more extensive than Joe Public realized.

They talked a bit about their lives since Tess had moved out of Paradise Hill and Michael went to Quantico to become an FBI special agent. Then, talk turned to the graveside service.

The waitress brought the rest of their food and they focused on eating and talking about her father. Tess was unsure whether to ask him about the other case – the case of Janine and her father's saving the news clipping and obituary.

She thought she'd picked his brain enough for one night, and was embarrassed to ask him about it.

But she couldn't let it go.

When they finished their meals, she leaned forward and looked down at the table, keeping her voice soft so the people at nearby tables couldn't hear her.

"There's something else I wanted to ask you about," she started.

"Sure," Michael said, folding his hands on the table, mimicking her posture, a smile on his face. "Ask away."

"What would you think about a man saving news clippings about a young woman's death and her obituary for four decades? Plus, practically every violent crime and case of arson in town?"

Michael frowned. "Someone you know?"

She lifted her shoulder, her face heating in embarrassment. "My father. I found a scrapbook and some clippings in his closet. I thought it was weird."

"What girl?"

"Janine Marshall."

"I know that case," Michael said, perking up. "A really old cold case. Never found a body. Police thought she ran away, got caught up in the sex trade."

"Yes," Tess said. "I asked my mother if my dad knew the girl, but she said no. Janine was apparently from 'the wrong side of the tracks.'"

Tess watched Michael's expression change from curious to nonchalant, as if he was forcing his expression to be innocuous.

"I wouldn't worry. Maybe he knew the girl. Maybe he was interested in police business. It doesn't in itself mean anything."

"So, what do you think happened?" she asked. "To Janine?"

He leaned back in his chair, holding his beer in his hand and running his fingers over the raised logo of the beer company.

"Every year there are hundreds of thousands of child abductions. Most of those are noncustodial parents or other family members taking kids without letting the custodial parent know, and most of them come home safely. Nationwide, only about a hundred and fifteen each year are stranger abductions, but it adds up. Over forty years, that's a lot of missing kids taken by strangers."

Tess visibly shivered. "It makes me feel sick to my stomach."

"It's difficult to read about and deal with the families. We feel a real pressure to work a case really hard to find and recover the child before anything happens."

"How often do you rescue children from their kidnappers?"

"Not often enough." Michael took a sip of his beer and saw that it was empty. He held it out. "Want another?"

Tess smiled but shook her head. "No, but thanks. I have a long day ahead of me tomorrow. I just found out that my father was a hoarder. I hired a cleaning crew to come tomorrow to help me dig him out."

"Really?" he said. His expression was surprised. "An honest-to-God hoarder? What did he hoard?"

She shrugged. "He collected stuff from flea markets. I don't know if there's any kind of theme to it. Mostly junk. Old clocks. Signs from old gas stations. Dishes. Strange lamps. Clocks. Clothes – so many clothes that I know he never wore, because they still had tags on them. What would make him do that? I mean, I understand it's because of depression, but it's strange that he'd become a hoarder."

"Collecting and owning things – any things – must have made him feel better. Maybe that was why he kept the news clippings for Janine – a way of holding on to something of her after she died."

"But if he didn't even know her…"

"Maybe he did." He shrugged. "A lot of people in town would have known her. Students in her classes at school. Her neighbors."

Tess smiled sadly and exhaled. "I better go. I'm meeting the crew over at my dad's early in the morning."

They both chipped in to pay the bill and then Michael walked with Tess to the parking lot and over to her car.

"If you want to talk about any cases, I'm glad to offer what advice I can. I can't reveal anything that isn't in the public record, but I can help you understand the whole process if you need it."

"That sounds great," Tess said and opened her car door. "I'll call you if I have any questions."

Michael extended his hand. "It was good to see you again, Tess. Good to see you did well for yourself. Paradise Hill can be a hard place to escape."

"I had no choice in the matter. I didn't want to leave but my mom did. Were you aware that people thought my mother left because she thought my dad killed Lisa?"

"What?"

"Yes," Tess said, recounting what Andrea at the motel said to her.

"That's weird. They interviewed every adult male in the town, but your dad was never a suspect that I could see.

That's probably just gossip because of the separation coming so soon after Lisa's disappearance."

"That's what my mom said, but it shocked me when Andrea said it. I didn't know what to think for a while. Then, I found that news clipping and wondered if my dad wasn't a secret serial killer or something." Tess laughed nervously.

Michael shook his head, a smile on his face. "No, Tess. Your dad wasn't a secret serial killer."

"How do you know? You know that old saying – 'Who knows what evil lurks in the hearts of men?'"

Michael shook his head. "I spent a lot of time going over the evidence in the case, and your dad was never a suspect. Never."

"Phew!" Tess said and wiped her brow dramatically. "I feel better already. Sometimes I have too good of an imagination."

Michael smiled. "Well, the offer is open. Call me any time."

She got in the car, glad to see him and have someone inside the law enforcement world she could use for advice and information for her article.

She drove back to the motel, happy that she'd had dinner with him. His words had allayed some of the fear she'd felt about that news clipping.

It meant nothing after all.

CHAPTER TEN

H e knew it was a risk, but he took it anyway.

There were more important things than always feeling safe. Like scratching an itch – his itch to see something happening with the case. What he did would likely not lead them to solve the case, but it would stir things up. People would once more talk about the poor girl who went missing back in April … Only now, they'd all express how horrible it was, poor thing, murdered by some psychopath.

He could see their faces as the women covered up their mouths in shock when they heard the grisly details and the men shook their heads in dismay. There would be renewed interest in the killer and who among them could be guilty. Of course, no one would think of him. No one ever did. He was too clean cut, too responsible, too quiet, too polite. He had too good of a family.

He was invisible.

Which was just the way he liked it. Their failure to

suspect him gave him so much satisfaction. It proved that they were stupid and he was smart.

The FBI and cops often watched crime scenes to scope out the gawkers because killers often like to watch them work the crime scenes. It gave them a thrill. It really did, and he could attest to it. He'd visited pretty much every crime scene several times. No one questioned it, for he was above suspicion. His camouflage was good.

He stood with the other gawkers at the bottom of the hill and watched the FBI forensic team work. It was better than staying home and watching old episodes of *Caught on Camera* or playing *Grand Theft Auto* while he waited for something to happen.

A half-dozen people stood with him and he knew them all: Cathy from the marina, who filled up boat gas tanks and rented out slips. She was a wacky lady who loved to gossip about other people's business. Old Man Reynolds, a Vietnam War vet, had driven up in his beat-up Volkswagen, which looked to be held together with rope and duct tape. He stood right up at the perimeter tape and smoked cigarettes with no filter, watching the white-suited technicians go inside and climb up out of the fire-razed pit.

Then there were the MacDonald twins – Tweedledee and Tweedledum, also known as Tim and Bart MacDonald. Both of them a bit slow and unable to do much besides bag groceries down at the store. There were two other people he recognized, but they weren't nearly as interesting. Mrs. Peterson who spent most of her time walking her little poodle, whom she was now holding in her arms as if to protect her from the horrible truth of the case. Beside her stood her pot-bellied husband, Joe, with wispy white hair and round glasses that made him look like a college professor.

He stood beside Old Man Reynolds and lit up his own cigarette.

"What's goin' on?" he asked, glancing over to the old man. "Fire?"

"More than a fire. Found little Melissa."

"Dead?"

Old Man Reynolds gave him a withering look. "Did ya think they'd find her alive?" He shook his head and turned back. "Buried in cement. What kind of world do we live in?"

The old man made the sign of a cross.

"Buried in cement?" he repeated, as if dumbstruck by the very idea. "That's sick."

"Darn tootin' it's sick. What kind of bastard kills a sweet girl like Melissa and then puts her body in a barrel and fills it up with cement? What kind of monster?"

He shook his head, commiserating, all the while secretly gloating that *he* was that kind of monster. He took what he wanted and did what he wanted with it. So far, no one could stop him.

"Lots of evil in this world," he replied. He took another drag on his cigarette. "Very sad," he added, making sure to contort his face into a suitably empathetic expression.

They stood there in silence, watching as an FBI special agent wearing a blue windbreaker walked down to the perimeter tape where they stood.

"Hey, folks," he said. "I know people are curious about what's going on. This is just to let you know we'll be holding a press conference in a few hours to update folks on what we've found."

"Is it true you found little Melissa?" Cathy asked, stepping closer to the special agent, whose expression did not change.

"We did find a body, but won't be saying more until we notify next of kin. You can understand."

"Someone said it was her," Tweedledum said.

"You'll have to wait for confirmation until the family has been notified. I'm sorry, but that's all I can say right now. I'm going to have to ask you all to move to another location. We have a truck about to pull in the driveway and we need this space clear."

Sure enough, he turned and saw a large four-by-four stake truck driving toward them. On the back was a winch. They were going to hoist the block of cement onto the truck's bed and haul it to the police station.

Like the others, he stepped back while the agent removed the barricade tape that blocked off the driveway and waved the truck inside.

He watched as the truck drove up the driveway and then did a three-point turn in the space beside the cabin so that the winch was facing the interior. He was curious about how they'd manage to lift the cement block up onto the bed of the truck. Rumor had it that the block of cement had broken in half from the heat, and that meant the corpse had been exposed. That was likely how they identified Melissa.

It would be nasty.

There was no doubt that five months of confinement in the cement would have not been nice for the body. There would have been considerable putrefaction. He did not envy the technicians their job. Even if they were experts and had worked numerous cases of a similar nature, it would be difficult because of the girl's age.

Even that notion gave him some satisfaction.

Look on my handiwork and be dismayed!

If he drove a few of them into a nervous breakdown, he wouldn't be unhappy.

Speaking of nervous breakdowns, rumor down at the gas station was that Michael Carter had one when his wife of eight years left him and took his boys. She'd applied for sole custody, claiming that Michael worked too much and was away too often on an unpredictable schedule to have joint custody. That, along with a difficult case, supposedly led to Michael taking a leave of absence to recover from PTSD.

It gave him immense pleasure to imagine the pretty boy being broken. Michael was always so popular, a great athlete and student, he had been one of the stars of the high school football teams. It had always been Michael Carter this, Michael Carter that…

He was, in other words, everything a mother could want in a son. He couldn't stand the man.

Guilt about Lisa and his role in her disappearance still plagued Carter, so the story went. If only he hadn't allowed the girls to sleep outside he could have intervened when the girls were fighting and made sure Lisa didn't leave into the gaping maw that awaited – *him*.

But boys being boys, he was more interested in getting stoned than fulfilling his responsibilities.

Michael would feel guilt for a lifetime.

That made him feel superior. He never felt guilt. He took what he wanted and damn the torpedoes. So far, he'd only been caught for pissy stuff.

They had no idea…

He would so enjoy the next few weeks, as the police ran around like chickens with their heads cut off. There were a few tidbits of evidence he could sprinkle around town that would send them on the wrong path.

That would be so much *fun*.

The crowd of people moved back to their previous vantage point after the special agent replaced the barricade tape and went back up to the house. He wished he could be right there, watching and listening to the technicians as they worked to get the block of cement and body up onto the flatbed. He'd learned a great deal in the past few years and he believed he had perfected his technique.

His most recent mission was proof of that.

He hadn't left a single clue behind that could tie him to the murder. Not one. Even exposing the body and the location where he'd hidden it wouldn't bring them any closer to him. Everything he used was typical material you could buy at any Walmart or hardware store. He hadn't bought any of it. It was all the property of the new owner of the cabins. The man was such an incompetent, he probably hadn't even done a proper inventory of the materials he bought and were stocked in the shed behind the rental office.

He knew where everything was, how much of it was left, and had the keys to access it any time he wanted and no one knew a thing.

It was almost too easy.

Almost.

LATER THAT NIGHT, he couldn't settle down. He had an itch he needed to scratch, but right now, hunting would have to do. He didn't want to take another girl so soon after Melissa. At least, not in Paradise Hill.

Instead, he took his bike to the woods behind Tess's motel and hid it in the brush just off the service road. Then he set up his blind and waited.

She drove up about nine, getting out of her Honda and then entering her room. He saw the interior of the room only briefly, when she cracked the curtains in the main picture window after she got inside. Through his scope, he saw her pretty face as she glanced left and right as if checking to see if he was out there watching her. He knew she had no idea, but for some reason, she felt uneasy.

Maybe her sixth sense had picked up his presence.

Her blindsight.

Then, nothing. The light stayed on for about an hour, then flicked off. For another hour, he sat there in the blind, wondering when she'd go to sleep. He hadn't had a smoke for two hours and his lungs were starting to itch with need, so he decided to leave soon if nothing else of interest happened.

He could tell she was watching television; there was a flickering blue glow behind the curtains instead of the brighter yellow room lights. Then, around eleven, she turned off the television and must have gone to sleep. He could have gone home at that point, but he wanted to walk by her room. Check out her car. He weighed the risk. It would look suspicious if he was seen walking around the motel so late at night, but he could make an excuse of some kind if caught. He was going through trash looking for recycling. That would work.

He packed up his gear, tucked the scope and night vision glasses into his rucksack, and tucked it in a recess beside a fallen log. After covering it with leaves so that no one would find it, he walked back down the hill to the motel parking lot, hopping the fence. Then, certain that everyone was asleep, he walked nonchalantly along the building, glad he was wearing good-quality rubber-soled boots so that his footsteps were quiet. Almost silent. A wind had picked up, and what remained of the dry leaves on the trees behind the building rustled in the breeze.

It would help mask his presence.

He walked up to Tess's Honda and glanced casually inside, but it was clean. A box of tissues was perched between the two front seats. An empty coffee cup sat in the holder beside the gear shift. In the back was a file box, probably containing stuff from her father's house, if he was to guess.

He didn't know what he had hoped to see inside – something personal. Something he could use to construct a profile of her as a woman and as a person. People liked to think that psychopaths were heartless. He knew he was one, no question. He'd done the online quiz and if there was a scale for psychopathy, he'd be at the far end. Psychopaths, the experts said, depersonalized the people they harmed. They had to because if they truly thought their victims were humans with names and lives, they wouldn't be able to hurt them. But that was just plain wrong. He didn't give a crap about them. None of them. They were all just lives to consume. He liked to know as much about them as possible while he choked the life out of them. It made them all the more valuable.

He kept little bits of them as trophies, but he kept more than just physical mementos of his victims. He had a mental construct of each of them that he drew on, enjoying the fact that he owned them. He'd own them forever.

Before this was over, he thought he might want to own her as well, but at that moment, he wasn't sure if she was going to be worth the effort. Still, he enjoyed the hunt even if he didn't catch anything.

There was nothing in the car worth breaking into it to retrieve. What he wanted was something so personal, so much of a treasure, that it would be painful to the family if they knew he had it. That pleased him – the thought that they'd cry when they found out he had that one thing. When he got one of their girls, he took from them because he despised them. Their weakness. How easy it was to steal away their most precious possessions.

He walked past the car up to the small walkway that fronted the rooms and stopped outside her door. While the wind served to hide the sound of his footsteps, it also prevented him from hearing anything from inside. He stepped as close as he could to the door and listened, but heard nothing. No television, no radio. No sound at all.

He sighed internally and continued walking the length of the motel, going to the trash can at the end and taking a cursory look inside just in case anyone saw him and became curious – or alarmed.

Sure enough, just as he got back to Tess's room for one last look, a figure stepped out from the end of the wing. The light was bad, so he couldn't see the man's face, and he was glad he'd pulled up the collar on his turtleneck so that whoever it was couldn't see his either.

"Hey!" the man shouted.

At that, he ran, sprinting toward the trees, jumping the fence and hoping that his years of biking would give him the edge if the man decided to chase him. He glanced back over his shoulder to see if the man was following, and dammit, he was. Not nearly as fast, but there he was jumping the fence. He obviously wasn't as agile and struggled to get over.

He didn't have time to search for his rucksack because the man was gaining on him.

"Hey, you! Stop!" the man yelled.

Cursing to himself, he took off, preferring to leave his

rucksack to be found than for him to be confronted or possibly caught by whoever it was chasing him.

He ran and ran, easily increasing the distance between them, until finally he came to his bike and hopped on driving down the back roads bordering Paradise Hill.

He'd escaped, but only just. It had been five months since he'd gone hunting. He'd taken too big a risk, and now he'd have to lie low for a few days to see what came of his close call with the man from the motel.

He wouldn't make that mistake again. If he took Tess – and he still wasn't sure if she was worth the effort – he'd make sure it was a clean catch.

No witnesses.

No evidence left behind.

He'd perfected his technique over the years, and he was not going to change now.

CHAPTER ELEVEN

Tess was woken soon after she fell asleep by a knock at the door of her motel room.

She sat straight up in a panic, her heart beating rapidly. The room was almost pitch black, the only light coming from the clock radio on the bedside table. Had she been dreaming?

The pounding came again, and she realized there was someone at the door. Swallowing back her fear, she stood up, pulled on her sweater and went to the curtains. When she glanced out, she saw two people – Andrea with a jacket pulled tightly around her, and a tall man wearing a baseball cap and a sheepskin jackets.

"Yes?" she said, unwilling to open the door.

"Are you okay?" Andrea asked, pointing to the door, gesturing for Tess to open it. "We need to talk to you."

Tess hesitated, not really wanting to open it. She finally relented, because it was Andrea.

"What is it?" she asked, standing in her nightgown and sweater. She turned on the overhead light. "Who are you?"

"Sorry to bother you, ma'am," the man said. "I'm Paul Douglass. I'm staying in the room down a ways. I just happened to look out my window and saw a man outside your door. He stood beside your car and was looking inside, and then he stood real close to your room. He was strange, wearing camo with his face covered. I wanted to make sure you were okay."

"I'm fine," Tess said. "I was sleeping and didn't hear anything."

"I chased him and found this," the man said and held up a backpack.

"What is it?"

"Looks like spying equipment. There's some night vision glasses, a scope of some kind. Plus a hunter's portable blind."

"Maybe he was hunting in the woods and came to the motel looking for someone?" Andrea offered, glancing between Tess and Paul.

The man shook his head. "No, he ran when I called out to him. He didn't want to get caught."

Tess nodded, unsure of what to think. "What should we do?"

"I'm calling the police. I'll turn this over to them – maybe they can find the owner. Give him a warning about hanging around hotel rooms."

"Thanks. Do you think it's safe to stay here?"

Andrea waved her hand. "The doors have double locks. I'm sure you'll be okay."

Tess forced a smile. "Thanks for letting me know."

She closed the door and stood in the entry for a moment, frowning as she thought about someone lurking around her door. In truth, she wished they had let her sleep, because now she'd be creeped out and would probably have a hard time falling back to sleep.

She went to the small kitchenette area with the microwave, coffee maker, and bar fridge, and took out a bottle of water. There was nothing to do now but turn on the television and watch late news. There'd be repeats of the earlier news show and she hoped it would bore her so much, she'd be able to fall back to sleep.

THE NEXT MORNING, the cleaners showed up early. Tess had only barely managed to wake up and get ready before a call came from the manager to let her know the cleaners were waiting outside her father's house.

She yawned and checked her watch. It was only seven thirty. She thought she had fallen asleep sometime after one in the morning. That meant she'd slept for six and a half hours, which was good, considering the interruption the previous night.

"I'm so sorry. I thought you said eight. I'll be right there."

"That's okay. They're a little eager to get to work," the manager said. "They get paid by the project so the sooner they get done, the earlier they get off for the day."

"I'll be there in ten."

"I'll let them know."

Tess ordered a coffee at the coffee shop on her way out of the motel. As she waited for her coffee, Tess noticed Serena Hammond, who stared at Tess quite intently while she stacked dishes in a dishpan. Selective mutism wasn't a common anxiety disorder. Tess had read about it when taking a psych class in college, but she'd never met anyone with it.

After she got her cup of takeout coffee, Tess drove to her

dad's house. When she arrived, the crew of three workers – two women and an older man – were leaning against their truck, smoking. They stood up straighter and the older of the two women threw her cigarette to the ground and stamped it out with her foot.

Tess parked and walked up to them. "Sorry you had to wait. Your boss said eight."

"No, our apologies," the man said. "I'm Grant Masterson. This is Elaine, my wife, and Kallie, our daughter. We thought you were living here and wouldn't mind us getting started earlier."

"Oh, I couldn't live here. Come on in, but hold your nose because it stinks inside. I took out the worst-smelling food that was rotting in the refrigerator but there's still trash in there that's festering."

"Don't worry," Grant said with a rueful chuckle. "We're used to it. We clean the grease traps out at the restaurant. We're used to a bad stink. Have these to help." He fished into a bag and pulled out a portable mask. He handed Tess one and she accepted it gratefully.

"Thanks," she said, holding it up to her face and pulling the straps over her head. "I'll need this."

For the rest of the morning, the crew began the process of de-junking Tess's father's house. They went through each room and then decided on a course of action, working on one room at a time, starting with the kitchen. They sorted everything into trash, items that could be sold or given to charity, and stuff they couldn't categorize. Tess would have to go through those items and decide for herself whether to keep them or throw them away.

Her father's junk looked like it came from flea markets he'd visited over the years. Many of the items still had the sale tags on, with the price and sometimes even the date. He must have spent hours and hours visiting local flea markets and garage sales, collecting other people's junk. Then he sat alone among the junk and watched an old color television from Tess's childhood. He didn't buy himself new appliances or electronics. He kept the old ones and spent his money on things he never used.

What a sad end to his seemingly lonely and miserable existence.

A FEW HOURS LATER, Grant came out of the back of the house, a cardboard banker's box in his arms. "You might want to see these," Grant said, his mask pulled up onto his forehead. "I found it in the rafters above the hall closet. Looks illegal."

Tess frowned and took the box from Grant. She sat on the sofa, where she'd pushed aside a pile of blankets and old clothes. Moving the junk on the coffee table out of the way, she set the box down and gingerly opened the lid.

Inside was a collection of print pornography.

It wasn't just your ordinary run-of-the-mill porn featuring young women in various poses, stark naked and doing all manner of things to each other or to men. Tess had seen quite a lot of that in her time working the crime beat researching sex crimes. This was much darker.

Women bound and gagged, fear in their eyes.

Barely legal girls wearing school uniforms in various states of undress, and at the bottom of the pile, even worse. Foreign language magazines with images of children naked.

She flipped through one of the magazines, but closed it when she came to a particularly troubling image of a girl and an adult man. It was explicit. In addition to the magazines, there was a file folder containing Polaroids. Those were the worst – the magazines looked somewhat posed and artificial, but the Polaroids were all too real and explicit. Adult men and small children.

The bile rose in Tess's throat, so she closed the folder and sat for a moment, breathing in deeply to try to counter her nausea. She shoved the file back into the box and closed the lid, her heart beating faster.

"Should I call the police?" she asked when Grant came back into the room. "There's child pornography in there."

"I would. I mean, your father's dead but they might want to know that he was buying this stuff." He pointed at the box. "It must be pretty old. There's a lot of dust on the top of the box. It hasn't been opened in years, I'd wager. No finger marks besides my own and yours."

"Why would he keep it?"

Grant shrugged. "He was a hoarder. They keep everything."

Tess decided to call Michael. He'd know what she should do.

"I'll call a friend from the FBI. He works in the Violent Crimes Against Children task force."

"You mean Michael Carter?"

Tess nodded. "Yes, he's back in town for Kirsten's delivery."

"I remember Michael. He was a great football player. Quarterback for the Spartans. One of the all-time scorers."

Tess smiled. "He was."

Grant went back to work, leaving Tess alone with the box of pornography. She stared at the offending box. You didn't just happen upon child porn, that much she knew. You had to seek it out to find it – especially print porn. It was guarded by pedophiles, passed around by small groups of people who trusted each other and sent their materials in plain brown manila envelopes with no return address. For her father to have print child porn, he must have gone looking for it.

That thought made her sick. Was her father a pedophile? Some of the porn was violent, but that had involved older women who looked to be past the age of consent. The fact that the lid had gathered a thick layer of dust suggested he hadn't opened the box for a long time. Maybe he'd been into it at one time but stopped?

Her mind worked hard to find some way of excusing her father's behavior. He'd never touched her in an inappropriate way – ever. He was always aloof, gone for a week or two at a time when he was doing long-haul trucking. When he was at home, he was friendly if somewhat distant, but he never abused them or even raised his voice. It didn't fit with the man she knew – but then again, neither did the hoarding.

She took out her cell phone and entered Michael's number. When it connected, she bit her lip, wondering how to bring up the matter. Embarrassment filled her at the thought that her father had child porn in his possession, but she needed to talk to someone about it.

Michael answered on the third ring.

"Tess," he said, and she could hear the pleasure in his voice. "I was just going to call you. I heard from my friend at the police station that there was a prowler around your motel last night. Are you okay?"

"I'm fine. The night clerk and another customer woke me up to check on me. The customer chased the man away and found a backpack with hunting stuff."

"I checked it out. We can talk about it if you want."

"I'm fine, really," Tess said.

"Is that why you called me?"

"No. I found something at my dad's house that I wanted to talk to you about, given your job with the FBI."

"Ask away. Anything I can do to help. Can you talk on the phone or do you want to meet?"

"Can you come over? I'd really like you to see it and give me your advice."

"Sure," he said and hesitated for a moment. "I'm just down at the coffee shop doing some reading. I'll be by in a few minutes.

"Thanks," Tess said and ended the call.

She slumped back on the sofa and glanced around at the piles of junk. It would take days to sort through everything. She yawned, feeling overwhelmed. Would she ever be able to finish? Tired and defeated before she'd even started, Tess worried that she'd never get through it all. She realized she was still in a kind of emotional shock.

For the next fifteen minutes, Tess tried to work at clearing away the junk on the sofa and coffee table so Michael would have somewhere to sit when he arrived. Old magazines were stacked in piles on the coffee table next to old newspapers; some of them were still wrapped in plastic to protect them from the rain, never read. Blankets – knit, crocheted, and velour – covered the old sofa, which was threadbare beneath the covers. Tess didn't want to even touch them. They looked dusty and had cat hair woven into the fabric.

Had her father owned a cat?

Tess got up and checked around, looking for a cat food dish or litter box. What else would account for all the cat hair she was now finding in tufts mixed with dust bunnies under the furniture and in the corners?

She couldn't find any recognizable cat dish and there was no litter box but there was a bag of cat food in a cupboard. Perhaps he'd had a cat in the past. She took out her cell and called over to Mrs. Carter's house.

"Hi, Tess. What's up?"

"Sorry to bother you, but did my father have a cat?"

"Not that I know of," Mrs. Carter replied. "He liked cats, but I don't think he actually had a cat live with him. Why?"

"There's a lot of cat hair in the house and a bag of cat food in a cupboard. I can't tell if he had a cat dish; maybe he used his own dishes. There's no litter box so he didn't have a house cat."

"He did make a point of feeding the strays," Mrs. Carter added. "Maybe he took one in recently that I didn't know about. He tended to keep to himself."

"The expiration date on this bag of cat food suggests he bought it recently. It doesn't expire for months."

"That's curious. I didn't talk much to him in the last year. For all I know, he had a cat and I never saw it. Maybe it was his cat that the kids killed?"

"Who can say? Unless someone comes forward to report a missing cat that matches the one the police took down, we'll never know. Why don't you come by tonight for supper?"

"That sounds nice," Tess said. "Will Michael be there?"

"He will. I thought you two could talk shop."

"I'm sure we will, but I'm also sure he shouldn't. He's supposed to be on leave."

"You know Michael. It's his life."

They said goodbye and Tess ended the call. She hoped the magazines weren't evidence that her father had been a pedophile, but there were only a few options possible.

The boxes had been stacked in the rafters above the hallway. A half-dozen banker's filing boxes filled with old bills and credit card statements took up the narrow space. Inside were bank statements, and other receipts. He'd hoarded those, too. You were supposed to save seven years' worth of banking information for tax purposes in case the IRS audited you, but these boxes contained records going back twenty-five years in some cases.

Her father just could not let go of things. She sat with one of the filing boxes and flipped through the files, looking for any important documents. The rest she'd put in storage somewhere – she might need the documents if her father hadn't filed his taxes. While she was going through a file of receipts, she found one for a storage unit her father had rented five years earlier. East Washington Storage Ltd. had a facility on the outskirts of Paradise Hill. The receipt said he'd bought the contents of the unit unseen at auction and had a five-year lease for it, paid in full, expiring later that year.

What a strange thing to do.

It was one more space she'd have to clean.

The list of contents for the storage unit included a bed frame, some fishing equipment, old car batteries, electrical cords, a cement mixer and a few shovels. There were also sealed boxes of unknown contents.

Tess frowned. Why would her father buy the contents of an old abandoned storage unit? She slipped the receipt into her bag, intending to visit the business when she had a chance to see if there was any information on who had owned the unit before her dad bought the contents. Although there was no way to tell what was in the boxes referenced in the sales order slip, perhaps the box with the magazines had been in the storage unit when he bought the contents.

There was no way of knowing, but Tess wanted to find

out why he had them and whether he had bought them or simply inherited them.

She heard a car door slam and went to the front door. Michael was just walking up the sidewalk. She hoped he could help her figure out her father's involvement in the Janine Marshall case, if any.

One thing was clear to her. She hadn't known her father.

Not at all.

CHAPTER TWELVE

Michael had been surfing the internet when Tess called, ruminating about Melissa Foster, so going to the house to check out what she found would give him an excuse to pull himself out of the case. He shouldn't become involved, on doctor's orders, but he was helpless to stop.

The preliminary cause of death had been strangulation, which was a common method of killing child victims, and which had been the method used to kill little Colin Murphy. She had also been sexually assaulted. It sickened him to think of the monster choking the life out of Melissa, most likely while he sexually assaulted her.

He pushed it out of his mind, trying not to focus on it. He tried to see it as just a piece of evidence to put into the file, to use in the future when comparing MOs.

He drove up to Ron McClintock's house and saw Tess pull the drapes aside at the front window. She opened the door and her face was paler than usual. Something really upset her.

"Thanks for coming," she said and opened the door wide.
"No problem."

Michael followed Tess through the junk surrounding the front door to the sofa.

"Don't mind the mess," she said and pointed to an old sofa. "Have a seat."

Before he did, he reached out and touched her arm.

"Hey, are you okay?" he said and squeezed. "I mean about last night. You sure you feel safe staying at the motel?"

"I'm fine," Tess replied, waving her hand. "There's another customer a few rooms down who will be there for a week, so I won't be totally alone."

Michael sat and leaned back, watching Tess, wondering how she was really doing. "Chief Hammond told me a man dressed in camo jumped the fence and stood outside your room."

She nodded. "They woke me up to make sure I was okay and said they'd found his backpack with hunting gear in it, so maybe he was a hunter who got lost."

"Like I said, he didn't have a rifle," Michael said. "If I had to guess, I'd think this guy was hunting humans. Usually, hunters have weapons, but he had nothing. No ammo."

"That's a scary thought. Especially since he was standing outside my door. Do you think he was stalking me?"

He shrugged, trying hard not to appear alarmed.

"You should be careful, regardless. If you want, I could take a room next to yours just to be safe. Actually, I'd like the excuse to get out of my mother's place." He laughed. "I'm sleeping in a single bed with my feet sticking out of the end."

Tess shook her head firmly. "You don't have to do that. I'll be fine."

"I'm serious. I'll do it no question if it helps you sleep at night."

"No, really. Thanks for the offer."

Michael realized she was stubborn about the matter so he didn't push, but he decided that he'd get a place anyway, and stay there at night. Tess may not care, but he did.

He turned to her. "So, what did you want me to see?"

"This." Tess picked up the box and put it onto the tabletop in front of Michael. "One of the cleaners found it in the attic. It has some illegal material in it. Child porn. Violent porn." She handed him some latex gloves, which he slipped on.

He lifted the lid off the banker's file box and looked inside, picking up a couple of the magazines. He flipped through them, recognizing right away they were old print porn from several decades ago. He didn't say anything right away, wanting to hold off judgment until he'd seen them all, but they were clearly child porn, some suggestive, some explicit. He thumbed through them, one at a time.

"This is definitely illegal," he said finally and closed the magazine featuring underage girls and boys. He examined the publishing marks and pointed to some text at the bottom of one page on the inside cover. "This was produced in Europe in the 70's. Sweden. This looks like it's from that era. Not recent, in other words."

"The lid's really covered in dust," Tess said and pointed to it. Michael checked the box and noted a layer of dust on top of the file box lid.

"Looks like it wasn't opened in a long time."

"I'm hoping it wasn't," Tess said. "You can't imagine how it makes me feel to think my father was looking at this crap. It's vile."

"That it is," Michael said as he examined a few other magazines. "I can send this to the Seattle FBI office and ask members of the task force about it. We have a few experts in child pornography. Nothing will be done about your dad, of course, now that he's dead, but it can go into evidence. Researchers will be able to use it to build a database of the kind of child porn out there. The other stuff? The BDSM porn is pretty standard. Most of it's staged. I've seen material like it before."

"If he'd been alive when I found it? What then? Would they charge him with possession of child porn?"

"Yes. If it was his first offense, he'd probably get off lightly. Your dad doesn't have a record, does he?"

Tess shrugged. "I have no idea. I never thought to check, to tell you the truth, but now I wonder."

"I can check for you," Michael said. "I can talk to a colleague and have him check into it."

"Thanks," Tess replied. "Any news on the Melissa Foster case?" Tess asked.

Michael stood up and put the lid back on the box of magazines, then removed his latex gloves. "Preliminary autopsy says strangulation as the cause of death. She was also sexually assaulted. This wasn't a case of punishment that got out of hand. Clearly, she'd been sexually abused and murdered."

She made a face of dismay. "Monster." She said nothing for a moment, obviously upset at the news. "You're on vacation. You shouldn't be doing this, should you?"

"It's no problem. I'm more concerned with you."

"I'm fine," she said and pointed to the mess surrounding them. "I'm recovered, but now I have to finish going through all this crap he collected."

He nodded and glanced around.

"It's hard to imagine why someone would want to let junk pile up all around them, but it's a sickness. People can't help themselves." He picked up the box and went to the front door. "If you need anything else, give me a call."

"Thanks," Tess said, walking him to the door. "I will." She gave him a smile and he returned it. When he got onto the porch he stopped and turned back.

"When's the funeral?"

"Graveside service," she said. "Monday at eleven. Just a few words by Pastor Greg. My father was an atheist."

"Okay. I'll be there for moral support if Kirsten isn't pushing out her baby."

"You're going to be at the actual birth?"

"Of course," he said, grinning at her expression. "When she starts to push I'll go outside, but I want to be there when I can. I was with Julia for both our boys."

"How are your sons handling the separation?"

He shrugged. "They're upset. I get to see them two week-ends a month."

"It must be hard for you."

"It is," he said, lifting the box. "I'll let you know what my contacts in the pornography unit say about these."

"Thanks. I'm coming over tonight for supper. Your mom invited me."

"Oh, that's nice. See you later, I guess," Michael said with a smile.

He put the box in the back of his vehicle, then drove off, pleased that Tess would come over and the two of them could discuss the cases. He was puzzled that Ron McClintock would buy child porn. Not surprised. He stopped being surprised about the level of perversity in the world years ago.

HE DROVE to Chief Hammond's office, dogged by a nagging sense of impending revelation that wouldn't go away. When he was working a case and putting the pieces together, coming close to the moment when he knew he liked someone for a case, he grew more excited, and that was how he felt now.

There was no reason to feel that way, since he wasn't working a case, but that same gut sense of excitement mixed with dread was brewing in him. That same sense of certainty that he was close to the truth.

When it came to Ron McClintock's stash of violent and child porn, he was puzzled. Ron seemed like such a mild-mannered type, happy to sit around and listen to people bull-shit, but Michael knew that mild facades often hid deeply troubled interiors.

He couldn't help but think about the Foster girl. Her case was cold with no arrests, and no suspects. Considering that there were several cold cases from around the region, Michael was starting to suspect a serial killer was responsible. There was a slight possibility that someone from out of town had just passed by, picking up the girl and killing her, leaving her body in the cabin, but that was unlikely. In most abductions, the perp was a local resident. Most of the time, it was a noncustodial parent or family friend. Occasionally, it was someone in the neighborhood who took the child after watching them for a while. Only very rarely was it a transient passing through. You started with the family and worked your way out.

In Melissa's case, the family had been ruled out. The father was out of town. The mother had been partying until late with friends who all attested that she was with them. The mother had stumbled into the house late and found it empty. According to the mother, and corroborated by the aunt, the girl was supposed to go and stay with her aunt if her mother was out late.

The mother figured Melissa had just gone to her aunt's when she saw that she was not at home. She hadn't bothered to check until late the next day, and by then the trail was cold.

At first, police thought the mother might have done it, considering the time that had elapsed between the last time Melissa was seen alive and when the mother finally reported her missing. But there were too many people who had seen her at the bar until closing to charge her.

Besides, there was no body.

Local police had worked the case with help from police in Seattle, but even after tracing hundreds of leads and potential sightings, there was nothing to attach to any suspect.

Practically every man in town had been interviewed as a potential suspect, but even the local pervs had alibis for that night. It was like a ghost had entered the town and whisked Melissa away, leaving no trace behind.

No one saw her walk away with anyone. No one saw any strange cars around the playground.

No one saw anything.

Michael wanted to sink his teeth into the case and find the killer, especially now that he knew how she died. He wouldn't be doing it in an official capacity, but he was going to talk to local police, review the case, and see what he could contribute, if anything.

It would make him feel less ineffectual

The PTSD diagnosis was hard to take, but he eventually had to accept it. Working the Violent Crimes Against Children task force had taken its toll. He'd seen too much horror in his years at the FBI and that, coupled with his recent separation and loss of easy access to his children, had resulted in the need to take time off.

"Don't even look at any cases while you're off," his supervisor said on his last day in Seattle. "Do anything but think about cases. You need some downtime. Everyone on this task force needs it now and then. If you don't, you risk a complete breakdown."

Michael had promised to stay away from any news of the cases the task force was following, yet here he was, less than two weeks into his leave, already getting back into a case.

He couldn't help it. The girl's murder preyed on his mind. Whenever he had a spare moment, his thoughts turned to her and what happened to her. What were they missing?

Why had her case gone cold?

CHAPTER THIRTEEN

He paced his room, back and forth, his mind working fast. He'd lost the backpack with his scope and blind, plus the night vision goggles. Luckily, they were standard-issue hunting gear you could get at any outfitter, or even Walmart. He always wore gloves when he used them so there'd be no prints to identify him. There was nothing to tie the items to him, although everyone knew he was a hunter. Heck, most of the men in town hunted at some point in their lives, so that meant about three hundred suspects, including every adult male his age.

He wouldn't be a suspect. That much he knew for sure. Still, his nerves were all on edge, and he couldn't stop making fists, wanting to punch something, someone. But at the same time, he welcomed the potential drama. He'd grown bored with his mundane existence – working every day, having a beer with the guys on Friday nights, playing video games the rest of his time off. Something had to happen or he'd go crazy.

He waited until it was dark enough and then walked to the motel.

Luckily, it was located on the outskirts of town, backed onto an empty space and behind that was only forest. He could watch her from where he stood, hidden in the dense underbrush that was still covered in foliage. Around him stood an ancient fir forest, evergreen, and so wearing his camo coat and pants, and his camo hat ensured that, like a hunter, he'd be invisible to his prey.

Her room was on the wing of the motel facing the forest. "Mountain View" was an appropriate name for it was the only draw to the small building. Behind them, the base of the Cascade mountains began, stretching up to Mission Peak.

He couldn't see inside her room because thick drapes obscured his view, but he could watch her movements and see when she left and returned. He'd brought a sleeping bag, and since he had the next day off work, he decided to stay out all night if necessary. He imagined he was on a mission somewhere in the mountains of Afghanistan, watching an enemy target, waiting for an opportunity to strike.

He wasn't going to take her. But he was interested in what she was doing. She was a crime reporter. Crime was his career. They were meant for each other.

She left her room about seven fifteen and that was his opportunity. He tucked the scope into his rucksack and left his blind, walking down the hill to the parking lot. The fence was easy enough to jump and then he was there, walking along the row of motel rooms, most of them empty because Paradise Hill's economy had taken a dive in the fifties and had never recovered – all that was left was a bit of fishing and hunting. That was it. Some folks worked in the logging industry, but there wasn't much else keeping the town alive and it had slowly shrunk until it was at its all-time low population.

He itched to get inside her room, see what she was working on, check out her personal items, but he had no idea how long she'd be gone. There was only one other customer in the motel that night that he could see, a few doors down – he could see a car parked there, but the lights were off. He had a lock pick tool and could slip inside if he wanted. He already checked the local area for any video monitors, but saw none. In the next lot beside the motel was a warehouse, but there was a tall fence surrounding it and it was several hundred feet away. He walked along the perimeter of the fence and still seeing no video monitors, he decided to go inside her room. If she came back and he was in the room? He'd freestyle, knock her out and leave.

So, he walked back to the door to her room, slipped up the scarf to cover the bottom of his face and quickly picked the lock. It was an older motel and had not been renovated. If the room had one of those electronic keys, he would have been out of luck, but thankfully no one had invested any money to upgrade the locks.

It was a piece of cake while he worked the tool, and in less than thirty seconds the tumbler turned and clicked. He was in.

It gave him a sexual thrill to consider waiting for her in the closet or bathroom when she came home, then springing out, scaring her and then slowly choking the life out of her.

He saw that one small bedside lamp was on and considered turning it off and using his night vision glasses, but he didn't want to make any changes that would draw attention to the room.

The first thing he did was take in a deep breath to smell

her. Women had a specific scent, he'd found, in addition to their perfume and shampoo. While he preferred them younger, it wasn't as much the woman he desired as having her under his control. He fantasized about having her tied up and unable to fight him. He could do anything he wanted to her then, and she could only stare up at him, tears in her eyes, wishing that she'd been nicer to him way back when. Back when she could have been nice instead of ignoring him or worse – laughing at him.

He'd seen her and her little friends laugh at him when he'd walk by them. He remembered it, oh, he remembered every single slight and there were many.

He opened her laptop, but it was locked and he had no idea how to guess her password. He didn't know her well enough to use birthdays or favorite actors or other personal details. He closed the lid and went through her clothing in the single suitcase on the stand. A few pairs of panties but nothing fancy. Nothing worth stealing. If she'd had used panties, he would have stolen those. Wouldn't she be confused when she got back home or went to wash them, wondering where they went? She'd think she was losing her mind, certain that she'd stuffed them in the side pocket.

Maybe another day.

He touched her bras and ran a hand over the silky night-gown – black, with thin straps. He'd like to see her wearing it, but preferably with her hands and feet tied to the bedposts, only there weren't any. He'd have to rig up ropes to the bed legs instead. Not as picturesque, but serviceable nonetheless.

There were several pairs of jeans, some blouses and socks. She wasn't fancy except for her nightgown. Boring, actually.

He checked his watch and saw that five minutes had passed. Better to leave now and come back another day than to wait around too long. He made sure everything was in the same place it had been when he arrived and left the room, closing the door behind him. Then he walked back to the fence, hopped over it and made his way back to the small blind he'd set up. He wished he'd picked up a coffee on his way, but he didn't want to leave behind any trace evidence and – specifically not anything with his DNA on.

He had work to do.

CHAPTER FOURTEEN

The next day, Tess wondered how he did it – how her father could live amidst such a mess. His bedroom had been just as bad as the rest of the house, with piles of clothing, boxes of junk, and bags of garbage everywhere.

He kept everything. Every damn thing.

A bag of grocery receipts. Years' worth stuffed into a plastic bag plopped on his chest of drawers. All from one grocery store which delivered groceries for shut-ins and the disabled. She knew he wasn't truly disabled. He did have a back problem – something about spinal stenosis – but he could walk. He chose not to. He had stopped leaving his house a few years earlier, according to Mrs. Carter.

Tess regretted that she hadn't kept better track of him but he'd never shown any interest in reestablishing a relationship with her and frankly, they had grown so distant that she didn't either, although there was a huge hole inside of her where a loving father should have been.

That much her therapist had shown her.

Not having a father figure for most of her adolescence and young adult years had taken a toll. She'd had unrealistic expectations for the men in her life and had been sorely disappointed by the men she did date. She'd start out with stars in her eyes, hoping this was the one who would be a good romantic guy, but inevitably, they'd disappoint her.

June, her therapist, said it was because she hadn't had a father when she'd needed him most and so she created an idealized father that no man could ever live up to.

So, one day a few months ago, after the most recent breakup with a guy who disappointed her, Tess decided to swear off men for a full year. She wouldn't date. She wouldn't look. She'd keep her head down and do her job, devote herself to her calling of helping the researchers and sleuths at The Missing solve old cold cases and write about it in her article for the *Sentinel*.

It was hard. It was lonely, but she realized she had to do some personal work on her expectations for men if she was ever going to be able to have a healthy relationship.

Tess stuffed the bag of receipts into a larger trash bag and moved on to the next pile of junk. Just as she was opening a bag to see what was inside, Elaine, the cleaner's wife, who was working in the attic, came in. She had something in her hands – a box that looked like it was meant to store books.

"I found something you have to see."

Tess stood up and went to examine the box that Elaine held. Inside was a large glass jar, of the kind restaurants would purchase from a wholesaler. The jar was surrounded by newspapers that had been crunched up into balls for packing material.

"What is it?"

She set the box on the bed and started to remove the

newspaper. When most of it was gone, she lifted out the jar and saw that it was filled with what looked like grey dust and bits of charcoal. She looked closer and saw something white poking out of the top.

"Oh, my God," Tess said and put the jar down. She glanced up at Elaine. "Is that what I think it is?"

The woman nodded, an expression of horror on her face.

"He must have had someone cremated and that's the…" Elaine said and hesitated. "The cremains."

"It must be," Tess replied and picked the jar up, turning it around to see if there was at least a label. "I don't know much about his family but maybe one of them?"

In fact, she knew practically nothing.

"If it was a friend or one of his family, you'd think he'd keep it in a better container," Elaine said, shaking her head in disapproval. "They have nice urns at the crematorium. Not too expensive either."

"I know," Tess said and scrunched up her face. "Oh, my God, I think I see a tooth."

Her eyes wide, she turned the jar around and showed Elaine the white bone-like piece pressed against the side of the jar.

"I saw that," Elaine said. "That's why I brought it to you. I think it's definitely human."

Tess stood and examined the jar with a growing sense of horror. She knew what she had to do.

"I have to call the police about this."

Elaine nodded, her brow furrowed. "You think it's evidence of a crime?"

"I have no idea but this isn't normal," Tess said and turned the jar around. "I want to know who this is and why they're in my father's house. Maybe it's an old aunt or someone from his family, but I'd still like to know."

Elaine laid a hand on Tess's shoulder. "Don't get too worried. Maybe he couldn't afford a nice urn. I doubt he killed someone and burned their body in the barbecue."

She cracked a grin and that made Tess feel even worse. Coupled with the scrapbook of murders and the porno she had a bad feeling about the jar. The first thing she would do would be to call Michael and get his opinion on the jar and its contents. Then, she'd call Chief Hammond and offer to bring it down to the station.

She'd be happy to get it out of the house and let the experts figure out who it was and why they ended up in a glass jar in her father's attic.

"I'm calling Michael," she told Elaine. "He might think the FBI should have it. He took the box of magazines and turned them over to the Child Exploitation Unit of the task force. He'll know what to do with this."

She glanced at the jar and peered more closely at the tooth. "If there's a tooth and bone, the crematorium didn't do a good job of burning the body. They might be able to get a DNA profile from it and figure out who's inside."

Elaine nodded and made a face. "They should get their money back, whoever paid for the job."

Tess nodded, but she had a bad feeling that the cremains were not of a family member or anyone close to her father. She had the feeling they were the burnt remains of the girl from Paradise Hill who had gone missing some forty years earlier.

Janine.

The girl in the news clippings that her father – or

someone – carefully cut out of the newspapers and taped in a scrapbook.

Tess went back into the bedroom and tried to focus on sorting through her father's junk but she just couldn't concentrate. She kept coming back to the idea that everything was tied together – the scrapbook of news clippings about Janine and other crimes. The box of violent and child porn. Now, the large jar filled with human remains.

She didn't think some funeral home had just done a poor job at cremation. She feared that her father had killed Janine and burnt the body up to hide the evidence, and had kept it hidden all these years in the rafters of their home. Could that even be possible?

Could the quiet man, the trucker, and then the hoarder he became be a cold-blooded killer?

He had died only a few days ago. Could he have been the man responsible for some if not all of the missing girls from Paradise Hill?

With a knot in her gut, she took out her cell and called Michael. He answered on the second ring.

"Tess," he said, his voice sounding pleased. "I was just thinking of you."

"I'm sorry to bother you again," she replied, no sure how to broach the subject.

"No, no problem. What's up?"

She sighed heavily. "I found something else I think you need to see."

"More pornography?"

"No," she said and chewed on a fingernail. "There's a couple of things, actually. Can you meet me at my motel room before dinner?"

"Sure," he said cautiously. "Care to tell me what you found or are you unable to talk about it?"

"It's crazy, but I think I found a big glass jar full of burned human remains."

There was a brief silence. "Do you mean cremains? In a glass jar?"

"One of those big industrial jars you find in restaurant kitchens. It's clearly human remains. I can see a tooth among the ashes. And a bone of some kind. I don't know anything about cremains. Do they usually contain teeth and bones?"

He cleared his throat. "Usually, the funeral director will remove any metal pieces – bridges in the mouth, metal hips, screws, plates and the like that may have been in the body at the time of death. They grind down the rest so there aren't any visible bones or teeth. It's to make it more palatable to the bereaved family and friends, in case they want to divide up the cremains. At least, the funeral directors I've talked to in the past have done that. I suppose it might be possible for a budget operation to skip that step but that would probably only be if they were disposing of the cremains for someone who didn't want to keep the ashes."

Tess made a face and thought about the whole distasteful business. She wasn't sure whether she wanted to be buried whole or cremated. The thought of the remains not being completely consumed in the fire made her a bit queasy.

"If you want, I could send the teeth and bones to our forensic lab for DNA analysis. They may not be able to do a complete profile, given the degradation of the sample due to the heat, but they may be able to match the sample to you or your father to see if it was someone related to him. A family member he might have had cremated that you weren't aware of."

Tess appreciated that Michael was doing his best to make her feel better about the whole business, but it wasn't working.

"This is really creeping me out."

"Don't think that way," he said softly. "There's probably a simple explanation. Your father likely had possession of one of his family member's remains – or even a friend. You've been out of his life for a long time. Who knows what relationships he might have had, or what might have happened in the time since your mother left and took you kids with her?"

Tess sighed. "I guess. But if you add it all up – the scrapbook of clippings about Janine Marshall's disappearance, the child porn, and now the ashes, it seems pretty suggestive."

"It is suggestive, but not conclusive. It could all be just circumstantial. Think of it this way. He likely knew Janine from school. When she disappeared, he was upset and followed the case, collecting clippings. Maybe he was an crime buff, like someone else I know…"

"Yeah, I know. But still…"

"But still, maybe the porn was stuff he found or inherited from a friend. You never know. Unless he had a bill of receipt for the porn somewhere, or we find stuff on his hard drive, you can't say for certain that those were actually his or that he had a preference for it."

"And the cremains? I would have thought your spidey sense would be on high alert."

She heard him sigh again. "Right now, my spidey sense is supposed to be on medical leave."

"I'm sorry to put this on you," she said softly. "I should call the chief and see what he says."

"No, don't apologize. I'm the expert. I have connections. I

135

can get that sent to the crime lab in Seattle and see what it is we have, okay?"

"My father probably could have found a great urn cheap at one of the thousands of flea markets and garage sales he attended in his life, if that was the case."

"Maybe he forgot about it. Considering all the junk, that's not a stretch."

"Okay," she said and swallowed back another objection. "If you want, I can bring it over to your mom's place. You can pick it up there."

"Sounds like a plan."

"You sure it's okay?" Tess asked, not wanting to impose.

"No problem. We can have dinner and talk about the case."

Tess smiled. "I'd like that. The prospect of a takeout meal eaten in my motel room just doesn't really appeal, especially considering that creepy guy who was standing outside my room."

"I told you I'd get the room next to yours if you want me to. I mean it. No need to stay alone and worry. I have an Agency-issue sidearm, have taken numerous self-defense courses, and I know how to take down a suspect, in case you didn't realize it. Plus, I've got big muscles."

She heard him laugh and laughed with him, imagining him in a pumped-up state.

"No, that's fine," she replied, a huge grin on her face. "I'm fine. I'll see you at your mom's at six?"

"Six is good."

They both hung up and Tess sat for a few moments and smiled to herself, unable to get the image of him being all protective out of her mind's eye. There was no doubt she'd feel safer if he stayed in the next room. Hell, she'd feel safer if she had a weapon herself, but had yet to take a firearms course and was afraid to get a gun without knowing how to use it.

Given her line of work, though, she was beginning to think it might be a good idea.

SHE SPENT another hour in her dad's house going through boxes of junk, sorting through his life, wondering whether he was a killer or whether everything was just a strange coincidence. When the cleaners left for the day, Tess stood in the front room and surveyed the much tidier area. There were piles of plastic tubs with magic marker identification on the sides: Junk. Save. Sell.

She glanced out the window at the sinking sun and saw a truck parked across the street. There were a lot of new people living in the old neighborhood. Some moved into their parents' houses and took over when they died. Others moved into the neighborhood from even seedier areas of town.

She stepped closer to the window and tried to make out whether there was someone in the truck. She saw a dark figure inside. Whoever he was, the man had looked right inside the house and into her eyes. Then the truck drove off and although she tried, she couldn't make out the license plate.

She stood frozen for a moment, wondering whether he was the man who had been standing outside her motel room. That thought unsettled her and her heart rate increased, adrenaline surging through her body.

Was someone stalking her?

CHAPTER FIFTEEN

Michael waited at the front door for Tess to arrive. The house was filled with the aroma of tomato sauce and the air was moist from pasta cooking on the stove. He'd just finished making a salad and spreading garlic butter on the sliced French loaf.

"How is she doing?" his mom asked from where she stood in the kitchen stirring a pot of sauce. "Even though they weren't close, it's hard to lose a father."

"Seems like she's doing as well as can be expected, but there have been a few revelations about him that are a bit unsettling."

"Oh?" she replied, her eyebrows raised. "What do you mean, unsettling? Do you mean that girl at the motel asking if her parents divorced because of Lisa? I told her that was just gossip. Her parents had been on the outs for a few years by the time Lisa went missing. Her mother was really afraid, that's all. She wanted to leave and he didn't. There wasn't enough left between them to keep them together."

Michael shook his head. "Not just that, but she did ask me about it. I'll let her tell you if she wants."

"Oh, come on now. Don't you tease me with news and then don't tell me what it is…"

"Really, Mom," he said and shook his head, wiping his hands on a cloth. "It's her story to tell. Let her tell you if she wants. I shouldn't have mentioned it."

She gave him a look – the look that said she was frustrated with his reticence to talk about himself, or anyone, for that matter, on a personal level. It was her job as a mom to try to get him to talk, and he understood that, but he wasn't going to indulge her desire to gossip. He shouldn't have said anything about Tess's father. It was a momentary lapse. He hoped she wouldn't push Tess for information. He kicked himself mentally. Tess would be upset if she hadn't wanted anyone to know.

Since he'd been off work, he felt lethargic, his mind like sludge. Only the reopening of the Melissa Foster case interested him and made him feel alive once more. He was addicted to his work, he realized. Most special agents lived for their work. It was more than a job.

He needed a few months off to recover and get back into the right mindset, but he knew he'd return just as eager to deal with cases as he had been before the Colin Murphy case. Many of the special agents on the task force commiserated with him. They'd each had their own *bête noire* – a black beast of a case that threatened to send them to the bottle or into therapy. It was going to happen sooner or later. During training, Michael's supervisor had told him that one day, there would come a case that would almost break him. He'd have to give himself permission to grieve or rage, but then he would have to move on and realize that there was only so much an agent could do, and be as professional as possible.

Move on to the next case. There would always be a next case. As long as there were sick fucks born and as long as there were as many freedoms and as much anonymity as there was in modern America, there would be serial killers and gangsters and psychopaths causing mayhem.

In other words, suck it up, buttercup.

He saw Tess walk down the street to the house was carrying a file box. Inside, he knew, was the jar of ashes – the badly processed cremains of a family friend or some unknown victim. He hoped it was the former and not the latter, because it would be difficult to explain otherwise.

The truth was that Michael was starting to suspect that Tess's father had a more storied past than anyone ever suspected. The pornography, the scrapbook, and now the cremated remains found in an unmarked jar suggested he had been involved in something in the past. Only DNA tests would tell who the victim was. If it was Janine, that would suggest her dad had been the killer.

He had a hard time believing that Tess's father was a killer despite the fact he did fit the profile. He wasn't around much back when Tess had lived in Paradise Hill, and even when he stopped long-haul trucking after hurting his back, he was antisocial. He'd kept to himself, especially the last decade, according to Michael's mother, who kept tabs on the doings of everyone in the neighborhood. He had a failed marriage, was a white male in his fifties, had traveled a lot during his adulthood. There were many men like that, of course, but few had kept scrapbooks of crimes, had violent and child porno hidden in their attic and the burnt remains of someone in their closet…

Michael left the house and met Tess on her way as he watched her trying to balance the file box in one hand and a vase in another.

"Here," he said, reaching her side just as she made it to the sidewalk. "Let me take that." He took the file box from Tess and caught her eye. "Do you want me to put it in my car and take it with me? If you don't want to talk about it, I mean." He gestured with his head toward the house.

"No, it's all right," she said and waved her hand in dismissal. "They'll find out anyway, if it's anything serious. Might as well find out now as later."

He held the door and the box for Tess as she went into the house.

"Hello, my dear," his mom said as she put down her ladle and went to greet Tess. "Come in, come in."

They hugged and Tess handed his mom the vase. "I brought this for you. Thought it was one of the nicer pieces my father owned."

"It is nice," his mom said, taking the vase and turning it around in the light. "It looks like leaded crystal. Thank you, sweetheart. Would you like a glass of wine? Some coffee? What'll you have?"

Tess appeared overwhelmed for a moment but then smiled and turned to glance at Michael. "What are you having?"

He shook his head. "Just a beer."

"I'll have the same."

He held up the box. "Where do you want it?"

Tess bit her bottom lip. "Put it in the living room. You can check it out in there, I guess."

"What's that?" his mom asked, all ears and eyes.

"It's something I found in my dad's house," Tess said,

shrugging, her cheeks red like she was embarrassed. "I asked Michael to take a look."

"Well, tell me. What is it?"

"It's a jar of human remains."

Michael almost laughed at the look on his mother's face.

"What?" She covered her mouth with both her hands. "Oh my God, Tess." She glanced between them. "Michael?"

"Just relax, Mom," he said and held out his hand to signal her to stop making a fuss. "We have no idea what it is until we get some tests done. I offered to check it out, send it to the forensic lab in Seattle to find out if there's a match in the system."

"Do you think it's Lisa?"

He frowned at her and glanced to Tess, who looked horrified. "Mom! No. It's not Lisa. I don't know why you would even suggest that."

"Well, back then there was gossip that her mom thought Ron was implicated in some way."

"You said that wasn't true," Tess said, frowning. She glanced at Michael.

"I said I didn't think it was true, but other people did. They said your mother thought so, but I never believed it. But with this…"

"We don't know what this is. Until we do, we have to assume the poor man is innocent."

His mom shrugged and took Tess's arm.

"You poor dear, finding that, what with all that's happened recently. Come and have your beer."

Tess glanced at him, a look of exasperation in her eyes.

"Go ahead. I'll take a look."

He went to the living room and sat on the sofa, placing the box in front of him on the coffee table. He opened the lid and pushed aside the crumpled newspaper. Before he lifted out the jar, he unfolded one of the newspaper pages and smoothed it on the top of the coffee table, checking the date.

"It's from 1992. That was before Lisa, so we can all relax. This likely isn't her, unless your dad started collecting newspapers back then."

Tess sat close beside him, her hands clasped in front of her like she was anxious.

"Can I see?"

She took the sheet of newspaper and examined it. Then she unfolded another and another, checking to see if the dates were the same. He should have thought of that himself, but he had been more interested in proving it wasn't – or was – Lisa inside. She was quick. He thought she'd probably make a good analyst, if she ever wanted to go into law enforcement or the FBI.

"This is from a different date," she said and held out another sheet. "From 1979. Who keeps old newspapers like that?"

"Janine went missing in '78."

Tess glanced at him, wide-eyed. "I saw stacks and stacks of old newspapers in my father's house, but not any from 1978."

"How far back did they go?"

She shrugged. "I didn't check them all, but the oldest was right around the time we moved out. Maybe my father started hoarding after we left."

She took another crumpled wad. "This is 1996." She read over the headlines and then dropped it onto the coffee table, her movements suggesting she felt defeated.

He took hold of the jar and lifted it out of the remaining packing material, then set it on the coffee table.

"What I don't get is why someone would store remains in a jar like this if it was a family member. If my father could afford to go to flea markets and garage sales every weekend and buy twenty dollars' worth of junk, he could afford to buy some kind of vase more appropriate for cremains." Tess shrugged. "If they are cremains and not the burnt remains of a murder victim…"

"Tess," he said and squeezed her arm. "Don't jump to conclusions. Only go as far as the evidence takes you, no more. That's one of the things we learn in the FBI. Stick with the evidence. So far, we have a jar of human remains. We don't know who it is. We don't know how the person died. We have nothing to point us in one direction or the other. I'll send this to the crime lab and ask a friend of mine to do a quick analysis of the DNA and see if there's any match in the system. Then we'll draw conclusions, okay?"

He raised his eyebrows, wanting to calm her fears about her father.

"But the scrapbook and—"

"So far," he said and squeezed her arm again. "So far we have a scrapbook of the kind a young man who was interested in crime would make. It may be no more than that. We have a box of pornography that looks like it hadn't been opened in years. We have no idea of its provenance. None. If we find nothing on your dad's computer, maybe he bought something that contained the porn without him knowing it. Because he's a hoarder, it never got thrown out."

"Or maybe my father was a sick bastard who killed young girls."

He shook his head in dismay. "Do you really think that? Did your father ever do anything that would make you suspect he was a secret serial killer?"

"You can't know," she said. "They don't look any different from the guy next door."

He had to admit that she was right.

There were many sociopaths out there who lived apparently normal lives except when they were kidnapping and killing people. The rest of the time, they had jobs, they had families, went to PTA meetings with their spouses. That was the truly scary thing about serial killers. The majority looked absolutely normal on the outside. Only on the inside and in their secret places did you see their true evil.

"No, I can't know that for sure, but…" he said and caught her eye. "We can't know anything for sure until we get back the analysis of the remains and his computer. Plus, I'd like to know more about the magazines. Really, this is just so much circumstantial evidence."

"Would it be enough to put my dad on your radar, if you were looking for a killer?"

He sighed. "Yes," he said truthfully. "I would put him on my list, but let me tell you something I've learned after a decade of working for the FBI and interviewing potential suspects. So many people have these kinds of things in their pasts. Things that they wouldn't want anyone to know about. It doesn't make them serial killers. Knowing your dad, I just don't see it. Not yet, at least. I could be convinced if I had more evidence. Like a DNA match to one of the missing girls. Until then, let's hold our conclusions. It could be your Uncle Ned from Hoboken."

She finally nodded and he continued to examine the jar. Inside were the remains of a human – no doubt. He saw one tooth, partially attached to a fragment of upper skull, pressed against the side of the jar.

What concerned him, and what he didn't say to Tess, was

that he could also detect something that looked a lot like charcoal produced in a wood fire. Crematoriums didn't use wood to cremate bodies. They used gas. That resulted in a specific kind of burn to the body. Much cleaner. Then the remains were ground mechanically to ensure a more uniform composite.

These looked like they had not been ground, for he could see pieces of charred bones and he suspected that if he poured out the remains, he'd find pieces of the bigger bones – hip, knee joints, the jaw. Vertebrae. Whoever burned this body had tried to smash it up, but not the way a crematorium did. He had a bad feeling about the remains.

Now it was even more imperative to send off the jar to the crime lab in Seattle. He had a growing sense of unease about Tess's father. The man may have been mild-mannered on the outside, but if he did this, there may have been a very sick serial killer deep inside. Ron McClintock might be the serial killer that Michael was increasingly sure had been working in the area for decades undetected.

"You let me send this to Seattle," he said and squeezed her arm again. "I'll let you know what they find. It's probably nothing, but in the meantime, maybe you should contact your dad's side of the family, see if anyone died in the past two decades that he might have the remains from. If so, that would make things a lot simpler."

"I will," she said and gave him a weak smile. "I've been calling to let them know he died and when the service is. There are so few of his relatives still alive or living in Paradise Hills. Some of them will be coming but most won't. Most of them probably had no idea he was even sick, let alone dead. He lost touch with his side of the family as well as with us."

"He was a lonely man."

"He was." Tess covered her eyes and bit her lip. He slipped his arm around her shoulders and pulled her against him. She'd had a real shock. Shock upon shock, in fact. Not only had her estranged father died a horrible lonely death, apparently he'd liked child and violent porn, had been obsessed about murders and crime, and had a burned-up corpse – possibly of someone he killed – in his attic. It had finally become too much for her.

He knew the feeling. Overwhelmed. That was how he'd felt when little Colin was found and he'd gone to see the body.

"It's okay," he said, pulling her closer. "We'll get through this."

She turned her head into his shoulder and let him hold her for a moment. He liked having someone in his arms again, even if it wasn't in the best of circumstances. He and Julia had been estranged for so long before she left that he had forgotten how nice it was to hold a woman in his arms and comfort her.

It felt good.

CHAPTER SIXTEEN

Tess pulled away from Michael, feeling like a total fool for crying in front of him, but it had just struck her like a freight train how lonely her father had been for so long. With everything that had happened – with her father's death and the things she found in his house, the stalker – it overwhelmed her.

She wiped tears from her cheeks. "I'm sorry. I'm not usually so emotional." She stood and turned to him. "Shall I get us a beer?"

"Let me get it," he protested but she stopped him.

"Let me. I need something to do."

Finally, he nodded. "Sure. They're in the extra fridge."

She left the living room and went into the kitchen where Mrs. Carter was busy draining the pasta.

"You kids hungry? Supper's almost ready." She turned to look at Tess, and noticed her red eyes.

"Oh, sweetheart," she said and came to Tess, pulling her into her arms. "I know it's hard to lose a parent. Even one you barely saw."

Mrs. Carter patted her affectionately on the back and, finally, let go.

"I'm here for the beer," Tess said, trying to smile.

Mrs. Carter nodded and pointed to the door to the attached carport. "The extra refrigerator is outside. The beer's in there."

Tess went outside and opened the refrigerator door. Inside were a dozen Millers. She grabbed two and went back, eager to get the caps off and have a drink. She wanted to relax and stop thinking of everything. A couple of beers would do the trick.

She went back inside the living room and saw that Michael was on the phone. She handed him a beer and he placed it on the coffee table beside the jar of remains, holding his finger up for a moment.

"Thanks," he said into the cell. "I appreciate the heads-up."

He ended the call and slipped his cell back into his pocket.

"That was the chief. Positive ID of Melissa is now official. Her body was well-preserved inside the cement. Whoever put her in it knew to shake the barrel enough to remove almost all the air bubbles. There were no big air gaps, besides the one that caused the crack in the heat. Body was only moderately decomposed. Autopsy confirmed that she was strangled to death and sexually assaulted. It will be a few days before the toxicology and lab reports come back."

"Why toxicology?"

"Sometimes victims are drugged." He cleared his throat. "There's another piece of news. That bracelet found in her hand? It was a charm bracelet. Melissa's mother said she didn't have one. But one of the other missing girls did."

Adrenaline surged through Tess. "Who?"

"Zoe," he said. "Zoe Wallace. Went missing a decade ago. She was wearing a charm bracelet when she went missing. It was one of the pieces of evidence we were using to identify her, in case her body turned up.

"So whoever took Melissa also took Zoe."

"Exactly. And the only reason Melissa had that bracelet in her hand was because her killer wanted us to know he did both. I'm starting to think our killer wanted the body to be found. And the bracelet. He's bored."

Tess shook her head slowly. "He's a sick bastard." She glanced over at his mom. "Sorry."

He smiled. "Don't worry. She's heard worse from me."

Tess sat beside him again. "There's something I didn't tell you," she said.

He turned to her, his expression expectant.

"What?"

"I thought I saw someone parked on the street outside the house watching me."

He frowned. "Did you recognize who it was?"

She shook her head. "No. He looked like he was wearing a hoodie so I didn't see his face, but I felt that he was looking right at me through the living room window. Then he drove off."

"Did he drive off fast or slow?"

"Slow."

He nodded. "Did you see his license or the make of the truck?"

She shrugged. "No. It was a black truck. Big. I couldn't tell much else."

He exhaled. "Might have been someone who knew your father and was just passing by."

"Or it might have been the guy who was looking into my motel room…"

"My offer stands."

"I know." She said nothing for a moment while they both took a sip of beer.

"If you don't feel comfortable staying at the motel, maybe you could stay here and I'll trade places with you. I can stay at the motel and you can take the spare bedroom."

Tess frowned. "No, you don't have to do that. It was probably just someone who knew my dad and was driving by to take a look, like you said. I don't want to put you out."

"It's no problem," he said. "I'm used to sleeping in small-town motels. Put a mattress under me and give me a dark room, and I can sleep anywhere."

"I'll let you know if I change my mind."

They sat for a moment and Tess took a long sip of her beer, wanting to relax and mellow out a bit.

"So, tell me what you know now about Lisa's disappearance. You must know more than the rest of us. Anything you can tell me that the public may not know?"

Michael shook his head. "Not really." He glanced down at his beer bottle and Tess thought he was probably feeling guilty for his role in the whole matter. He met Tess's eyes. "Of course, I've gone over that night a thousand times in my head. Probably ten thousand times."

"I know," Tess said, sympathy for him filling her. "I feel the same. If only Kirsten and I hadn't been so mean to her over that stupid teddy bear. She would have stayed and our lives would all be different."

"If I'd been more responsible, I wouldn't have let you girls spend the night in the tent. But Kirsten was insistent, and we wanted to be able to drink. We were such stupid, selfish, irresponsible jerks. I can't believe we did that. And look at the huge consequences it had for everyone."

He had a haunted expression in his eyes. "If we had come out and asked how you guys were, we would have seen that Lisa was gone, and that might have made a difference. If I'd known she went home, I would have gone over right away. Her mom wasn't supposed to be off work until really late. I would have made her come back and stay at our place. She would still be alive today. Who knows where our lives would be now?"

Tess shrugged. "Who can say? I might not have become a crime reporter. You might not have joined the FBI. My parents might not have divorced."

Michael was silent for a moment. "I guess my life is pretty good, all things considered. I mean, yeah, Julia and I split and she has the kids, but I love my job."

"You're on medical leave…"

"Yes, but I couldn't leave it now. It's my calling."

"Same here," she said, thinking about her own history after Lisa disappeared. "I get upset by the stuff I read about missing children, but I can't not do this. Before Lisa went missing, I wanted to be a movie star. After, I wanted to be a cop."

He smiled at her. "Movie star?"

She laughed. "I was ten. I wanted to be Mulan."

"How come you didn't try out for the police force?"

Tess made a face. "I'm afraid of guns."

He laughed with her. "Mulan had a sword. I could easily get you unafraid. Once you've taken a gun handling course, you'll feel more confident."

She shook her head. "I don't know. I was always worried that someone would take it from me and use it against me."

"A self-defense course would take care of that. It happens that I'm a good self-defense instructor on top of being an expert marksman and all-around hero."

He gave her a grin and she smiled back, thinking that he was usually quiet and not given to boasting about himself or joking. He was trying really hard to make her feel better.

"I'm sure you are."

They were silent for a moment. He was probably thinking the same thing she was – that they had both failed Lisa. That if they had been more responsible or nicer, Lisa would be alive and the world would be a different place.

Mrs. Carter came out into the living room, her apron in her hands.

"Supper's ready. Come and sit at the table."

Tess followed Michael into the dining room and sat across from him. For the next hour at least, Michael tried to direct talk away from Tess's father and the remains, and toward other matters – and for that, Tess was thankful.

"Eugene is taking the kids this weekend so maybe we can have a nice meal together with Kirsten and Phil. You'll get to meet him. He's such a nice man."

"Better than the deadbeat," Michael muttered, half under his breath.

"Now, Michael. Don't you be like that. Eugene is a good man. He's changed from when you knew him. He's a straight arrow."

Michael grunted but said nothing more. It was clear he didn't like Kirsten's previous husband.

"That would be great," Tess said, curious about Kirsten's new partner. "Although I'd love to see her kids."

"It's Eugene's weekend, so I expect he won't want to give it up. He only gets them three weekends out of four."

"I'll probably be here for a couple of weeks, so I'll see them before I go back to Seattle."

"Then it's settled. I'll make a roast and we can have a nice meal together."

Tess smiled, glad to have the chance to see Kirsten again.

AT ABOUT NINE, Tess yawned behind a hand and smiled at Mrs. Carter.

"I should go. I have some reading to do. My dad had all these files and I want to figure out what I have to keep and what I can throw away. I want to see if there's a will tucked away in the files so we won't have as much problem settling up the estate. Plus, he has all these journals he wrote when he was growing up and a file full of short stories."

Michael stood up from the sofa. "If you want, I can come with you, check out the motel room."

"Really," she said and smiled, waving her hand in dismissal. "I'm a big girl, and I'm not worried. Besides, I think someone moved in earlier today just two rooms down, so there are more eyes on the place. I'm fine."

Michael followed Tess to the door and waited while she pulled on her shoes. "I'll talk to the chief tomorrow and call my contacts in Seattle. We'll probably send the jar to Seattle tomorrow. They can look at the jar itself as evidence as well as the contents."

"How long will it take to get results?"

Michael shrugged, leaning against the door. "Depends on how much of a priority it is. Coupled with the magazines and the scrapbook, I'd say they might put it on a front burner."

Tess exhaled in frustration. "I guess none of us really knew my father."

"Have you talked to your mother?"

Tess shook her head quickly. "I don't want to until I know something for certain. No need to alarm or upset her unnecessarily."

"See? Now apply that to yourself."

Tess smiled at him. "I will. Thanks for doing this for me. I really appreciate it."

"No problem. See you on Monday? The graveside service is at eleven o'clock, right?"

Tess nodded. "Yes. I doubt there'll be too many people in attendance."

"You might be surprised. I saw the announcement in the local paper. You might get quite a few attending. Your dad lived here all his life."

"He did," she replied. "Thanks again. Tell your mom thanks for supper."

"I will. Talk later."

She went to her car and got inside, wishing all this was over and done with so she could go back to Seattle and her life. She felt out of sorts being here in Paradise Hill, away from her usual life of work and friends. Her apartment in the city, her walks along the waterfront. Her visits to the newsroom to discuss stories with Kate. Spending time at the courthouse listening to cases.

Maybe she'd be in Paradise Hill for another week and then she could return, put this all behind her.

As she drove away, she hoped that everything she'd found in her father's house was innocent and she could forget everything to do with the house and its contents.

She passed the house, which was now dark. Tomorrow, she'd go back to the house. She was almost finished with the bedrooms.

She hoped there was nothing more to find.

TESS STOPPED at the gas station to fill up her tank and went inside to get some chocolate and a newspaper. She'd always been a news hound, but since she had returned to Paradise Hill, she'd been too busy with the house to spend much time reading other than the headlines in her newsfeed. She picked up a copy of the local newspaper – the *PH Express* – and brought it up to the clerk.

"Sorry to hear about your dad," the woman behind the counter said. "I'm Marcy, by the way. I knew your dad as a customer for a long time. He used to come in here every Saturday for a *US News and World Report*. Said it was the only paper he read."

"He did?" Tess replied, frowning. "He had stacks of newspapers in his house so I assumed he read pretty much every newspaper there was."

"No," she said and rang the chocolate through the till. "He said most papers weren't fit for the bottom of a birdcage so he didn't bother."

Tess didn't reply, wondering where all the newspapers had come from if her dad hadn't read them.

"I hear you work for a paper up in Seattle," Marcy said.

"I do," Tess replied. "The *Sentinel*."

"We don't get that one here," she said. "We get a few of the national papers and the local paper. That's about it."

"It's really focused on local stories," Tess offered.

Marcy smiled and watched while Tess used her bank card to pay. When the transaction was complete, she handed Tess her bag.

"Have a nice night."

Tess smiled and left the store. While she drove off, she thought about the stacks of old papers in her father's house. It didn't make sense. Why would he buy a whole bunch of papers if he didn't read them?

She couldn't figure it out. Just another mystery about her father.

TESS PARKED her car and was glad to see another car a few doors down. At least if someone was hanging out around her car or door, someone might see or hear. She hauled in her backpack and newspaper, and was careful to lock the door and put on the chain behind her.

She did some research for the article for about an hour, going back all the way to Janine in her quest for all the missing girls and women from the area. There were a few who were deemed truly missing, and others were determined to be runaways who had been seen working the streets of larger cities in Washington and Oregon. Those she crossed off her list, although she couldn't be sure that some of the girls hadn't been kidnapped as part of the sex slave trade.

Around ten, she felt thirsty and decided to go to the drink machine for a bottle of water. The vending machine was down the row of motel rooms and around the corner next to the main office. She searched through her change and found the right coins, remembering that it was $2.50 per bottle – which was far too expensive. She kicked herself for not buying a bottle or two when she was at the convenience store earlier.

She slipped on her sweater and went down the row of motel rooms, noting that there was a light on in the room two doors down. She glanced up at the mountain behind the motel. In the dark, it loomed like a huge black hole. Above, the sky was dark and full of stars. With the moon already setting behind the peak, it would be a good night for stargazing if you were into that.

When she got to the machine she saw that the water was sold out. Since it was so late, she didn't really want to drive to the gas station again. Then she remembered that there was another vending machine in the main office. Luckily, it was open all night, so she went inside and said hello to Andrea.

"How are you doing? Everything all right? No more strangers hanging around?"

Tess nodded and waved her hand. "No. I'm fine. There's someone just a room away from me now, so I'm not worried."

"Yes, I put them there so you wouldn't be all alone. A nice older couple on a trip to the Scablands."

Tess smiled and held up her bottle of water. "Got what I came for. The other machine's out of water."

Andrea nodded and picked up her pen. "I'll let them know first thing in the morning."

Then Tess made her way back to her room, passing the older couple's room and wondering what they looked like. Not many people stopped in Paradise Hill; there were better, classier hotels just down the road another fifty miles. Maybe they were tired and so they stopped instead of driving through.

She opened her door and went inside her room, closing the door behind her. Before she could flip the safety lock, she heard something from the bathroom — a creak that didn't sound right. Frowning, she wondered if it might be a mouse — but then a tall figure wearing a ski mask came at her, not stopping until he had her in a choke hold. She screamed without even thinking but before she could get her hand on the doorknob, he had a hand over her mouth, holding on to her from behind.

She struggled, kicking back at his legs until she heard him grunt, but he merely tightened his grip on her.

Then he slammed her head against the wall and that was it.

Darkness.

CHAPTER SEVENTEEN

Michael didn't feel right leaving Tess all alone, even though she protested that she'd be fine. Although she insisted she didn't want him to, he decided to take a room close to hers, and convinced Andrea to provide a cover story for him in case Tess asked about the new customers.

"If she asks, tell her it's an old couple or something. I don't want her to know I'll be staying here at night. I just don't like to leave her all alone after what happened the other night."

Andrea waved her hand. "I understand. I don't blame you. That was scary. Even I got the creeps from it."

He parked a rental car at the spot down from Tess's so she wouldn't recognize his truck, and had his mom drop him off so he could slip into the room without Tess noticing. She wouldn't even know he was there, but he'd feel safer knowing he was just a dozen feet away from her room.

About ten o'clock, he saw someone pass the room and glanced between the drapes, seeing Tess as she passed by. She must be going to the vending machine. He waited by the door, listening for her return. When his cell rang, he cursed and went to grab it from his jacket pocket, not wanting to miss when she went back to her room. He'd go out after he heard her return and check out the motel grounds to make sure nobody was hanging around watching her room.

He finished the call from one of the officers working the Melissa Foster case and then hung up, going back to the window and pulling the curtain back. She must have already come back, so he put on his jacket and left the room, planning to check out the perimeter.

The scream of fear was unmistakable and came from Tess's room.

He didn't even think. He just acted, running to the door and shouldering it once, twice, and then three times, managing to push the door open. Inside, he saw a dark figure looming over Tess, who was on the bed on her back, a smear of blood on her forehead.

Michael threw himself onto the man's back, pulling him back off Tess, then slamming him against the wall, banging the man's head. Tess's attacker wore a ski mask, which Michael tried to grab as the two wrestled each other. The intruder managed to pull free from Michael's grasp and ran out of the room.

Michael ran after him, peeling out of the room and following the man up the hill behind the motel. He lost the man in the darkness, and stopped about three hundred feet into the forest.

Cursing, he ran back to the motel room and found Tess sitting up on the bed, holding the corner of a sheet against her forehead.

"Oh, God, Tess," he said and knelt beside her, pulling the

sheet away from her forehead. She had a cut which was bleeding quite freely, so he covered it once more with the sheet. He grabbed his cell out of his pocket and dialed 9-1-1, connecting with the operator and asking for police and an ambulance to be sent to the motel.

"Are you all right?" he asked, brushing hair off her forehead. "You've got a nasty cut."

"Thank God you came by," Tess said, tears in her eyes. "If you hadn't…"

"Shh," he said and pulled her into his arms, comforting her. "I was staying in the room two doors down. When I heard you return to your room, I decided to check out the motel grounds and heard you scream."

He heard the wail of a siren as the ambulance approached. It came to a halt right outside, the lights flashing in the darkness. A police car pulled up beside it. The EMT came right over to Tess to check her out. Michael stood up and went to speak with the police officer, who had entered the room with his hand on his sidearm.

"Did you get a good look at the man who attacked her?"

Michael shook his head. "He was wearing a ski mask. About six foot, six-two. Medium build. Wearing all black and gloves. I chased him into the forest but lost him a few hundred feet in."

The police officer nodded. "I'll call in and report it. Have a few of the patrol cars to search for a suspect." He glanced around. "Did he steal anything?"

"I think he was after her," Michael replied, watching the EMT apply a bandage to Tess's head. "Someone's been watching her. We reported a prowler the other night."

"Yeah, we got the report. You figure it's the same guy?"

"Yes. Ms. McClintock said she thought someone was watching her today at her father's house."

"We'd like her to give a statement down at the precinct. You know the drill."

"That I do. I'll bring her down."

The police officer began speaking into his radio as the EMT stood up and approached Michael.

"She has a nasty bump and a cut. Looks like it needs stitches. You can take her down to the ER or we can. Up to you."

"I'll take her."

Once everyone was satisfied that Tess was okay and that they knew what protocol was, the police and EMTs left Tess and Michael alone. Andrea, the front desk clerk, came down with her sweater wrapped around her and examined the door.

"I'll call my nephew. He does work for us and can fix this in no time."

"I'll move Tess's things," Michael said. "She'll stay at my mother's place for the night," he said and raised his eyebrows when Tess looked like she wanted to protest.

"Okay. I completely understand. Do you want to keep the room once the door is fixed?"

Tess started to speak, but Michael interrupted.

"I think that, considering what happened, Tess should stay at my mom's for the rest of her stay." He gave Tess a stern look and she backed down. He knew she would try to stay in her motel room, but he was having none of it.

Once that was settled, Michael moved Tess's possessions into the rental. She was still shaken up, as could be expected, and let him take over.

"We should go to the ER and get that treated," he said

and helped her with her jacket. "Then we can give a statement at the station."

"Okay," she said and let him lead her to his car. "You're the professional." She finally smiled at him and he knew she was starting to calm down.

"I'm sorry to put you through all this," she said and placed her hand on his arm. "It's the last thing you need while you're on medical leave."

"Don't even think of apologizing. None of this is your fault. Besides, we're old friends. Been through hell together, right? Who better to go through hell with you again?"

He helped her inside the truck and fastened her seat belt.

"I could use a little less hell, thanks."

"Me, too, but somehow, the universe has other plans for us – and they don't seem to be relaxing ones."

THEY DROVE to the ER and, after registering and filling out the insurance forms, Tess was brought into a treatment room to get her cut stitched. Once she was stitched up, she was sent off with a fresh bandage on her forehead and a prescription for Tylenol with codeine, which she promptly threw in the trash.

"Hate codeine. Makes me zoomie."

Michael laughed. "You don't like being zoomie?"

She shook her head. "Nope. A beer or two is all I can handle, thanks."

He then drove her to the police station and sat down with her while the duty officer took her statement. Tess went to the waiting room and then the officer quizzed Michael, going over what happened.

"It happened really fast. When I finally got the door

open, he had his hands around her neck and was on top of her on the bed. I grabbed him from behind and we struggled. I think I slammed him pretty hard against the wall but he managed to escape. He might have a bruise on his head so if you want to tell your guys that, they can check."

"That's good to know. We'll check around with our usual suspects. See if any of them have a fresh bruise."

"Thanks," Michael said. "There's really nothing else to tell you. I think he had brown eyes but the room was dim so I didn't get much of a look at him, even considering the ski mask."

"Hey, you do what you can. She's lucky you were watching over her."

"Yeah, she didn't want me to but I took a room anyway."

He narrowed his eyes. "I suppose she'll be more willing to take precautions now. She needs to be extra careful until we catch whoever did this."

Michael shook the duty officer's hand and went to collect Tess. She was sitting with her eyes closed, her arms wrapped around herself.

"You okay?" He sat beside her, his arm around the back of her chair. "We can go now. I called Mom and she'll fix up the third bedroom for you."

Tess opened her eyes. "Okay. If you insist."

"You wouldn't really consider going back to the motel, would you?"

She shrugged. "I doubt whoever it was would come back. They'd be expecting that I'd have someone staying with me. I'd probably be safe."

He stood and held out his hand. "I want you to stay at my mom's. She has an alarm system. I'll be there in my old bedroom, sleeping on my twin bed, surrounded by my trophies and Batman posters."

He cracked a grin and finally, she smiled and took his hand, standing up.

"Okay, I give in," she said and dropped his hand. "I'll come along without resistance."

"Resistance is futile."

She laughed and he knew she was going to be okay. Shaken, understandably. But she'd be okay. He hoped she'd be recovered sufficiently by the memorial service to deal with what would no doubt be a very emotional day.

Even if she hadn't been close to Ron, he was her father. Losing your father was hard. Michael knew that all too well.

THEY ARRIVED at his mother's house just before one in the morning. Tess yawned as he carried her suitcase inside. His mom was waiting in her robe and slippers, her hair already up in her curlers for the night.

"Oh, Tess, you poor dear," she said and hugged Tess. Tess appeared glad to have some mothering so Michael left them and took Tess's suitcase into the sparc bedroom next to his. He put it onto the bed and switched on the bedside lamp. Then he checked the windows, making sure the locks were on and the blinds were pulled down.

The last thing he wanted was for Tess to feel nervous. He went back to the kitchen where his mother was fixing Tess a cup of tea. The two sat at the island and Tess was telling her about the ordeal.

"I have to go back to the motel and get a few things," he said and squeezed Tess's shoulder. "I'll be back in fifteen."

She glanced at him, smiling softly. "Thanks for everything. Sorry to put you through this."

"Don't even mention it," he said and pointed at her. "It makes me feel a bit less useless."

Then he left, feeling somewhat better that she'd be staying at his mom's place until things with her father's house were wrapped up.

In the meantime, he was going to spend a few days looking for whatever sonofabitch had the audacity to break into a motel room and attack Tess. She'd reported a black pickup parked outside her dad's house earlier in the day. He'd begin by asking Lawrence back in Seattle to pull all the black pickups in town and then he'd drive the streets, looking for an owner with bruised cheek or black eye.

That would be a start...

CHAPTER EIGHTEEN

He ran until he came to the empty lot behind an abandoned warehouse and watched to make sure no one was driving in the local area. Most FBI special agents were fit motherfuckers and Carter was no exception. Luckily, he was a fast runner and had gotten a head start, and he knew the woods better than Carter did. Since the moon was just setting, he had enough light to find the road in the darkness and the junker car he'd taken from his uncle's yard.

He knew enough not to hunt using his own vehicle. Luckily, he had dozens of stolen plates and his uncle kept several old cars in the back lot. He swapped them out whenever he needed cover.

Once he got back to the station, he coasted into the lot, parking in the back, where all the vehicles were kept. He removed the plates and placed them behind a stack of old parts removed from the junkers when they were brought in. His uncle kept the parts in case he ever wanted to restore an older vehicle. He never went into the stack so it was a perfect place to store his stolen plates, taken from cars and trucks around the state on his travels.

They were useful. If someone took down the license plate, it would come back to some stolen vehicle or stolen plates from another location. They had gotten him out of a lot of potential jams in the past.

He glanced in the mirror over the sink in the garage's washroom and checked out his forehead. There was a definite bruise beginning to flower over his left eye. He'd get a black eye as a result. That might be a way to identify him, so he had to think quickly.

What to do to escape detection...

HE STAYED in the garage that night, not wanting to go back to his place in case his movements were noticed. He also didn't want to walk around with the bruise on his head. Carter could identify him from it if they ran into each other.

No, he had to create a diversion. Luckily, he was expert at subterfuge and had relied on his wits for most of his adult life. When you were a hunter, you needed a blind. He had many blinds. He blended right in. No one would ever suspect him.

Before dawn, he walked back to his uncle's grocery store. Once there, he changed into a pair of company overalls and took one of the company delivery trucks onto the highway. It was his day to pick up the fresh produce shipment from the next town over, and this would give him the cover he needed.

He drove onto the highway and took it to Yakima, which was much less sleepy than Paradise Hill. Just before he got into the town's center, he took out his cell and sent his uncle a text that he was picking up the delivery early.

Then, instead of taking the curve in the road, he went straight, down the ditch, and crashed his vehicle into a tree.

The old delivery truck had no air bags. He wore the seat belt — the old type that didn't cross over his chest — because he wasn't an idiot, but the force of the collision sent him forward, striking his head on the side of the door frame.

He wasn't driving too fast — just fast enough that he managed to injure himself.

Bingo.

He saw stars, and when he felt the blood dripping down his cheek, he knew he'd created enough of a diversion that no one would wonder about his blackening eye.

It was a painful way to achieve his end, but there was nothing else he could think of that could provide him cover for the black eye besides staying home for a week. He couldn't stay home sick. People would come by and check on him. His aunt would bring food and medicines, her mustard poultice and that damn Vicks VapoRub, insisting that she spread the hideous concoction on his chest and under his nose the way she had when he was growing up. He'd tried that ruse once before when he'd needed to lie low, and had made a note to himself not to use it again unless he truly wanted to be stuck inside, accepting all the ministrations of his prying and interfering relatives.

He couldn't ask for a week of vacation while the bruise healed. His uncle would protest because he'd recently taken a couple of weeks, using that to cover his tracks from five months earlier.

No, covering up the bruise with this accident was the only way.

He sat in the delivery truck, momentarily stunned, then he rummaged for a rag in the glove compartment and pressed it to his forehead. He searched for his cell, but it had been thrown onto the far floor and was out of reach, so he waited for someone to notice the wreck and call the police. The front of the delivery van was crumpled, and steam escaped from the radiator – no doubt punctured by the shredded hood.

Finally, a car drove by and stopped next to the truck. A man got out who looked to be a mechanic. Dressed in a dark blue greasy uniform, he had probably been driving to his job at the garage. The man was in his mid-thirties with a shaved head and baseball cap turned to the side. He ran over, his expression alarmed.

"Hey, buddy, are you okay?" The man glanced at him, eyeing his bloody rag. "You want me to call the ambulance?"

He nodded without speaking, pressing the rag against his face.

He did feel a bit queasy at that moment, and even a bit dizzy. He had hit his head hard on the side of the door frame and had maybe overdone it, but timing a crash to achieve just the right amount of damage was no easy feat. The pain didn't bother him. He was immune to it and had been his entire life. As a former wrestler in high school, he'd suffered a lot of bruises and breaks. He'd been in fights – probably more than his fair share, all under the cover of learning MMA. He'd been in car accidents before. He could take some pain, and this was far less than the mental pain he'd feel if he actually got caught for attacking the bitch.

No, he couldn't have that. He didn't want anyone rooting through his past in any detail. Sure, he'd covered his tracks damn well over the years, but too-close scrutiny could turn up some material that would be damning. Luckily, he appeared above suspicion.

He'd survive this and come through it white as snow.

When the ambulance drove up a few moments later, he had to laugh to himself. They'd never expect that he was hiding evidence of his late-night expedition meant to scare the bejesus out of little Miss Priss, Tess McClintock.

She was like a magnet to him. He wanted to teach her a lesson. He'd done some research on her; she'd become some kind of internet sleuth trying to solve cold cases, including the ones he was responsible for, and that was not acceptable.

He wanted to do something to chase her out of town and send her back to Seattle. She could fuss about the missing girls there, if she cared so much. Leave Paradise Hill, and him, alone.

If he couldn't run her off, there were other ways he could get rid of her.

The EMT came over with a black medical bag in hand and opened the truck's door on the driver side. The angle at which the truck hit the tree meant it took some effort to get the door open but they finally managed. She looked him over as he remained seated, checking for broken bones. Finding none, she peered at the cut and then asked him if he felt he could stand.

He nodded, and she helped him out and led him over to the back to the ambulance, where he sat while she examined his head wound.

"You got quite a cut there. It'll need stitches and there's some tissue damage around it. You should get checked for a concussion. We can take you to the local hospital."

He nodded, not wanting to go, but it would provide good cover for the bruise. Just then, a patrol car from the local police drove up. The officer got out and walked over, spoke with the EMT, and then turned to him.

"Can you tell me what happened?"

He shrugged, trying to act guilty. "I was texting my uncle and I guess I didn't see the curve in the road."

The officer shook his head. "Texting while driving is a violation and carries a fine of up to $234 and a note on your license."

"Crap."

The police officer took down the details of his license and registration, and then wrote out a ticket.

"I need to call my uncle," he said. "I was driving to the warehouse to pick up a delivery of fresh produce. He'll need to send someone else to pick it up."

"Okay."

"My cell is in the truck on the passenger side floor."

The passerby went over and found the cell and brought it over.

"Here you go," he said, handing the cell to him. "If you don't want the ambulance, I can drive you to the hospital. It's not far from here."

He shook his head. "No, thanks. I'll go in the ambulance."

He wanted everything on the record so he would be above suspicion.

As the ambulance drove to the hospital, he laughed to himself. When she frowned and asked him why he was laughing, he shook his head.

"Just a joke I read on my Facebook feed."

She nodded in understanding.

ONCE HIS CUT had been stitched and cleaned up, he waited for his uncle to come pick him up from the hospital waiting room.

His uncle was suitably concerned about him, bending down to look at the bandage and tut-tutting about him texting and driving.

"It's just not like you to text and drive. You should have waited until you got to the warehouse."

"I know," he said, feigning remorse. "I got a ticket and have to pay a fine Almost three hundred bucks."

His uncle shrugged. "We'll stop by and check the truck but I'm told it's a write-off. It was old and needed to be replaced, and this will give me an excuse, I guess."

"Sorry," he said. "I just wanted you to know I was going early to get the shipment."

"I know, I know," his uncle said and laid a hand on his shoulder affectionately. "You're a hard worker. Always put in the extra effort."

As they drove to the warehouse to check out the wrecked delivery truck, he smiled to himself. He was in a crash in the next town doing his job like a good little worker bee.

His usual cover...

CHAPTER NINETEEN

Saturday morning while Tess slept, Michael took the jar of remains to the police station.

Chief Hammond was extremely interested in seeing the jar, his face wary.

"Now, where'd you get that?" he asked when Michael opened the box and removed the jar, setting it on the chief's desk.

"The cleaners found it at Ron McClintock's when they were going through the attic. Apparently, he was a hoarder. His house is filled with junk. They also found a box of pornography, including some child porn. And," he said, feeling bad for Tess but needing to inform the chief about his finds, "a scrapbook filled with clippings about the missing girls in town going back to 1978."

"'78? You mean Janine Marshall?"

"Yes. Plus the other three, as well as a number of cases of arson and armed robbery."

"We don't get much of those in these parts," Hammond

said, leaning back in his chair behind his desk. "They make big headlines and folks talk, as they will."

"I could see the scrapbook being the product of someone who might be interested in law enforcement. I know I was, especially after what happened with Lisa Tate. Even Tess became obsessed with cold cases after that. You could argue that both our careers were shaped by that night."

"It had a big impact on a lot of us. I knew her family personally. It tore up more than one family."

Michael nodded, thinking about Tess's family.

"So I need to send this to the crime lab in Seattle. I have a friend who works in the forensic unit who can do a quick DNA profile and check the system to see if we have any matches. If the families haven't already provided DNA samples, we can ask for some so we can rule the remains in or out."

"You opening up a case?"

Michael nodded. "Informally. Tess is going to contact her family and ask if anyone knows whose remains they might be before we do anything formally. These could be the badly-processed remains of a family member, but I'm really thinking they're not. I'd say these were burned in a wood fire rather than propane like they do in a crematorium."

Michael turned the jar around and pointed to a hunk of charred wood.

Chief Hammond nodded and examined the jar closer.

He frowned. "Before you get too far ahead of your skis, we're not sure this is evidence of anything yet except a bad cremation job."

Michael nodded, shrugging. He didn't want to argue with Hammond. He wanted to stay on good terms with the lawman because he could grease the wheels for the FBI in town.

Hammond peered at the jar over his reading glasses, turning it around and examining the material inside.

"Hmm. I agree with you about these being burned in a wood fire rather than in a crematorium."

Michael nodded. "My thoughts exactly. My friend in Seattle's going to work overtime to process a sample."

"It would be great to see some developments in the cases, especially for young Melissa. I'm sure the family's really suffering now, knowing that she's dead and not being held alive somewhere or working the streets in Seattle."

"It's hard for them, no doubt," Michael said. "Now that we've linked Melissa to Zoe Wallace, we may be able to connect them both to Lisa Tate. Three girls in twenty years. All close in age. All from troubled homes. Five others in the surrounding counties that match the victim's age and MO. Sounds like a serial case to me."

Hammond nodded and leaned forward, his eyes narrowed. "You found child porn in Ron's attic and a jar of badly burned remains. Sounds like Ron is our chief suspect."

Michael put the jar of ashes back in the container. "Except that whoever started the fire at the cabin did so after Ron died. So, I honestly don't think Ron did it."

"Could be an accomplice."

Michael shrugged. "Could be. Can't rule anything out at this point."

"Where did you find the pornography?"

"In a file box in a closet. Looked like the box hadn't been opened in years, from the dust covering it. Do you know how long Ron had been hoarding junk?"

Chief Hammond leaned back and pursed his lips. "I can't

really say for sure. These things start slowly, from what I hear." He thought for a moment. "After he hurt his back, he stopped going out. That was almost a decade back, and he really became more of a hermit afterwards. He stopped golfing and fishing with us. Gave up the cabin he used to rent in the summer. Sad life after Laurie left him and took the kids. Never recovered."

"What did you think of Ron?"

Chief Hammond pushed back from the desk, leaning back, hands behind his head. "He was quiet. Not a big talker. More of a listener. I guess truckers, especially long-haul truckers, are used to being alone a lot with their thoughts. He'd been happy enough when Laurie lived with him. She was the one who ran the house, because he was away so much. But when he was home, he was happy. He was one of those men who seemed content to listen to other people talking. You know what I mean?"

Michael nodded. "Sure," he said. "I had a friend like that growing up. Liked to sit and listen to the rest of us bullshitting"

"That's what I mean. He didn't do much himself, but just sat there absorbing it all."

"Did he show an interest in crime? Police work?"

Hammond made a face. "He liked to hear me talk about cases when we went fishing. Would ask me about this or that. Nothing suspicious, like. Seemed to be interested in a passing way more than anything. More like he was trying to be a good friend listening to me talk. And he was clean as a whistle in terms of a record. A bit of drinking and driving as a teen, but we all did that. Might have had a speeding ticket or two but nothing more. He was, as far as I was concerned, a law-abiding citizen."

"That's good to know." Michael frowned. "I wonder about that scrapbook, though. Do you know anyone who keeps one like that? Did you when you were a young man?"

Hammond laughed. "Back then, I was more intent on breaking the law than studying it. I was a wild one, frankly. Luckily, my dad got me out of a lot of scrapes or I would never have been able to get into law enforcement. I was no Boy Scout. Never did anything seriously criminal, but you know what teen boys can be like. Lots of anger brewing under the surface. Lots of hormones. Sometimes it gets out of hand and that leads to petty criminal stuff – vandalism, joy-riding, shoplifting, arson."

"Arson?"

"You know what I mean. Lighting garbage cans on fire. That kind of thing."

Michael shrugged, not really convinced that arson was something you could write off. Vandalism didn't usually threaten people's lives, but arson could and did kill people. Intentionally or otherwise.

In general, the Chief was right. Often, young men of a certain age had too much anger and desire bound up in them and the outlets were drinking, fighting, driving fast, and the occasional misdemeanor. It didn't mean they'd go on to live a life of crime.

God knew he had done his share of drinking, smoking pot, and driving while impaired during his youth. He was lucky to have escaped anything serious, and had gotten off lightly when he'd been caught with open booze in his car while driving. Never got charged because his dad was a respected member of the community.

Tess's dad didn't sound much different. He had no record

and had lived a crime-free life – or at least, he'd never been charged with anything. There was a difference.

That didn't mean he couldn't have been a killer who'd merely gotten away with it. It was always possible, although there were usually clues if you knew where to look. Some serial killers never committed a crime other than their murders. Others lived a life of crime that spanned the criminal code, ending in serial murder. It depended on the type of murderer they were. Some were what law enforcement types called "organized," and some were "disorganized." The public was more familiar with the organized serial killer, the ones who planned well and covered their tracks. Fictional killers like Hannibal Lecter, or real-life serial killers like BTK.

The disorganized kind were usually caught quickly, because they left behind many clues and were not well enough organized to cover their tracks. They were often ne'er-do-wells who couldn't seem to get their lives in order, and typically had a long string of failures – failed school, failed jobs, failed marriages, if they were married at all. Often, these men lived alone and generally spent their time on the sidelines of life, in the shadows, living among the refuse.

Ron McClintock had a steady job most of his adult life, had no criminal record, had married and had children. He had divorced, true, but so did half the population. Yes, he became a loner, but he might have been simply broken by the divorce and loss of his kids and family life. And he had several incriminating pieces of evidence in his home but each one, taken by itself, could be explained away, depending on the circumstances.

If there was a serial killer at work, with an accomplice or alone, he was the organized kind. You didn't get away with murders over twenty – or forty – years if you weren't extremely careful about your work. He had most probably also killed the others in neighboring counties, and that was the first thing to check. Too often serial cases languished because people didn't connect the dots. The task force was intended to overcome that kind of jurisdictional entropy.

There were several cases in Yakima and Kennewick, which were close enough to Paradise Hill that they might be linked, depending on the MO. Two older girls in their teens fit the bill, if Janine was included. But one younger girl who was around the same age as Lisa and Zoe was definitely a case to look into.

In total, there were nine cases in Paradise Hill and the surrounding counties he liked for the Paradise Hill Killer, which was how he was thinking about the man. Whether it was Ron McClintock or someone else, the girls were too close in age and too similar in their case details not to link together.

But he just didn't see Ron McClintock as the killer, despite the fact he had those three strikes against him. It didn't fit with what he knew about serial killers, but he had to hold out the option. He didn't know everything about the man. It was possible he'd find out more as time went on that excluded him from – or included him on – the list of potential killers.

The oldest case, Janine, didn't seem to fit with the others. First, she was older by three years older compared to the other girls. And second, she had gone missing after a party with a group of kids she went to school with. They had all been cleared.

In the end, he concluded that Lisa, Melissa, and Zoe were more likely linked than Janine, but until he knew more, he couldn't be sure. He was supposed to be off work but this was too close to his heart to ignore. If there was any connection to Lisa, they wouldn't let him work the case even if he were back in the office. This he'd have to do as a private citizen.

He and Tess were both emotionally invested in the case due to that night back in '98. They both felt a pull to the cases, and it seemed fitting and right that they be the ones to solve them. But he knew he'd have to talk to his supervisor and come clean about his suspicions – because the attack on Tess and the fact she had someone stalking her meant the killer might be on their tail.

He had to be responsible and protect Tess, even if neither of them could let go of the case.

CHAPTER TWENTY

Tess spent the morning in bed.

It wasn't that she was sick, but the adrenaline had all left her body and she was weak. To be honest, the burial was on Monday and she didn't want to face the prospect of burying her father. She would spend Sunday lazing around, but today, she had work to do.

Mrs. Carter came in to her room about eleven when Tess still hadn't gotten up and come out.

"Are you okay?" she asked, opening the door and peering inside.

Tess turned over in bed.

"I'm fine. I'm just sleepy for some reason."

Mrs. Carter came over to the side of the bed.

"I just wanted to check in case you had a concussion and weren't doing well."

"No, I didn't have a concussion," Tess said. "I haven't slept well for the past couple of nights. I want to sleep a little longer, if you don't mind. This bed is so nice and warm."

"You go right ahead," Mrs. Carter replied with a smile. "I

have some bacon and sausage in the oven keeping warm. You can eat when you get up."

"Thanks."

Mrs. Carter went back out and closed the door behind her, leaving Tess alone in the darkened room, wrapped up in the thick blankets.

When Tess returned to Paradise Hill, she still had fond memories of her father from when she was a child. The memories were few and far between, but they existed. Most of the good memories were from holidays – Christmas, birthdays, Easter, vacations to the coast, ice fishing in the winter up north. Her father didn't talk much, but he was there in the background, smiling like he was enjoying himself. He'd be gone for weeks at a time and then home for a week straight, before heading out again for another one of the long hauls that took him away from them.

That had to have worn on her mother, but for Tess, it meant her father was something special. When he was on his way back from a trip, everyone was excited. They cleaned the house and planned special meals for him that he loved – roast beef, ham, turkey, lasagna, steak with corn on the cob, barbecue ribs with homemade coleslaw. He ate so much fast food and truck stop café food that Tess's mom went all out when he was back in town between trips. Tess still loved those foods best because they reminded her of her father's return from the road.

He'd often bring them gifts from his trips. Tess still had the jewelry he brought home for her – bracelets and necklaces, earrings and girly things she treasured. When her mother complained about the cost of all the gifts, he always said he got them for next to nothing because they were stuff he picked up at flea markets and garage sales he visited where he stayed overnight, when he had time to kill before picking up another load. Now Tess wondered if his tendency to hoard hadn't started all the way back then when he was away from home so much and spent his off time stalking garage sales. He didn't spend much and insisted that Tess's mother shouldn't fuss about the cost.

Her mother still did fuss, because she held up half the sky, as she always said. She worked shifts at the grocery store because Tess's dad didn't earn enough to support the family on his own, no matter how long he stayed on the road. As a result, they were solidly working class. There was never much left over and never much that went to waste.

Tess got a scholarship to study at Washington State U, because her grades were so good, but the scholarship covered tuition and books. She had to work to afford to live in the dorm because they had never saved any money for her education. Thad had a small savings account started for him but Tess missed out. By the time she was ready for college, their savings had dwindled as the economy in that part of the state had failed.

These days Tess had a pretty decent income working for the *Sentinel*, all things considered. Thad made better money working up in Alaska, but he still hadn't married and was living a bachelor's life in Anchorage. He didn't plan on coming down for the burial. If Thad wanted his job, he had to work his twelve days without stop. They were flown up to the site and flown out. No exceptions. He couldn't get time off for a death in the family even if he'd wanted to – and he didn't. He had no love for his father, having parted on bad terms back when Lisa went missing. Thad thought that their father should have moved with them to Seattle. He could have found work there as a long-haul trucker, but it just wasn't in his father to leave Paradise Hill. He'd been there all his life and it was his home.

Tess would have liked Thad to come just for the support, but she knew he had nothing good to say about their father, so it was probably just as well. For an hour, Tess tossed and turned, unable to rest as she passed things over in her mind. Finally, she sat up in bed and stretched. She was wide awake now despite trying to go back to sleep, so it was time to get up. She grabbed her bag and went to the main bathroom, locking the door behind her.

She examined her face in the mirror. There was a bruise over her eye and a red mark on her neck where the attacker had grabbed her by the throat. Seeing it, she remembered that moment of fear and panic set in. She had to grip the counter and breathe deeply. It took a moment, but then her heart rate slowed and she no longer felt ice in her veins.

The last thing she needed was to be afraid and start panicking every time she thought about what happened. She had to be functional for the next forty-eight hours so she could get through the burial.

After that, it would all be over and she could return to her real life back in Seattle. The only thing left to figure out was why her father had such incriminating material in his house. Who was the person in the glass jar? Was her father interested in child porn?

Was he a serial killer?

With that on her mind, she had a shower and got dressed, trying to make herself look somewhat presentable.

AFTER BREAKFAST, Tess went to her father's house to finish working on the bedroom. The cleaners had the weekend off, so it was Tess on her own working away at the mess. Mrs. Carter had been out at the store and left Tess a note that she'd be back in fifteen. Tess should have waited but she wanted to get started, so she left a note on the kitchen island and left.

She was still spooked about the attack but couldn't do anything about it, so she closed the living room curtains and went back to the hall closet to finish clearing out the boxes of junk inside. She rolled her sleeves back up and put on a mask because of the dust.

In the first box was a pile of receipts and unopened advertising mail – offers from a local pizza shop, national ad campaigns for payday loans and big chain stores, several years old. She frowned – none of the businesses had franchises or outlets in Paradise Hill. It was as if her father had collected other people's junk mail, from other cities in Washington. She checked the address on the few that were addressed to *The Occupant* and saw that they had been sent to an address in Kennewick, closer to the southern border.

Had her father stayed at the house when he was a long-haul trucker? As far as she knew, he'd stayed in his rig, sleeping in the back, so why did he have this mail from Kennewick?

Puzzle after puzzle. There was a lot she didn't know about her father and it unnerved her that he may have had a life that he kept from his family.

She took out her cell and called her mother.

"Tess," her mother said when she answered. "How are you, dear? How are the preparations for the burial?"

Tess hadn't called to tell her mother she'd been attacked. There was nothing her mother could do and it would only upset her, so she'd decided not to say anything.

"They're fine. Hey, look," she said, trying to word her question just right. "I found some old mail in a box in Dad's closet. It was for Kennewick. Did he have an apartment there when he was driving long-haul?"

"I don't believe so. At least I don't think so, but you never know, right?" her mother replied, sounding tired. "He was gone for a couple of weeks at a time. I used to wonder how he could stand sleeping in his rig all that time, but truckers are a different breed."

"It wouldn't surprise you if he had an apartment in Kennewick?"

"Sweetheart," her mother said, her voice sounding frustrated, "I gave up being surprised at what your father did years ago. I stopped thinking about him entirely when we left. As far as I was concerned, he was out of my life and that was fine."

"You weren't upset?"

"Of course I was," she replied. "But your dad made his choice. He chose Paradise Hill. I wanted to leave so you could be safe. He may have got an apartment after we left. Who can say?"

"Okay," Tess said, not wanting to get into an argument with her. "I have to finish up here. I'll talk to you after the burial."

After they said goodbye, Tess went back to the window just as Michael was driving down the street toward the house. Just knowing he would be there eased her anxiety.

For the first time since she arrived back at her father's house, she relaxed.

CHAPTER TWENTY-ONE

After spending another few minutes at the chief's office going over the details of the Melissa Foster autopsy, Michael packed up his things and drove to Tess's father's house.

His trip back to Paradise Hill was supposed to be therapeutic. He was supposed to stay clear of law enforcement business altogether – but things hadn't worked out the way he planned. Instead, he'd become embroiled in a cold case that was hot once more. Melissa. Then there was Tess and the man stalking her and harming her, not to mention the strange findings at her father's house.

Yes, there had been serial killers who escaped detection for years. In fact, most serial killers escaped detection. Research suggested that at any given time there were fifty serial killers at work in the US alone. Only a few were ever caught and brought to justice.

Dennis Rader was one example – the BTK killer, who bound, tortured, and killed women over decades. He was a pillar of the community, was married with children. There were others. Sure, if you looked closely, you'd find something in their past or in their secret caches of trophies that looked innocuous at first glance. But Michael believed that if you knew what to look for, and if you could get access, you could figure out who was a serial killer based on their computer hard drive, their internet searches, and their possessions.

He'd spoken to the chief about who might have attacked Tess, but neither of them had come up with anything solid. It could be just a local creep who went too far, intending to rape her. Paradise Hill was small but even in a town with so few people, there were bound to be a couple of sociopaths. If one percent of people had antisocial personality disorder, that meant at least a dozen in town the size of Paradise Hill might be the type to break the law – to steal, rape, or even kill.

Those were scary statistics but they were reality. Michael was all about facing harsh reality. He'd learned the hard way that there was evil in the world, the day Lisa had left the tent and went home in the dark to whatever fate awaited her. He'd spent so many hours – countless hours – wondering what happened to her, what horrible things someone had done to her and where she was buried.

Was hers the body in the glass jar? Or was it Janine?

What horrors had both girls suffered? He knew only too well what kind of bad things might have happened to them before they died. He'd seen bodies, photos, and films. Sometimes he couldn't sleep at night and had to take a sleeping pill to get the images out of his mind.

So he completely believed and accepted that there were several psychopaths in Paradise Hill who might have wanted to hurt, rape, or even kill a pretty woman like Tess. Men who hated women so much that they wanted to inflict pain on them, choke the life out of them after brutalizing them. It sickened him, but finding and stopping those men also motivated him. It was his life's work.

He drove up and parked behind Tess's vehicle, glancing up and down the street to check and see if anything seemed out of place. There was nothing so he tried to relax just a bit. He knocked at the door and was greeted by Tess, who was wearing a face mask and safety glasses.

"You look like you're in a hazardous waste zone," he said with a smile.

"The dust is terrible in the closet. Just in case there's any black mold, I didn't want to expose myself to it."

She removed the mask and glasses, then smiled back at him, closing the door behind him.

"How are you?"

She shrugged. "As well as can be expected, all things considered."

"You'll be rattled for a few days because of the attack. You should start getting over it when things are over with the burial and service."

She nodded. "Do you think my attacker will show up at the service? Don't they like to attend those kinds of events?"

Michael shook his head. "Not with a bruise on his head. It would be a dead giveaway."

"If he does have a bruise," Tess replied, her voice sounding doubtful.

"I knocked him a good one against the wall. He'll have some kind of mark." Michael could see Tess was upset, so he changed the subject. "Found anything interesting?" He glanced around the living room.

She nodded and led him to the sofa, where he saw a pile of junk mail on the coffee table next to a bin filled with it.

"He saved all this junk mail from years ago when we still

lived with him, but it's from an address in Kennewick, not Paradise Hill. I asked my mother if he rented an apartment when he was on the road, but she wasn't sure."

"Hmm, that's curious. Signs he was a budding hoarder?" Michael sat on the sofa, picking up the flyers and mail, sorting through it. "Rent in Kennewick is pretty low so he might have been able to keep an apartment there without your mother knowing."

"Why would he? He always bragged about his great rig and how it was like a hotel room in the back."

"Maybe he was sick of not having a shower or kitchen."

"Maybe," Tess replied.

"But why Kennewick? He could have just driven the distance and stayed here. It sounds suspiciously like a second home."

Tess nodded, and he could see the resignation on her face.

"I just can't imagine him doing that."

"It may have been junk mail he got from an item he bought at one of those flea markets. Maybe in a box of something he bought. In an old desk. An old filing cabinet. You can't know unless you get access to his banking and find receipts for rent at the Kennewick address."

She nodded. "I have a box of bank and utility receipts. I'll check there first. He saved everything. If he was paying rent in Kennewick, I should be able to find out."

He shook his head, unable to stop himself from smiling fondly at her. She was so much like him. He'd get something in his mind and be unable to get it out unless he followed it through to the end. She had to find out whether her father was leading a second life, one way or another.

He watched her put the mask back on and lower the protective glasses.

"Here," she said and handed him a mask out of a package. "If you're going to stay, you can help."

He took the mask from her, hooking the loops over his ears and pinching the nose to tighten it. "I don't suppose you have another pair of protective glasses?"

"As a matter of fact, the cleaners left some behind." She went into the kitchen and sorted through a box, and brought him back a pair.

Then she went back into the closet, and for the next hour they checked through boxes, setting aside any that had files. When they had stacked a dozen boxes beside the sofa, Tess sat and began sorting through them. He sat beside her and dug into a fresh box.

"This one looks like it has bank statements," she said and lifted out one of the thick expandable file folders. "There are a bunch of receipts from different businesses. My father kept everything. And I mean everything."

For the next hour, the two of them fished through the files. The receipts Michael checked were for a variety of items – mostly things Ron had bought at sporting goods stores in neighboring towns, including rifles and ammo, camping gear, fishing rods and tackle, and portable propane tanks.

"Did your dad do a lot of fishing and hunting?"

Tess glanced over at the pile of receipts Michael had already gone through.

"Some," she said, and pulled one out of a pile. "But not recently. Not since he hurt his back."

"When was that?" he asked, checking the dates on the receipts.

"Ten years ago," Tess replied. "He had a car accident

when he was out hunting and stopped long-haul trucking when he couldn't stand the long drives due to the chronic pain. He started to work for Hammond Delivery doing local deliveries. Then he stopped working altogether when his back pain got too bad. They think his chronic pain masked his pancreatic cancer symptoms. What he thought was back pain turned out to be untreatable cancer. When he finally was diagnosed, he had only weeks to live."

"That's sad. What a horrible cancer to get," Michael said, imagining Ron at the end, sick, skin and bone. A corpse waiting to die like Keith, one of his co-workers. "I've seen it before. One of the guys at the Seattle office died of it. Not a nice way to go."

Tess nodded, her expression sad. "I wish he would have told us. I would have come out to look after him, despite everything. He was still my father."

"He probably didn't want anyone to see this place," Michael replied, glancing around at the still-messy room. "I'd be really embarrassed if this was my house."

They worked away for a while in silence. He supposed they were both thinking about her father and his fast and painful death. He opened a new batch of receipts and found one for a storage unit just outside the city. The receipt was for approximately five years earlier and indicated that Tess's father had purchased the contents sight unseen.

"Look," he said and showed her the receipt. "Your dad was one of those treasure hunters who buy the contents of abandoned storage units sight unseen."

"I know," she said and took the receipt from him. "I saw another receipt from a box in his room. Some of these boxes might be from a unit he rented, but who can say?" She smoothed the receipt out, running her hand over it to remove the wrinkles. "We should go see what he has in the storage unit."

"You should take it easy today," Michael said, his tone chiding. "We can do that after the burial. It's going to be an emotional time for you."

"I'm fine," she said and gave him a look of impatience. "Really. We weren't close in the last decade. It's going to drive me crazy if I don't figure this out and find out whether he was a pedophile child killer or not."

"Tess," he said and reached out to touch her arm. "I'm almost certain that he's not a pedophile child killer."

"But not a hundred percent sure."

He shook his head. "No one can ever know what's in someone else's heart. But there would be more clues if he was. Not a box of old European porn that looks like it hadn't been opened in years. Not a scrapbook that might have been made by any school kid interested in police work."

"And the burned remains in a glass jar? What does that tell you?"

He shrugged. "Like I've said, you can't get ahead of the evidence. They'll start to process the sample tomorrow and have a preliminary analysis in a few days. Then we can start theorizing. Right now, it's not enough to draw any conclusions. All of this," he said, pointing at the boxes surrounding them, "it could all be circumstantial. He might have bought it all sight unseen and then never got rid of it. Even the remains."

"You're probably right," she said with a heavy sigh. "It's just so strange to find this house the way it is and all these incriminating things. I don't know what to think."

He squeezed her shoulder. "Don't think anything. Hold your conclusions until we have more evidence."

She nodded and held up the receipt. "Then there's this," she said. "A bank account statement. There are checks attached and one is for rent at the address in Kennewick. It's from five years ago."

Michael took the statement from Tess's hand. Sure enough, there were a dozen checks stapled to a bank statement and one of them was labeled rent, and the address was in Kennewick

"I guess he had a second life after all. Maybe it started after your mother left him?"

"The junk mail was dated from a decade before. He's been living a double life for seventeen years. Not long after my mother left, in other words."

"Maybe he kept a place in Kennewick because he had a girlfriend there."

"Maybe," Tess said, but her voice sounded doubtful. "If so, he never told us about it."

"He probably wouldn't tell you. He'd try to avoid it. Kids don't take it well when their parents get new partners, in my experience."

Tess removed another sheet from the box. "Here's another statement and another check. This one is from 2000. He had that apartment for a long time."

"It's not against the law. I wouldn't worry too much about it."

"It's evidence," she said and looked in his eyes.

"Evidence that doesn't say much other than he had a place in Kennewick. That's it, Tess." He took the receipt. "This was after your parents split. Maybe he rented it to get away from this place."

He glanced around at the house. At one time, it had been nice enough, as small bungalows went. Three bedrooms, a combined living and dining room, and a kitchen with a pass-through to the dining room. A decent-sized backyard that backed onto the mountain. Lots of trees, and a playground and small park only a few houses down.

A lot of people would be happy to live in a house like that – at least, before it became a hoarder's nightmare.

"Maybe," she said, and he heard her sigh heavily once again.

They went back to work, sorting through boxes, looking at contents and deciding what to do with them.

"Why don't you let me take you away from all this?" Michael said. "We'll go out and get some supper. Tonight's rib night at the Grill. I know you love ribs. Plus, they have a really nice beer on tap." He raised his eyebrows.

She finally smiled, and this time it was a real smile, her eyes crinkling at the corners.

"Beer sounds really good right now," she said and plopped the sheet of paper onto the coffee table. "I'm just about dried out with all this dust. And I do love ribs."

They packed up the boxes, closed the place up, and drove to the Grill. As they sat down in the booth by the window, Michael thought he could get used to having Tess around. They worked well together and had some of the same obsessions.

Then he shut that part of his brain off and focused on the menu. Tomorrow was another day and then they had the burial. That would be a stressful time for Tess. He'd do what he could to make things more bearable for her.

It was the least he could do.

CHAPTER TWENTY-TWO

He spent all day Saturday recovering, with a nasty headache from the knock on his forehead. The hospital gave him some pain meds, but he wasn't going to get caught up in the opioid epidemic. He didn't have a concussion, just a nasty bump over his eye and a cut that had needed five stitches. Plus, he'd sprained his arm when he had tried to brace himself during the crash. He had his arm in a sling, because even supporting the weight hurt.

Damn…

He hadn't expected that much damage. He'd merely wanted an excuse for the black eye. Still, the fact that it had happened while he was working in another town meant he had a great alibi. No one would suspect he'd attacked Tess the night before because they'd be too focused on his tireless efforts at his job. They'd praise him for working even on a Saturday.

Above and beyond.

Back at the apartment, he paced the room. Normally on Saturday after he picked up the delivery, he'd go to the diner and have lunch – hot beef sandwich with gravy, his favorite – and then drive around town, delivering groceries to the addresses on his list, checking out what everyone was doing in the process. But his boss had given him the day off.

It sure helped to have your uncle as your boss.

Clint Walker called him Saturday night, wondering if he was planning on coming to the bar for a game of darts, but he bowed out.

"How's your head? We heard you crashed the delivery truck in Yakima."

"Yeah," he replied. "Was texting my uncle."

"You're usually such a law and order type."

"Too much beer at Moran's last night, I guess."

"That'll teach you – not," Clint replied with a chuckle. "It was a bender night for all of us, I guess."

"Yep," he replied. "I was still a bit hungover when I picked up the truck and drove to Yakima."

"Don't drink and drive," Clint said with a rueful laugh. He'd had a few DUIs before, and knew of which he spoke. "You take it easy tonight. We can restart the match next weekend."

"Thanks," he said. "I appreciate it. Don't want to lose my trophy."

"That's for sure," Clint said with a laugh.

That was a good omen. Clint thought he'd been there to the bitter end with the rest of them, probably falling asleep in his beer like he usually did.

He tried to rest easy the remainder of the night. However, his plan to cover his tracks required more effort, and he'd have to pay Mr. Garth Hammond a visit if he wanted to escape detection.

HE LEFT after dusk and parked down the street from Garth's house, watching to see when he left the house for the bar. Garth was a regular feature at Harry's, the local watering hole. Never missed a Saturday night.

He had a plan to cast some shade over Garth. It would require that he had his timing down just right. Garth usually left for the bar around nine o'clock and walked the four blocks from his house to the bar.

That was his chance.

He drove to a street a few blocks over from Harry's and parked, then walked down the poorly-lit back alley behind the bar and waited. Sure enough, Garth appeared, walking down the street at just after nine, hands in his pockets, whistling like everything was right with the world.

He waited in the shadows and when Garth passed the entrance to the back alley, he jumped Garth, throwing a good hard punch to the man's left temple. Totally cold-cocked, he dropped like a rock.

That was all he needed to see -- Garth on the ground. He ran to the end of the alley and stood behind the dumpster, watching to make sure Garth did in fact get up.

He came to and pulled himself up, rubbing his head and glancing around.

"What the fuck?" he said, stumbling a bit as he dusted himself off.

Then, like the good old boy he was, Garth went inside the bar. He'd have quite the story to tell the guys.

He could hear the conversation in his mind:

"What the hell happened to you?"

"Someone cold-cocked me on my way inside."

"What? Did you see who?"

"No. I was walking along, minding my own business, when out of

the blue, someone hit me. Knocked me out. When I came to, I was lying on the ground."

"No shit. You gonna report it?"

"What the fuck am I going to say? A ghost hit me? No fucking way. Give me a beer and I'll be fine."

They'd all get drunk and his tale of being punched out by some bogeyman in the alley would become a legend. A tale told by an idiot, full of sound and fury…

But the existence of the mysterious attacker and the bruise over his eye would be a piece of evidence that would be added to all the others. If push came to shove and they were both questioned by police about their whereabouts on Friday night, and how they got their bruises, guess who's story would be more believable?

At least, that was the plan.

ON SUNDAY, he was feeling better, and decided to venture out before the boys came for the afternoon. Most people went to one of the churches for Sunday worship in the morning; he did too, now and then, to keep up appearances. He didn't believe in God. If there were a God, He wouldn't have let him do what he did and get away with it for so long. So, he didn't go to service every week but at least once or twice a month, especially when he wanted to cover up something or have an alibi. He went enough that people assumed he was a believer but not enough to be slavish about it.

That was it. Appearances were all people cared about. They didn't care about the truth. That they could take or leave, depending on whether it suited their prejudices. Mostly leave, especially if the truth was harsh.

And it was harsh.

People were sheep. They were fucking sheep. Wolves like him were the ones who ruled the world. He took life when he wanted to. Nothing was done to him – no bolt of lightning came down from on high to stop him from choking the life out of a girl if he wanted. Nothing could stop him from doing what he wanted to her.

When he was alone with a girl, he was God. He decided on life and death – and it was pretty much always death. There had been a few he'd let go because he was just not into it but they were usually the dregs of society and would never be able to either identify him or incriminate him. Besides, the whores he frequented on occasion were used to being pushed around and abused, so high on crack and meth that they didn't care as long as they got their money or drugs.

There were enough wolves out there that the police could never find and stop them all.

The police were stupid.

He was smart.

In fact, he decided to go to church and show his face so that people would be all the more sympathetic to him.

"Poor boy! Look at that, tsk tsk tsk..."

By the time he sat in the pew, heads were turning to check him out. No doubt *Maureen* had already spread the word about his accident. He nodded to a couple of people he knew who were related to his mother, then focused back on his hymnal, hoping none of the congregation would stop by and say hello.

No such luck.

"How are you, dear?" Mrs. Benson asked, scooting in beside him while her husband took a spot a few pews forward. "Your mom told us about the accident. Texting and driving is dangerous. I always tell the girls not to bring their cell phones when they drive, but you can't tell some people anything. I told them…"

Mrs. Benson droned on a few more minutes. He fantasized grabbing her by the throat and choking the breath out of her so he could get some peace, but he just smiled and nodded, pretending to listen to her inane chatter.

He wasn't reckless.

He murmured something to her about regrets and learning a lesson, and how he had decided to put his cell away when he drove from now on. That he'd gotten a ticket and would be paying a hefty fine. That he was on the mend and had gotten off quite lightly, all things considered. That she should see the front end of the delivery truck and the tree.

"You should come by for Sunday dinner. We're having roast with mashed potatoes and corn. You're always welcome."

"Thanks," he said. "I have the boys this afternoon and then they're going to their grandma's for supper. We'll see how I feel."

She nodded and laid a hand on his arm. "I understand. The invitation is open. We'll see you if we see you."

Not if I see you first.

She got up and toddled over to her husband and sat beside him, whispering to him. Mr. Benson turned and nodded to him, smiling perfunctorily. They were friends – friends of his adoptive-father, Joe and Maureen, not his real father and mother.

His real father was the town ne'er-do-well, who couldn't seem to keep a job and was always getting into scrapes with the law. Drunk and disorderly, theft, driving under the influence. He'd been in and out of cells on a regular basis, and had several bastards living with their mothers or, like he had done, with other family members. Then pappy was caught for armed robbery and went away for a decade, holed up in Connell at the Coyote Ridge Correctional Center. The bastard wanted him to take the rap for that one, too, but he refused.

His real mother was dead, but while she was alive she'd been the black sheep of her family and the two of them were a pair, their lives thrown away to drugs and street crime. Luckily for him, his uncle had taken him in when he was five, but he'd had five hellish years of living with his mother and her collection of boyfriends who variously abused him or neglected him, depending on their tendencies.

It paid to be the bastard of a girl from the right side of the tracks. He'd escaped his real father's fate. He'd kept his nose as clean as he could during his non-hunting times.

When he was hunting, that was another matter altogether. Hunting couldn't help but break the rules. If he got caught – and he knew he would eventually – his crimes were the kind that men would talk about for years to come. Maybe even use him as a case study to teach the FBI special agents about serial killers.

That would feel good.

It would feel freaking fantastic. All his life, he'd been invisible. The quiet one. The one who disappeared into the woodwork.

Soon, one day soon, he'd be a legend.

For the time being, he'd keep hunting until he no longer got any reward from it. At that point, he'd lure them in and maybe kill a few FBI special agents in the process. Just to shove their faces in it.

How upset they would be when they found out it had been *him* all along...

HE WENT to the coffee shop and sat at his usual place, ordering his usual plate of hot beef sandwich and coffee. His instinct was to hide out, but if he followed his usual Sunday routine, everyone would think he was just a good old boy, doing his usual thing. Nothing to see here folks, besides the black eye and bandaged arm.

Move along.

The guys from work crowded around him, checking out his eye and the bandage, joking how he looked like some woman had given him a black eye and that the crash was just a cover story.

He laughed with them, of course, playing along like it was a good yuk.

Wouldn't they be shocked if they knew the truth...

After they left him alone, Cam McPherson sat on the stool beside him and looked him over.

"Heard you got in an accident in Yakima. Totaled the old delivery truck, right?"

He laughed ruefully and shook his head. "Yep. I'm living proof that texting and driving don't mix. That's the end of my public service announcement."

Cam laughed. "You should have taken the new one. At least it has air bags."

"Yeah, should've."

"Hey, did you hear that Garth was jumped on Sixth Street, just behind Harry's?"

"No shit?" he replied, his eyes suitably wide with shock. "Someone mugged him?"

"Yeah, but they didn't steal his wallet or anything. Probably just some freak out to kick ass. Prove himself bigger and meaner than everyone."

"Probably. Must be a pussy because Garth's pretty easy pickings."

"Yeah," Cam said with a nod. "Eats like a pig but skinny as a rail."

They talked for a while about the Seahawks-Cowboys matchup and about the latest vehicle Cam was refurbishing. When his food arrived, Cam slapped him on the back grabbing his takeout coffee and donut and leaving the coffee shop, much to his pleasure. For the rest of his meal, he ate in relative peace, broken only when someone deigned to say hello and point at his black eye.

"Heard about the accident. Never can be too careful. Take care."

He gave them all the requisite smile and nod, and when he'd finished his plate and paper, he left the coffee shop, satisfied that he'd done his part to maintain the camouflage that would keep him out of prison.

The boys came over for the afternoon, and while they had planned on going for a drive to one of the cabins and have a bonfire, he used his injuries as an excuse. Instead, they spent the afternoon playing video games, the three of them bonding over running over street prostitutes in Grand Theft Auto.

The only moment when he felt the least bit unsure about his ruse was when he dropped the boys off at their grandmother's for Sunday dinner and he had to be civil to Carter and Tess. Luckily, he had an airtight alibi for his wounds and so he shrugged it off, enjoying being so close to Tess that he could smell her perfume when he passed by.

Carter had been his usual uncivil self, barely giving Gene a good word. Fuck him. Maybe one day, he'd have the pleasure of taking the sonofabitch out. When he was good and ready.

Until then, he put on his congenial facade and smiled like he was just a good old boy.

It seemed to do the trick.

Ron McClintock's burial service was scheduled for Monday. He wasn't planning on showing up, even though he had been a kind of friend to him. Older men like Ron seemed to want to befriend him – especially those who knew his provenance as a bastard. He didn't complain. It made them less likely to suspect him. In fact, he cultivated their friendships, as he had Ron's. They knew his bastard of a real father. They knew the story of his mother spreading her legs when she was only fifteen and getting knocked up with him. Of her living with his real dad for a few years until things fell apart and Dear Old Dad was arrested and sent to prison for fraud. Of how his mother had been lost to meth and had neglected him for a good couple of years before his aunt and uncle intervened after she died from an overdose.

It was good old Uncle Joe and Aunt Maureen who stepped in and rescued him, giving him the best kind of camouflage you could ever hope for.

It was satisfying in a way he couldn't explain that he went under their radar – everyone's radar – for so long. No one would ever suspect him. It was almost as good as the hunting itself.

Almost...

No. He wouldn't show up at the graveside service. He had the accident to excuse him from attending. He'd tell his aunt that he had a bad headache and all the ladies would coo and cluck and worry about him and his concussion when they saw him in the store or gas station.

Poor dear...

He knew eventually he'd get caught. But not for a while. There was no sign on any front that his cover had been blown.

He aimed to keep it that way.

CHAPTER TWENTY-THREE

Sunday afternoon, while Mrs. Carter was at church service and Michael was busy with the police going over the Melissa Foster case, Tess spent some time alone at her father's house. After an hour of packing and trashing, there came a knock at the front door. Tess glanced up from the bin she was working on as a chill go through her.

She checked her cell, but there was no message from Michael, Kirsten, or Mrs. Carter.

She went to the window and pushed the curtain aside. On the street was a van with *Hammond and Sons Services* on the logo.

She went to the door and saw that it was Garth, the young man who had been with John Hammond the day she arrived. He had a plastic-wrapped basket of flowers in his arms. Most importantly, he had a red contusion on his forehead.

"Hello, Tess," he said. "Got a delivery for you."

"Thanks." She didn't open the door. "You can leave it on the front step."

He shrugged and placed the bouquet on the step. "Never got a chance to personally say I was sorry about your father. He was a friend of my dad's. Used to work for us."

"How did you get that bruise over your eye?" She peered at him through the glass window in the door.

He held a hand up to his eye. "Oh, this? You won't believe it, but someone jumped me out of the blue on my way to the bar last night."

"Really?"

"Yeah, I was walking down the street on my way to Harry's and wham! I was cold-cocked and out cold. Woke up seeing stars."

She watched him to see if he seemed sincere but couldn't tell.

"That's terrible," she said, forcing herself to seem sympathetic. "You can leave the flowers, thanks." She gave him a perfunctory smile and then watched him walk down the sidewalk to the vehicle and didn't leave until he'd driven off back up the street toward the town center. She should have given him a tip for the delivery but she did not want to open her door to him.

Garth Hammond had been her attacker.

It had to be him, but of all the nerve… To actually show up to her father's house with that bruise over his eye?

That sounded just like what a sociopath would do, gloating in how he was able to attack her and get away with it.

She carried the basket of flowers into the living room where she set it down on the coffee table. After peeling away the clear wrapping paper, she found the gift card:

From an admirer

HE HAD to be sending her some kind of sick message.

She examined the flowers more closely and saw that they were roses – not the kind of flowers you would usually send for a funeral or bereavement.

She called *Hammond and Sons Services* intending to find out who sent it. She entered the number on her cell and spoke to the receptionist, who gave her the number of the florist. When Tess called that number, the woman refused to tell her who had sent the flowers.

"I need to know," Tess said, impatient with the woman. "Is there no way to tell who paid for the flowers? They had to have used a credit card."

"I'm sorry but I can't tell you eve if I knew," the woman said. "It looks like it was paid using a gift card by a national florist that does online ordering. That's all I can tell you. You'd have to take that up with them. We just arrange the flowers and get them delivered to the addresses we're given. We don't handle the actual purchase or delivery, and even if we did, which we don't, I couldn't tell you. It would violate our customer's privacy."

Tess hung up and called Michael's cell. It rang a few times before he answered, sounding pleased to hear from her.

"Tess, hello – how are you? I stopped by to check on you between meetings and Mom said you were still sleeping."

"I think Garth Hammond is my attacker."

"What? Why?"

"He just showed up at my fathers with a delivery of roses."

"Yeah, John also does local deliveries besides landscaping."

"He had a bruise over his eye."

"What?" he said, and his voice was immediately concerned. "Are you alone?"

"Yes. I have the doors locked."

"I'll be right over. You shouldn't be there alone, considering what happened."

"I have so much work to do here," she protested, glancing around at the mess. Despite a couple of days' worth of work, the place was still a hoarder's dream. "I didn't think my attacker would actually show up with a bouquet of flowers."

"Of course not. Just wait there for me. I'm going to call Chief Hammond and let him know."

"Okay. Sorry to drag you from your work."

"Don't apologize. Chief Hammond will probably send someone to have a little chat with Garth Hammond. If he has no good excuse for the bruise, they'll likely pick him up and charge him with assault."

"Good," Tess said. "He said he was attacked last night and that's how he got the bruise but how can he prove it? He said it happened in a dark alley and he didn't see who did it."

"Chief Hammond will know if he reported the attack. I'll let you know what I find out."

"Thanks. It'll make me feel better to think they have whoever did it."

"How are you feeling?"

Tess took in a deep breath. "I'm fine. Nothing but a bruise on my forehead and neck to show for it. I did start to have a panic attack, but was able to stop it before it happened."

"You should get some counselling to deal with that. I have a therapist and believe me, it really does help. I know it's not the manly thing to admit, but there you go. I admit it."

"It just means you're human. It's brave to admit that you're suffering and need help," she said.

"Luckily, the FBI is used to this kind of thing and has a really great therapy program in place for agents who experience traumatic events. You really should get a therapist."

"I'll consider it."

"Look, stay there and don't let anyone in until I get there, okay? I'll be ten minutes."

"I won't," she replied, and ended the call.

She sat amidst the mess, the flowers – which were now really creeping her out – on the coffee table. Part of her wanted to take them and throw them into the trash rather than look at them and wonder.

She went to the window and moved the curtain aside to check the street outside the house. Everything was quiet; there was no movement and no one on the sidewalk. She could see the Carter house from where she stood, and saw Mrs. Carter's car in the driveway.

She exhaled and tried to calm her fears.

MICHAEL ARRIVED within ten minutes and Tess was never so glad to see someone walking up the front sidewalk.

She opened the door and let him in.

"Hey, how are you?" he asked, taking her arm in his hand. "Tell me what happened and what he said."

They sat on the sofa and Tess described everything she could remember about the brief encounter with Garth.

Michael leaned back and shook his head. "I don't get why he'd show up and expose himself so blatantly. I'd have thought that he'd hide out with that black eye. Certainly didn't expect that your attacker would show up and actually confront you."

"Me either. He seemed totally nonchalant about his eye. Said he got it from being mugged last night."

"How fresh did his bruise look?"

Tess shrugged. "How should a two-day old bruise look?"

Michael pursed his lips. "Depends. Should start turning purple by the second day."

"It was still pretty red."

Michael frowned. "Sounds really fresh. Besides, from what I remember of Garth, he's on the skinny side and the man I fought with was well-built."

"I didn't have a good look at the man who attacked me," Tess said, her mind going back to that night. "It was dark. All I saw was a blur."

"He'd have to have balls of steel to come to your father's house and deliver flowers if he was your attacker, which suggests that whoever he is, he feels very safe and sure of himself. I would never have thought of Garth because he's skinny and kind of a runt."

"What did Chief Hammond say when you told him?"

"He said if Garth was attacked, he didn't report it. He'll send an officer by Garth's place and speak with him. If he has no alibi for Friday night and if he really did get the bruise on Saturday, he's not our man."

Tess glanced around the living room, which was starting to take shape, although it was still filled with junk. Only now, the junk was arranged in neat rows and stacks.

"There's so much left to do."

"Come to my mom's. I don't want you to be alone here," Michael said. "You should take the afternoon off, considering. Watch some Netflix. This mess will wait until Tuesday."

She turned to him and finally smiled. "Okay, I will. I am pretty tired."

It could wait until Tuesday. Maybe by then, they'd know whether Garth Hammond was their man.

TESS SPENT the evening at Mrs. Carter's and was curious to meet Kirsten's two boys, who were coming over for dinner with their grandmother and aunt while Kirsten and Phil had a dinner out -- perhaps one of their last before the baby came.

Around five thirty, a car drove up and out got a man and two young boys. Michael went to the door and let them in.

"Hey, you two. Give me a hug," Mrs. Carter said, corralling the two boys, forcing them to hug her. The oldest boy was fifteen and the youngest was thirteen. They had Kirsten's dark hair and were both lanky. Michael went over and gave the two boys a hug, rubbing the younger boy's hair affectionately.

In stepped Kirsten's ex-husband, Gene. Tess hadn't seen him in years, except in pictures Kirsten had posted online before they split.

Mrs. Carter pointed to Gene's head, which was bandaged. A shock went through Tess when she saw it.

"I hear you got in an accident in Yakima," Mrs. Carter said after shooing the boys into the living room where their XBox and controllers waited.

"Yep," Gene said, touching his head, a guilty smile on his face. "That'll teach me to drink late on Friday night and then text and drive the next morning. Darts match every Friday night. I'm the reigning champ and celebrated a bit too hard, I guess."

"You were celebrating late?" Michael asked, his voice light.

Gene shrugged. "Don't know what time exactly. After midnight, I guess."

"You remember Tess McClintock," Mrs. Carter said, pointing to Tess. "Kirsten's best friend from school."

"We met at the baby shower for Craig," Gene said and nodded at Tess. "Sorry about your dad."

Tess forced a smile. "Thanks."

Gene passed Tess and stuck his head in the living room. He spoke to the boys who were already sitting in front of the television.

"You boys help your grandma with the dishes after supper."

They two boys nodded, their focus on the video game they were already starting to play.

Then, Gene passed Tess, nodding to her again without saying anything.

"Phil's picking them up later?" Michael asked, staring at Gene intently.

"Nine o'clock. School tomorrow."

"Okay, see you," Michael said and held the front door open for him. "Thanks for dropping them off."

Tess waited until the door was closed and Mrs. Carter went into the living room to talk to the boys. Then, she went to Michael, who was watching out the window as Gene drove off in his car.

A blue Toyota sedan.

"Are you wondering what I'm wondering?" she asked.

Michael turned to her, a look of bemusement on his face. "You mean, isn't it curious how Gene got that bandage over his eye?"

Mrs. Carter came to where they stood. "Kirsten told me he got it in an accident in Yakima yesterday morning. He was supposed to get the kids but had to postpone until today."

Michael said nothing but raised his eyebrows.

Tess didn't say anything, either. Gene had an alibi -- he was at a bar until after midnight. He got the wound over his eye in an accident with his truck in Yakima.

Still, it was unnerving.

There were two men with bandages over their left eyes. Garth with his attack in the dark and Gene with his accident. Of the two men, Gene seemed more of a size to be her attacker, but Garth's story seemed less credible.

Tess tried to put it out of her mind.

THE FIVE OF them enjoyed another of Mrs. Carter's home cooked meals, listening to the two boys talk about their dad's accident and how they missed out their weekend with him because of it.

"We were going to go to the cabin and have a bonfire, but his accident meant we had to stay home."

"That's too bad," Mrs. Carter said. "Maybe next weekend."

They sat in the living room together and watched several episodes from The Walking Dead, so the boys could catch up.

Finally, Phil arrived at nine and he came in for a moment to talk to Mrs. Carter and thank her for taking the boys for the evening.

Tess watched Phil and noted how similar he was to Eugene. Both men were older than Kirsten by almost seven years. Phil was a real estate agent working in an agency in Kennewick. Eugene worked for his uncle and had his own security business, monitoring and installing security systems in residences and business in town.

Tess felt a bit jealous about her own lack of a romantic life, but she held out hope that she'd meet someone compatible soon.

She watched Michael with Phil, how they shook hands and talked together. Michael clearly preferred Phil to Gene.

Finally, the little family left and Mrs. Carter put on the kettle for some hot tea.

About nine that night, Michael got a call. He held up the cell to show her it was from Chief Hammond.

"Hello, Chief, how are you? It's Sunday night. Why are you working so late?"

Michael listened for a few moments, nodding his head, and giving a monosyllabic response. "Yes. Yes. Okay."

Finally, he shifted his position and turned to look at her, his expression unreadable but he didn't sound pleased when he spoke.

"So you're sure about that?"

He listened some more and then said goodbye. He turned off his cell and slipped it back into his pocket.

"Apparently, Garth claims he was attacked when he was walking to the bar after dark. He showed up at the bar with a red mark over his eye. He told the guys at the bar he was jumped on the way over. He had no idea who did it, and was on the ground and had no chance to fight back."

"Did he report the attack?"

"No," Michael said. "He said he didn't think it was worth the effort since he never saw who hit him."

"Do you think he's lying?"

Michael shrugged. "I don't know. He had a bruise on the side of his head – the same side as the man who I fought with." He shook his head in frustration. "But it doesn't make sense. If he was your attacker, he's pretty brazen for coming over to your place. Besides, he has an alibi for Friday night. He drank in the bar until midnight and then went home. He has friends who can put him at Harry's until then. That pretty much rules him out as your attacker since your attack was *before* midnight."

Tess sighed. "Maybe the others were wrong about what time he left?"

"Could be. Unless one of them comes forward to change his story, we're stuck with the fact that he has an alibi for the night you were attacked. I just don't see him for it, but I may be wrong. When adrenaline flows, you don't always notice the finer details of a situation. Maybe the guy I fought was smaller than I remember. We'll have to wait and see but Hammond isn't going to charge him with anything, considering his alibi."

Tess turned back to the television and pressed play on the PVR. She tried to settle in and watch the next episode but her mind was caught by the prospect that Garth wasn't her attacker after all. That meant someone else was.

Someone who was still walking around free. Like Gene. But he had an even better alibi.

Tess shivered, wondering who had attacked her and if they'd ever know.

CHAPTER TWENTY-FOUR

Tess woke the morning of the burial with a headache.

She'd struggled to fall asleep when she went to bed and had woken up several times out of a light sleep, her heart pounding. Michael said she could expect to experience nightmares. It was the trauma of the attack. Sometimes, people had delayed reactions and didn't show the stress for a few days after an attack like hers.

Tess figured that was the case.

She took a quick shower to help wake up, covering her bandage with some plastic and duct tape. When she was finished, she went to the kitchen where Mrs. Carter had a fresh pot of coffee brewing.

"How are you, dear?" Mrs. Carter said, coming over to give her a brief hug. "This will be a hard day for you."

"I'm fine," Tess replied, yawning and stretching. "Just a bit tired. Didn't sleep well."

"That's to be expected. You've had a scare and suffered

the loss of a parent. Those are two big hits at once. If anyone deserves a vacation, it's you."

"I have to get the house cleared up and put it up for sale. No rest for the weary, I guess."

Mrs. Carter nodded and pointed to the oven. "There's bacon and hash brown potatoes in the oven. You can fix yourself a couple of eggs if you like. I'm zipping out to pick up a few groceries – but I'll be back in time for the burial, of course."

"Thanks," Tess said and smiled. She held up her coffee. "This is what I really need. I'll eat when I get half of it down and my brain starts waking up."

Mrs. Carter smiled back, gathered up her bag and jacket, then left the house. Tess carried her mug of coffee to the living room to check on Michael, but he was out. She heard a ding from her cell and checked her messages.

MICHAEL: I'm down at the Chief's office checking on the case but will be back in time to pick you up for the service.

TESS: Thanks. You're supposed to be on medical leave and not get involved in any murder cases, if I remember what you told me.

MICHAEL: Suitably chastened. I know I should stay away, but this case is personal. Hope you had a good sleep.

TESS: I didn't sleep well but there's always tonight. Maybe after the burial, I'll be able to relax.

MICHAEL: Hope so. I'll pick you up at 10:45.

TESS: See you then.

Tess sat on the sofa and watched the news headlines for a while as she drank her coffee. When her stomach finally grumbled, she went to fix some breakfast, and when the time arrived, she dressed in her black suit and got ready for the service.

While she dressed, she wondered who would show up for

her father's burial. He'd been a hermit for the last few years, but before that, he'd been a community member all his life.

Most of all, Tess wondered if her attacker would be there and whether she'd know him if she saw him without his mask. The two suspects so far, Garth and Gene, both had alibis but without a thorough police investigation, she doubted either of their stories would be checked very thoroughly.

She shivered and watched out the window for Michael to arrive, glancing up and down the street to see if there was a black truck parked anywhere in sight. She'd be glad to have Michael with her at the service. He'd be checking out those in attendance to see who might match the description of her attacker. While it was often the case that attackers showed up at public events like a funeral or memorial service, so they could watch their victims and gloat, Michael didn't think her attacker would show up. Both Gene and Garth had shown themselves to her so perhaps neither of them were her attacker.

She couldn't imagine the attacker would be so ballsy to show up with a bump on his head. Her attacker probably wouldn't go out in public for a few days until whatever bruise he'd received had faded.

That made Tess feel a bit better, but she sure never realized how many people ended up with black eyes on any given weekend.

MICHAEL ARRIVED after Mrs. Carter came back with her groceries, and the three of them drove to the burial site. When they arrived, the pastor was already there, waiting to speak with Tess so they could go over the program.

After they went over the process, she thanked him for being willing to do the service, considering her father was an atheist.

"These services aren't for the dead. They're for the living," Pastor Greg said, patting her on the shoulder. "The living must go on and it comforts them to hear the gospel, even if the deceased wasn't religious. Most folks in Paradise Hill are Christians. They need to hear the good news when facing the death of one of their community members."

Tess smiled and glanced over at the gravesite. A mound of dirt was piled beside the open hole, and the casket had already been positioned over the grave. All that was left was for Pastor Greg to say a few words and invite others to do so as well. They'd lower the casket into the ground and people would throw flowers into the grave.

Tess would throw a single shovel of dirt into it; others could do so as well. Then it would be over.

A dozen foldable chairs had been arranged beside the grave and there were several bouquets of flowers positioned around the casket. It was as minimal as a graveside service could get, but Tess knew it was more than her father would have wanted.

Tess took a seat in the front row of chairs and waited while people drove up in their vehicles, finding spots on the narrow road that circled the cemetery. Dressed in their Sunday best even though it was Monday, they came to give Tess their condolences before taking their seats.

She smiled, shook hands, and thanked people for showing up. She was surprised to see how many people attended – far more than she would have imagined. There had to be about fifty people in all, and it made her feel a bit better. Even if her father had been a hermit, and perhaps a serial child killer, there were people who had thought enough of him to show up to his burial service.

Everyone who stopped by seemed to have a story about how they had known her dad. Chief Hammond arrived with his wife, and they filed by and shook Tess's hand.

"We all knew your father," Chief Hammond said, holding her hand in both of his. "He was a regular feature in most of our lives, up until the last five years or so. Our condolences to you, your mom and your brother."

Tess thanked him and turned back to the graveside, where Pastor Greg was getting ready for his service.

She looked around at the people gathered, amazed once more that so many people had showed up. It made her eyes brim, and she wished she'd had some time with her father before he died.

Then she noticed a man in a suit and tie, standing off to the side of the group. He was panning the crowd, recording the scene with his cell.

"Who's that?" Tess asked Michael, leaning in closer. "He's recording the funeral."

Michael glanced over to the man and shook his head.

"Don't worry about him," Michael said. "He's one of the FBI crime lab guys. I asked him to record the funeral, just in case someone with a bruise on his head shows up."

John Hammond showed up at the last minute, still wearing his work overalls. He stood at the edge of the crowd, his hands folded.

"There's John Hammond."

Michael glanced over to where Hammond stood. "He and your dad were tight most of their lives."

Tess nodded and turned back to watch Pastor Greg, who cleared his throat, waiting for silence so he could begin.

He spoke for about ten minutes, talking about the parable of the prodigal son and how, while Ron McClintock had been away from the church for years, he had asked for forgiveness before he died and that God always forgave those who truly repented.

"We're all sinners," Pastor Greg said. "God forgives all those who come to him. Let that comfort you when you face your own mortality. There is a paradise waiting for us if we only ask."

The attendants lowered the casket into the grave, and Tess threw in her single rose, where it landed on top of the flower arrangement. Finally, she shoveled a bit of dirt into the hole.

That was it.

Her father's life was now officially over. Michael took the shovel from her hands and added his own shovelful of dirt.

Several people came up to Tess to offer their condolences once more, including a number who had arrived after the service started. She didn't recognize any of them but they each introduced themselves as friends or old school buddies of her father's.

She managed to thank them all.

One man, Harold Kemp, came over and shook Tess's hand. Tall and stooped, he reminded her of Lurch from *The Addams Family*, which she'd watched as a child.

"Ron was quiet," he said, his eyes unfocused, like he was remembering. "Kept to himself mostly, but he was always there when you needed someone to take a shift. He said he had no life, so driving was all he had. Spent his time away shopping for collectibles. Never saw him much after he quit because of his back," he said. "Didn't even know he was sick."

The sound of his deep voice, truly and honestly sad at her father's horrible end, finally overwhelmed her, and she covered her eyes. Michael slipped an arm around her shoulder and she forced a smile, thanking Kemp for the kind words. Kemp finally left her alone to her tears. Michael took her elbow and maneuvered her toward the vehicle. She was glad he had taken charge, ending things when he must have seen that she was overwhelmed once more after that sad story about him and how lonely he must have been.

She got into the car and Michael closed the door for her, then came around to the driver's side. Mrs. Carter got into the back seat behind them.

"Well, that was a nice service," Mrs. Carter opined. "I was pleased how many people came out. He was such a loner after your mom left but people here are loyal and wanted to pay their respects."

That only made Tess feel worse, and she pressed the tissue against her eyes and tried to hold in a sob.

"Oh, dear," Mrs. Carter said, laying a hand on Tess's shoulder from the back seat. "I didn't mean to upset you. But it was really nice to see all the people."

"It was nice," Tess said, smiling finally, wiping her eyes with the fresh tissue Michael handed her. "I was afraid no one would show up except for family."

"He lived here all his life," Mrs. Carter said. "I'd expect a lot of folks to come even if they weren't the best of friends."

They drove back to Mrs. Carter's place and Tess sighed, feeling like that part of her responsibilities was over. Now all she had left was the house.

And the jar of ashes. The pornography. The scrapbook of crimes...

She turned to Michael. "How long before you get any results back from Seattle? About the remains?"

"A few days," he replied. "They have new technology that can take as little as twenty-four hours but usually seventy-two hours. My guy in Forensics said he'd process it right away and check the missing persons' database for any hits. Hopefully, we'll know by tomorrow. Thursday at the latest."

"What will happen if they get a hit?" she asked when the car stopped in the driveway. Her stomach was in knots at the thought her father might have been a killer. Even worse, a serial killer.

"If they get a hit, they'll see what links there are between your father and the victim." Michael got out and came around to her side, opening the doors for her and his mother. "But I'm not expecting anything. Really, Tess. Your father was not a serial killer."

She shook her head doubtfully.

"Tess…" he said, his voice slightly scolding. "There could be a completely innocent explanation for everything. I told you, those remains might be a family member whose ashes were badly processed…"

She shook her head. "Don't try to whitewash this. If it was a family member, I'm sure he would have marked it. You know, 'Aunt Tilly' or whatever. Besides, I contacted my Aunt Sharon, his sister in Idaho, and she said there were no family members that she knew of whose ashes he would have had."

Michael shrugged. "It could be as simple as him buying an old piece of furniture and the ashes being inside it. He may not have even known he was getting them when he bought the thing. He did buy the contents of storage lockers sight unseen, after all."

She nodded, but wasn't willing to write the remains off until the tests came back.

"Remember what I said," he told her, taking her arm and helping her out. "Don't get ahead of the evidence. Wait to hear what the crime lab says before you worry yourself about it."

"I'll try, but my mind keeps going to him being some kind of Dennis Rader, fooling us all."

He shook his head, taking both her arm and his mother's arm, walking with them up the driveway to the front door.

"I'm more interested in who wasn't at the service. We should make a list and see who might have a black eye."

"Garth didn't show. Neither did Gene."

"No, they didn't. When I think of it, both are as clean as a whistle," Mrs. Carter said. "Garth's practically a saint."

"A saint?" Michael said, his voice dismissive. "He was charged with theft and spent time in juvenile detention."

"That was his darn father's influence," Mrs. Carter said. "He's totally reformed. He volunteers at the Mission, serving Thanksgiving dinner to the homeless. He delivers groceries to seniors and shut-ins in the neighborhood who can't get out on their own. He got saved while he was in jail and repented. He's been a model citizen ever since."

"Model citizens can be just as evil as the worst among us," Michael said. "If you knew what I knew, Mother, you'd never say that. The men I've investigated who have done terrible things to little children…" he said, shaking his head sadly. "Some of them were paragons of virtue – at least in the public's opinion."

"Shush," Mrs. Carter said and shook her finger at him. "Don't speak like that about him. I just can't believe it would be Garth. He had a hard life. He was in foster care for a while until John got back on his feet. He's just lucky John Hammond got custody and not his mother."

They went inside and Tess plopped down on the sofa, listening intently to Michael and his mother argue about Garth's virtue – or potential lack thereof.

"Why not?"

Mrs. Carter came over and sat beside Tess.

"It's a sad story. John Hammond Jr's little sister Allison ran off with Daryl Kincaid, that rake. How many girls did Kincaid get pregnant? He liked them young."

"Interesting," Michael called from the kitchen, giving Tess the eye. "So did Eugene Hammond. He started dating Kirsten when she was fourteen."

"She was precocious," Mrs. Carter said with a frown. "Wouldn't listen to anything your dad or I said. We grounded her, took away privileges, but she found a way to sneak out and be with him regardless. When she got pregnant, at least he had the decency to marry her and he was a good father, no matter what you think of him, Michael. He always provided for Kirsten and the boys."

Tess could see a muscle in Michael's jaw pulse. He was holding back what he really thought -- that Eugene was a flake.

"John Hammond wasn't much better than Daryl," Mrs. Carter continued, in her element talking about the town's secrets. "He got Darryl's sister Heather pregnant when she was only thirteen. Had Garth, but they never married. John took him and raised Garth himself when Heather couldn't manage because of her drug problem. Very difficult situation, but John managed to raise him up pretty good, considering."

"Except for that small stint in jail," Michael countered.

"That was a foolish thing he and his father got involved

in, and you know it. It was Daryl's influence that got John in trouble. Now Daryl's in jail for aggravated assault and robbery. He's been away for ten years and John and Garth have both been living exemplary lives. Garth got a steady job and he's a volunteer, giving back to the community."

"If you ask me," Michael said, bringing Tess a cup of hot tea with a slice of lemon, "that apple doesn't fall far from the tree. Mom just doesn't like to admit it because Daryl Kincaid is her cousin and she's far too generous. Everyone thought Daryl was a good old boy, back before he started robbing grocery stores and gas stations. Not to mention setting fires."

"He set fires?" Tess asked. Arsonists were often psychopaths in the making.

"Daryl Kincaid is the worst of the worst. He's a psychopath, if you ask me." Michael said, echoing Tess's thought. He sat beside Tess after handing his mother her cup of tea. "He stole cars, shoplifted, theft, break and enter, armed robbery, assault, drug trafficking, pimping. He has a record as long as my arm."

Mrs. Carter nodded, her own cup of tea in hand. "John Hammond was his friend, but they pretty much parted ways after high school. John had problems with his dad, over who would run the business, but other than that, he's been a good father. Garth did have a rough period about a decade ago but he's exemplary now. He was only a young man back then and never had a mother's love," Mrs. Carter added. "You have to cut some people slack, Michael."

Tess sipped her tea and pictured Garth in her mind's eye. Totally ordinary. Blended in. Light brown hair. Brown eyes. A bit of a weak chin. Ears that stuck out a bit too far; hair short and buzzed on the sides like he was a Marine. Could he have been her attacker? Could he feel so emboldened that he'd deliver flowers to her doorstep, despite having attacked her a night before? He'd have to be a real sociopath if so.

She sighed. The more she learned about him, the more she thought Garth didn't sound like a stalker and someone who might break in and assault her – but that was one thing Tess had learned from her criminology studies.

If you looked at the photos of serial killers – taken not when they were in a lineup but were in their own environment – you would never be able to pick them out of a crowd. There was nothing you could see by looking at a person.

You really couldn't tell what went on in the hearts and minds of other people.

You just couldn't.

CHAPTER TWENTY-FIVE

H e would have liked to have attended the funeral, but wanted to avoid any attention that would inevitably be drawn to him because of the accident. Instead, he stayed off in the distance, three hundred yards away in the shadows of the forest, and watched the small group of people while the graveside service took place. There were a lot more people than he'd thought would show up. Ron McClintock had quite a few acquaintances, even if he'd had few friends.

Carter stood protectively beside Tess, his gaze lingering on her far longer than it should have. He had the hots for the redhead.

That much was clear.

It filled him with rage the way Carter looked at her and she looked at him. He'd take care of them both, if he had his way.

And he usually did.

AFTER THE SERVICE, he waited until all the cars had driven off and the two cemetery workers finished covering up the grave. Then he went to his parent's place for dinner, sitting with them and listening to them talk about Ron McClintock and what a strange, quiet man he was, and how broken he was after Mrs. McClintock took the kids and moved to Seattle.

"And poor Tess," his mom Maureen said, making a face while she ate her meal. "Imagine getting attacked like that in her motel room, what with her father's death and the burial to arrange. She must be so upset."

"Terrible," he said, taking a satisfied slurp of his stew. "Any leads on that?" he asked his father Joe, who seemed somewhat quiet.

Joe chewed thoughtfully for a moment and then shook his head.

"Not a single one," he said. "No one saw anything. We checked the security videos but so far nothing has showed up. Couple weren't working. Whoever attacked her was damn lucky, because there aren't any cameras covering the back."

"They ought to change that," he said, shaking his head in disapproval. "That creates a blind spot that a thief could take advantage of. I should talk to the owner about installing some cameras. I saw a couple of sweet cams at a good price online."

"You're should," Joe said with a satisfied nod. "I'll call him and tell him you'll drop by. Maybe people will start to take security seriously and install them in more of their buildings. You could have a real thriving business if so."

"You do that, Dad," he said. "I'd be glad to go by and check the place out."

He smiled to himself. Gaining access to the town's businesses and finding all their blind spots was a great accomplishment. It provided him with so much intel on what business were vulnerable and which were protected. He already knew the vulnerabilities at the motel, which was why he could follow Tess without concern.

"What happened, anyway?" he asked, watching Joe's face.

"According to the report Michael Carter gave at the station, the man was tall and well-built, dressed all in black. Wore a balaclava and had on latex gloves. Michael thought he knocked the guy in the head a good one, but so far, we haven't turned up anyone in town who has an injury that matches."

He watched his mother and father, amazed at how they could look at his face and not think to themselves that maybe he was the one who had done it.

Blindness of the loving family. They couldn't imagine that their beloved adopted son – the boy they'd rescued from a world of pain and raised as their own – could be a would-be rapist, let alone a serial killer.

It gave him a special kind of satisfaction to know he'd fooled them all. They looked at his injury and never connected the dots. Of course, they didn't. There were his texts from Yakima moments before the crash, police records of the accident, medical records of the trip to the ER for stitches, of the pharmacy order for pain meds. He had friends who would swear he'd been at the bar with him when the attack had gone down.

Nah, he was clear.

There was no evidence to link him to the murders. The evidence that did exist was never going to implicate him. It was set to implicate others. They'd be seen as the guilty parties, not him.

No, he'd planned it all out so well.

For two decades, he'd gotten away with it. He'd laid down a trail of crumbs leading to others while covering his own tracks, some of whom were now dead and gone and would be unable to defend themselves when the evidence turned up.

"Terrible business," his mother said, clucking like a hen over her stew. "What kind of man could do that to poor sweet Tess?"

He could have laughed out loud at that moment, but he knew that his dear parents would be shocked so he held it in. Both of them were sad, thinking of the death of one of their generation and the horrors of the world to see what was right under their noses.

Especially his father. The fucking Chief of Police.

Some cop *he* turned out to be...

CHAPTER TWENTY-SIX

Tess spent Tuesday at her father's house with the cleaners, going through boxes and cupboards, slowly making headway against the hoard. So far, she'd gone through two rooms and the cleaners were almost finished with the kitchen and bathrooms.

Tess couldn't believe the state of the bathrooms. Both were filthy and had malfunctioning drains; one of the toilets was broken, empty and covered in newspapers.

Around two in the afternoon, Michael drove up. When he entered the house, he rubbed his hands together almost in glee.

"What's up?" she asked, removing the mask and protective eyewear. She couldn't help but get caught up in his enthusiasm without knowing what it was for. "You seem happy."

"I am happy." He removed a folded piece of paper from his jacket pocket and held it up in front of her. "I have here in my hand the preliminary DNA analysis of the sample sent to the Seattle office."

"Oh God," Tess said, a surge of adrenaline making her heart rate speed up. "That's so fast." She reached out to take it from Michael, but he didn't give it to her.

"I have friends in high places. And sorry but you can't see this," he said. "This is official now. You might want to sit down."

She did, trying to prepare herself.

"What?"

He sat beside her. "Now, remember, this in itself doesn't mean your father was involved. But we have a positive ID on one of *two* DNA profiles."

"Two profiles?" Tess asked, impatient to hear the results. "Was one Lisa?"

He shook his head. "No. Not Lisa. It's Zoe Wallace. They don't know who the other DNA belongs to but there were clearly two DNA profiles in the sample."

"Two bodies? Who else could it be?"

"It's impossible to say. The only other girl from Paradise Hill missing in recent years is Melissa and they have her body."

"What about Janine? She's still missing."

"They don't have Janine's profile on file because that was forty years ago. I'm going to talk to her family and get a DNA sample so we can exclude or include her."

"Oh, God. So, it was *Zoe*..." She shook her head, her gut knotting at the thought that her father might have killed the young girl. If he had, then he might have killed them all.

"Tell me about Zoe. I haven't read much about her case yet."

Michael handed her the letter.

"You're not supposed to be reading that," he said. "So you can't let on I gave it to you."

She nodded and read it over. It detailed how the sample had been developed and checked against the database of missing persons in the US. She'd seen similar documents online when researching cases. It was all FBI forensic science-speak, but she understood the gist.

"Zoe went missing after leaving the park by her house. Kids played there until after nine and then they went home, one by one. Zoe was one of the last to leave."

Michael leaned back, his arm on the back of the sofa. She wondered if it was bad for him to talk about the case, considering he was supposed to be on a medical leave.

"She came from a broken home. Lived with her mother and two siblings, both older. Mother was a cocktail waitress who worked at the hotel in Yakima on the weekends. Her mother had been arrested when she was younger for prostitution, got pregnant several times from different fathers. The oldest sister stayed with them when she was out of town working. They didn't even miss her until the next day. The older girl figured she'd spent the night at a friend's, which was common on the weekends."

Tess shook her head in disgust. There were so many vulnerable children and predators who hovered around, waiting for a chance to strike.

"There were never any suspects?"

He shook his head. "Father had an alibi. Uncles as well. The local suspects were interviewed, but none of them stuck. She just disappeared on her way home. People said she ran away and I guess the police decided that was the most likely explanation."

"God, that's horrible. That sounds so much like Lisa."

"I know," Michael said, rubbing his chin. "Maybe if Curt and I had done our job, Lisa would still be here."

"Don't blame yourself," Tess said and reached over to squeeze his arm. "If Kirsten and I weren't so mean, she would have stayed in the tent with us."

"So many ifs," Michael replied. "People do things right nine times out of ten, but that one time they fail? A child dies. Now that we have Zoe's remains, we can start working on where her body might have been burned. Somewhere remote. At a cabin, maybe."

"My father used to rent a cabin every year. We'd go there and have bonfires, cook the fish we caught. I hate to think he used those bonfires to burn Zoe and whoever else he killed."

"Tess," Michael said, his voice insistent. He took hold of her shoulders and stared into her eyes. "Your father had Zoe's remains in his possession. How he came to possess those remains is key. Until we know how, we can't know for sure he was responsible."

"You have to admit that if it was anyone else besides my father, you'd be on him."

"That's right, but I knew your father. He didn't ever make me look twice."

"You're not infallible."

He sighed heavily. "Don't I know it. Look. Let's go out to the storage facility and talk to the owner. See if we can track the previous owners of the contents your father purchased. That may tell us a lot."

She nodded, deciding to humor him. It couldn't be good for him to be worrying about the cases and making up excuses to keep her happy at the same time.

"What's going to happen? What are the FBI going to do about the remains?"

"They're officially reopening the case. Barnes and Parker

will want to interview you and any of his friends, have access to your dad's house."

"Will you be involved?"

He shook his head. "I'm on leave. I'll still help out where I can, but I'm officially off duty."

Tess nodded and handed the letter back to Michael.

"I don't want to get you in trouble. As far as I'm concerned, I've never seen it."

She gave Michael a smile and he folded the letter up and slipped it back into his pocket.

"Shall we get a coffee and take a trip out to the storage facility?"

"Might as well," she said and glanced around the house. "None of this is going anywhere." She stood up, removing the mask from her head and placing it beside the safety glasses.

"Let's go," she said with a sigh. "I'd like to know who rented the storage unit he bought."

THEY LEFT THE HOUSE, letting the cleaners know to lock the doors when they finished for the day. Michael drove and Tess watched the streets as they made their way through town to the outskirts where the storage facility had been built years earlier. Rows upon rows of metal corrugated sheds side by side comprised the facility. Tess had been there once before when it had first been built; her father had wanted to rent a unit just because it was the new thing in town.

Had his hoarding started back then?

They drove up to the office and parked in the small lot. Tess followed Michael inside. He'd be more authoritative than she was when it came time to ask questions, so she let him lead, although her investigative reporting instincts kicked in.

"Hello," the clerk at the front desk said. "How can I help you?"

"Hello," Michael said and pulled out his FBI ID and flashed it in front of the clerk's face. "I'm Special Agent Michael Carter," he said in a deep low voice. Tess bit back a smile, not wanting to give away her amusement at his new persona.

"I know who you are, Michael," the young woman said. "I'm your second cousin Helen on your father's side. We met at Callie's wedding five years ago?"

"Oh, sorry," Michael said, wiping his brow theatrically. "I wasn't sure about the connection. Good to see you again."

He gave her a brilliant smile and Tess could almost see the young woman's heart rate increase. Michael was handsome, by any standard.

"What can I do for you, Michael?" she asked, her eyes bright.

"Well, Helen, we need to find out who rented a storage unit that Tess's father bought when the renter defaulted."

"Is this official FBI business?" she asked, her eyes widening.

"Yes, it is. I can give you my supervisor's phone number in Seattle, if you need to call him."

"No, that's not necessary. I trust you. Do you have a receipt?"

Tess handed her the receipt. Helen was happy to take it, and checked out the receipt number.

"Do you have records from five years ago?" she asked.

"We put everything on a database a few years back. Paid a lot of money for it, so I hope so. We have the required seven years of data in the database. For tax purposes, you know."

She gave Tess a big smile and clicked on her keyboard, then moved her mouse around.

"That unit was rented by John Hammond, Jr. He missed the renewal payment and then three subsequent attempts to collect. When he was asked to pay the outstanding amount, he was unable. Your father, Mr. Ron McClintock, paid the outstanding debt and accepted the contents, since Mr. Hammond couldn't afford to keep the unit. In fact, your father paid for the storage unit for a full ten years. It's still in his name. Do you want me to cancel it, now that he's, you know...?"

"You better, I guess. We'll have to hire movers to come pick up the contents."

"It's yours to inspect," she said. "We can issue a refund on the remaining amount of the lease, once we have a certified copy of the death certificate."

The three of them left the office and walked along the line of sheds to one near the end. Helen opened the shed, and Michael lifted the door to reveal the empty interior.

"It's empty," Tess said, glancing at Michael.

"It is. He must have removed the contents and never used it."

Tess nodded. "So my father came and took the contents five years ago?"

Helen nodded pertly. "He did. I guess John was on the outs with his father so no one agreed to bail him out of his financial troubles," she said conspiratorially, raising her eyebrows. Then she glanced at Michael. "I probably shouldn't have said that, but it's pretty common knowledge in town. They've been on the outs for a decade or more."

"That's okay, Helen," Michael said, his voice extra deep. "I appreciate the cooperation with the investigation. It makes our work a lot easier. If you need me to sign anything, I'd be happy to."

"No, it's fine. Besides, it's not like I told you a secret or anything. When someone defaults on a rental payment, and the unit is put up for auction, we do include a summary of the contents and keep the renter's name on file in case the purchaser wants to return any personal property to them. You never know what you might find inside. Even dead bodies." She rolled her eyes and laughed.

"Really?" Tess said, laughing with her although she felt a bit sick. "Wouldn't they stink up the place?"

"Not if they're mummified or encased in cement like that poor little Melissa. Isn't that terrible?" Helen said, crossing her arms. "Is that why you're in town?" Helen looked at Michael pointedly.

"I was on leave to be with Kirsten when she delivers her baby, but with finding Melissa's body, I'm working again."

Tess watched Michael, surprised that he was so willing to lead Helen on.

"Anyway, thanks for helping me out," he said, giving her another smile.

"No problem," Helen said, tilting her head to one side.

Michael closed the door and Helen turned to Tess.

"It's still yours for another five years if you want to keep it."

"No, that's not necessary," Tess replied. "I won't be storing anything here. Whatever I don't throw out or donate will go back to Seattle with me for my mom and brother."

"Okey dokey," Helen said with a smile. "We'll issue you a

refund as soon as we get a certified copy of the death certificate."

Michael and Tess walked back to the office with Helen. Michael opened the door for Helen and said goodbye.

"You really led her on," Tess said when they got to the car. "I hope you don't get in trouble for it."

"Nah," he said and waved his hand. "It's not like my supervisor would get upset if he knew. My leave of absence was wholly voluntary. I can end it any time I want."

"You're not going to, are you?"

He shook his head and opened the car door for her.

"Once Kirsten has her baby and she's doing well, I'll end my leave and start working on the cases."

"You feel well enough?" she asked, knowing it was a sensitive topic.

"I'm much better. For a while, I didn't want to be involved in any cases, but now?" he said and started the Jeep. "I'm back."

They drove off and Tess looked at the receipt in her hand.

"So, John Hammond owned the contents of the storage shed? What do you know about him?"

Michael shrugged. "He was a friend of both our fathers. Went to school with them. About the same age. John and his father were estranged for a while. John's younger brother is running the original business now that his dad is retired. John Jr. started his own business as a result. That has to hurt."

"What happened?"

Michael shook his head. "From what my mother told me, John wanted to change the business in a way that his father didn't approve. They fought about it. John tried to get his father declared unfit and removed from the company and that was it. John's father kicked him out. I guess John Jr. could no longer afford to pay his bills. That must have been when your dad bought the contents of the storage unit, probably to help John out."

"It doesn't help us out. There's no guarantee that the jar and porn were in the storage unit. The contents of the boxes weren't listed on the manifest."

"No," Michael said, pointing to the list of contents. "But it does say eight banker's boxes filled with miscellaneous content. The ashes were located in a banker's box. If anything, they might be John Jr's. He didn't have a bruise on his head, but maybe the man who attacked you is completely unconnected to the cases."

She nodded. "John seems like such a nice gentle man."

"I think," Michael said quietly. "I think the ashes might be Janine."

Tess turned to look at Michael. "Why do you think that?"

"The dates of the newspapers. If the murderer added Zoe's ashes to the jar, he may have put in extra newspaper to keep it from moving around in the box. We should check the dates on the papers. If they're from around the time Zoe went missing, that might explain the different dates."

"The cases were Janine, Lisa, Zoe and Melissa, right? In that order?" Tess asked, ticking them off on her fingers.

"Yes," Michael replied, turning into the driveway of his mother's house. "Plus, there are about five from surrounding counties that match the same age and MO. Girls between the ages of eight and fourteen, went missing at night, from a park or playground, never seen again. We have two, maybe three bodies now. Zoe. Melissa. Maybe Janine."

He put the car in park and got out. Tess followed him into the house, the receipt in her hand.

"What next?" she asked when they got inside and went to the kitchen.

"Next, we have a cup of coffee. I already talked to Janine's aunt to get DNA samples from her and sent them off to the crime lab in Seattle. The guys will be interested in that," he said and pointed to the receipt. "They'll want to know that Hammond was the renter. If it was Hammond's storage unit, it was probably Hammond's jar, not your father's. Maybe the porno and the scrapbook, too. That would exonerate your father. It wasn't his fault that Hammond possessed those items – he just inherited them when he bought the contents."

"Why would he keep them? Anyone could see the magazines were child porn. The ashes were obviously human remains. Why didn't my dad go to the police and turn those in? It makes him look guilty. Like an accomplice."

"Maybe unwitting. He may have never even looked. Maybe Hammond was happy to let your father keep those in his house. If they were ever discovered, it would be your father who looked guilty."

Tess poured some coffee into the filter and frowned while the water boiled.

She wanted to believe her father wasn't involved, but it was possible to argue that her father had to have checked the contents at least once. If he had, he'd have to have seen the porno and the human remains. If so, he should have gone immediately to the police. The fact that he hadn't meant he was complicit or was trying to protect his friend.

She couldn't believe her father had bought the contents sight unseen and never checked inside. No matter what the reason, neither was acceptable, given the potential crimes. Child porn was not acceptable, let alone murder. If her father thought John Hammond was responsible for the remains and pornography, he should have called the police right away, friend or not.

Of course, now that he was dead, Tess's father couldn't be charged with anything, but it would be important to investigate and close the case.

"What about talking to John Hammond? We could ask him about the storage unit and what was inside. See what he says."

Michael nodded. "We could. He can't deny that your father bought the contents. All he can do is deny that there was anything nefarious contained in them. Your father could have bought the contents and then used the boxes to store his own possessions."

"I thought you didn't believe my father was a murderer."

"I don't," Michael said. "I'm just playing the devil's advocate to make sure I cover all possibilities."

She sighed. "Will you come with me?"

"Are you sure you don't want me to go alone? I can do it, no problem. I don't have to give anything away about the contents, but I'd like to see how he responds when he learns we have the contents of his storage unit. That'll give away a lot. If he's totally nonchalant, and says or does nothing suspicious, that suggests the porno and remains weren't his. I have experience talking to suspects and I usually get a feel for someone."

"Do you think I should come?"

He shrugged. "Maybe you should. You might disarm him, as Ron's daughter. You can ask if he wants his possessions back, that kind of thing. Say you know the boxes were his and that you need to get rid of them, so you're making the offer. We can go from there."

She imagined how Hammond might respond if he was the killer and was faced with evidence.

"Let's go together."

He nodded. "That might be best."

Her nerves were on edge as they slipped on their jackets and headed out, wondering what he'd say when confronted with the manifest.

CHAPTER TWENTY-SEVEN

T he streets were quiet at that time of the afternoon so the drive to Hammond's business at the edge of town only took a few minutes.

Hammond had a small business, including tree trimming, yard maintenance, snow removal, and trash removal as well as local deliveries. He'd been a mechanic working for his father's fleet before he'd been disowned and blocked from the family business, but still had the same entrepreneurial spirit and wanted to run his own show.

Behind the building, which was a converted gas station with two service bays, was a junkyard filled with old cars and trucks, collected over the years from collisions on the highway and in town. The place was run-down and rusting, the paint peeling and the sign barely legible.

Hammond and Son

The original delivery business had been started by John's grandfather. Michael couldn't help but think of *Sanford and Son*, the old television series, when he saw the lot and buildings.

He parked in a slot and got out of the vehicle. Tess came to his side.

"Are you sure about this?" he asked, gesturing to the Jeep. "You could stay in the vehicle and I could do the talking."

"No," Tess said with a shrug. "He was my father's oldest friend."

They walked to the front door of the old office and went inside, the door jingling when it opened and closed.

A middle-aged man wearing a greasy set of coveralls, wiping his hands with a rag, came out of the service bay. Tess peered inside the bay and saw a car being restored, the hood open and a winch lowering a new engine inside.

"Can I help you?"

"We're looking for John Hammond."

"He's in the back. You're Tess McClintock," he said. "I'm Andy Hammond. Sorry about your dad."

"Thanks," she said and gave him a quick smile. "Which Hammond are you?"

He laughed. "John's cousin. There are a lot of us, that's for sure. Wait here," he said. "I'll go get him."

Clint disappeared into the back of the building.

Tess turned to him. "How many Hammonds are there?"

"Too many."

"The Hammonds are everywhere in Paradise Hill," Tess said, her voice sounding a bit nervous.

"Moving, tree trimming, deliveries, police work, politics, and one used to be the only auto mechanic in town," Michael replied. "They have it almost all sewed up."

He glanced around the place. It was old. Everything looked like it was from the 1950s – or earlier. Fading calendars featuring pretty girls in short shorts and holding wrenches suggestively. Peeling paint and yellowed wallpaper covered the walls.

In the service bay, by contrast, the equipment was modern.

From the rear of the building, he heard voices and then John Hammond emerged from a door. He was still wearing the set of filthy overalls that he had worn to the service.

"Hello," he said. "Tess. Sorry I didn't come by at the service and say anything. I'm not real good at crowds.""

"That's okay. I appreciate the fact you showed up."

Hammond smiled, his beefy face barely changing.

"Michael Carter, right?" Hammond said and extended his hand.

Michael shook the man's hand. "Yes. That's me."

He gave them another forced smile. "What can I do for you?"

"My father had some of your possessions in his house," Tess said, her voice soft. "I'm cleaning the house to get it ready to sell and came across the contents of a storage unit he bought about five years ago. It was your unit and I wanted to know if you'd like the contents back or if I can dispose of them."

"Storage unit?" he said and frowned. "Oh, yeah… " He rubbed his bald head. "Down at East Washington Storage. Bunch of old business records and stuff from my grandad's. Been in storage forever and I couldn't afford to keep it anymore. Your father helped me out. He said he was going to send the contents to the dump. You still have them?"

"Yes, they're up in the attic at my father's house. We're getting a load sent to the dump, so if you want, I can include the boxes or you can come by and pick them up."

Hammond pursed his lips and considered. Michael

watched his face. He seemed surprised that the contents of the unit hadn't been disposed of. At that moment, Michael sensed desperation from Hammond. Hammond hesitated far too long with his response and it was then that Michael knew.

He knew that Hammond owned the porno and/or remains. They were from his storage locker. Michael had never gotten a sense from Ron McClintock that he was anything other than a quiet family man, a harmless man of few words.

He got the opposite sense from Hammond. From him, Michael got a watchful sense of calculation, like the man was assessing whether Michael was a danger to him and what the best escape route would be.

Hammond ran a hand over his bald head again and glanced around like he was searching for an answer – or was planning to run.

Michael was sure the man was going to bolt.

"Sure," he said finally. "I could come by and pick them up." He laughed nervously. "I don't even know what was in that unit, to be truthful. Just a lot of junk from the old business."

That was a lie. Michael knew it as clear as day.

"I have the manifest, if you want it. I think there's some boxes and other items still up in the attic. I didn't get to check what's inside yet but I can if you want."

"No, no," Hammond said quickly. "That's perfectly all right. I'll come by later today and get them." He checked his watch and looked around – at what, Michael couldn't tell – and then spoke. "In fact, if you don't mind, I could come by right now."

"Oh, sorry," Michael said. "We've got an appointment with the real estate agent," he said and checked his watch.

"Yes," Tess said, quickly picking up on his intent. "We won't be able to get back to the house this afternoon. Could you come by tomorrow?"

"Gee, I'm kind of busy tomorrow what with some work I have booked," Hammond replied, grimacing. "How about I come by tonight? Can you meet me there after supper?"

Tess looked at Michael quickly, her brow furrowed.

"I guess," she said. "You could come with me, right?"

"Sure," Michael said and smiled broadly at Hammond. "You bring a truck and I'll help you load it up."

"Nah, you don't have to do any work. I'll bring Garth."

Michael shrugged. "I'm sure Tess will be glad to get rid of the boxes and stuff. Her father was a hoarder and it's been a nightmare going through everything."

"You'll be able to identify your things," Tess said. "We've been working for the past four days but have barely gone through half of the junk."

"Much appreciated," Hammond said and extended his hand for another shake.

First Tess then Michael shook his hand. Michael peered into the man's eyes, which were clearly evasive. His face was red and there was mottling on his neck, indicating he was upset that the contents of the storage unit were still around and not destroyed, as he'd thought.

That would shake him if the remains and porn were his.

Michael went to the door after Tess said goodbye and held it for her, following her out and over to the Jeep. They got inside and he started the engine, fighting with his desire to glance back and check out the storefront to see if Hammond was watching them.

He half expected to see the man with a shotgun, planning on killing them both to shut them up, but when he drove around and could see the window, Hammond merely stood there, watching, his face hidden by shadow, his hands deep in his overall pockets.

"He's guilty," Michael said.

"I know," Tess replied, her voice a bit breathless. "I got the sense he was desperate to rush over to the house and remove the boxes right away."

"I'll have to talk to the agent in charge of the investigation about Hammond. Maybe they'll have to visit him before tonight. If he gets all those boxes and finds the remains and porn missing, he'll know we're onto him. Who knows what he'll do? He could leave the state, leave the country."

As they drove away, Michael watched the building in the rearview mirror, expecting to see Hammond standing in the middle of the road with a shotgun pointed at them, but nothing happened. He relaxed as the building disappeared when they turned the corner.

Maybe he still needed time off.

"What now?" he asked, turning to Tess.

She sighed. "I need a coffee. And a donut."

"Not a beer?" he said with a smile. She was as tense as him.

"Actually, a beer sounds fantastic." She turned to him and smiled back. "That was intense. Was I a total fool to come along with you? For a moment there, I had the feeling he'd like to pull out a gun and shoot us both."

He nodded in understanding. "I felt the same way."

"You think he killed Zoe?"

"He's guilty of something, that's for sure. When he learned about the boxes? I could almost see him mentally freaking out. Now, it could have been the porn. Or the jar. Or both. Not possible to say yet."

Beside him, Tess exhaled heavily. "From now on, I'm letting you professionals handle the suspect interrogation."

He reached over and squeezed her hand. "You did good," he said. "You totally caught on when I wanted to delay and you ran with it."

"I felt like a deer in the headlights."

He laughed grimly. "I know the feeling. Let's go to the Chief's office so I can contact Nash, the agent in charge of the case. Then, we can grab a beer at the bar. They have some good buffalo wings."

"Sounds like a plan."

Michael drove to the police station in downtown Paradise Hill. It was an older building with an ornate façade and a heritage designation as one of the oldest buildings in town. They went inside and stopped in the entry.

"You wait here," he said, turning to Tess. "I'll run upstairs and talk to the Chief. I won't be more than ten minutes."

"I'll check my messages," Tess replied and pulled out her cell.

"Good. I'll be right back."

HE RAN up the stairs to the Chief's office, and checked in with his assistant at the reception desk.

"Is Chief Hammond available? I need to talk to him about a case for a moment."

"Sure, Michael. Go on in." She waved him through.

Chief Hammond's door was open and the man was seated behind a huge oak desk. He was on the phone but ushered Michael in with a wave of his hand.

"Sure thing," Hammond said into the phone. "I've got someone in my office but I'll get back to you."

261

Then he hung up and pointed to the chair across from his desk.

"Have a seat," he said. "What can I do for you, young man? Aren't you supposed to keep your head out of official FBI and police business?"

Michael rubbed his head, grinning guiltily. "You can take the boy off the farm but you can't take the farm out of the boy, I guess. There's something I wanted to tell you about the Zoe Wallace case."

"Shoot," Hammond said, leaning back in his chair.

"Those remains and magazines we found at Ron McClintock's house? I think they were from a storage unit that your cousin John couldn't pay the rent on. Ron bought the contents and had them stored at his house. He was supposed to dispose of the contents at the dump when he took possession, but I guess they became part of his hoarding problem and were upstairs in the attic for the past five years."

"John?" Chief Hammond said, frowning. He pursed his mouth and sat in silence for a moment, his eyes narrowing. "He ran into some bad luck a while back, but in general, he doesn't strike me as a serial killer."

"I agree, but if I had to choose between Ron and John, it would be John, no question."

Hammond nodded slowly. "I would tend to agree. I honestly don't see either of them for the murders. But if you say the remains were from Hammond's storage unit…"

"We just went to his shop and asked him about the contents to feel him out, and he definitely panicked when he learned the boxes hadn't been disposed of at the dump. I could see him change when he realized they were still there and that we may have had access to them. He wanted to come right over and get the boxes. Didn't want to wait."

"So he has no idea you've looked inside?"

Michael shook his head. "Tess pretended that she hadn't checked the contents. I could tell he was very concerned about them. He's coming over to Tess's father's place to pick them up tonight."

"You sent the remains and magazines to Seattle, right?"

Michael nodded. "I did. Maybe you could bring him in for questioning about the boxes. He's going to find out that they're gone and he'll know the police have them. He might run."

"He might," Chief Hammond said and rubbed his jaw. "I'll have to talk to the judge about a search warrant for his property. Who knows what we might find there. If he killed Zoe, and whoever else is in that jar, who knows how many he might have killed."

Michael nodded in agreement, thinking the same thing himself.

"I already spoke with Janine's aunt. Got a DNA sample and sent it off to Seattle by courier earlier so we can compare profiles with what's in the jar. We'll be able to rule out Janine that way. Results should be back in a couple of days."

"Good," Hammond said. "That case has been cold as Antarctica for close to forty years. Can't imagine that it's her but you never know."

"Hammond would have been seventeen when Janine went missing. If he's Zoe's killer, he could have started with Janine."

"That he could," Hammond replied. "I grew up with John. Amazing to think all of us have been going to bars and restaurants and weddings and funerals with him all these years. I fished with him and Ron McClintock and Daryl

Kincaid. Spent time at his cabin. Hard to believe he's a killer."

"He was definitely panicked at the thought those boxes were in Ron's house."

Chief Hammond sighed audibly. "I'll get back to you as soon as I've talked to the judge about a warrant. We'll go over and search the place, bring him in for questioning."

Michael stood and extended his hand to Hammond. "Thanks for your help," he said as they shook. "I'm know I'm not officially working the case, but I'm unofficially here in case you need me to do anything."

Hammond gave him a quick nod. "I'll take it from here. You go to your mom's and get in some R & R. You need it after your year from hell."

"It's hard not to follow what's happening."

"You did more than follow. You've really helped. Now go. Have a beer and relax. We'll take over."

Michael left the office and made his way out to the foyer where Tess sat with her eyes focused on her iPhone.

"Ready?" she asked, glancing up at him.

"Let's go get that beer."

As they walked out to the Jeep, he hoped they'd wrap things up as soon as possible with Hammond. He felt nothing but malice from the man when he'd learned the boxes from the storage unit were still in existence. It unnerved him and he'd only feel safe once they knew for certain whether John Hammond was the killer and behind bars.

CHAPTER TWENTY-EIGHT

The panicked call came in while he was sitting alone at home in his underwear, watching sports.

John Hammond wasn't making sense.

"Those damned boxes," he said in a breathless voice. "Ron didn't get rid of them like he was supposed to. Now they have them – we need to find them and get rid of them right away."

He knew exactly what boxes John meant, of course, from the moment he mentioned Ron. Hammond was freaking out.

"Slow down, slow down," he said, trying to calm him, barely able to keep a smile off his face. "What boxes? What the hell are you talking about?"

"The boxes," Hammond said, his voice breathless. "The ashes were in a box in my storage unit. When I had that trouble back in '13, Ron bought the contents of the storage unit and was supposed to put the stuff in the dump and get rid of it, but he didn't. He kept it in his damn attic. I got a visit from Tess and Michael Carter just now. They asked if I wanted to collect the contents or whether they could dispose of them. *Sheeeit*. I said I'd come by and get them tonight, but damn, I don't want to wait just in case they start poking around in those boxes."

"Why the hell did you call me?"

"Tess isn't going to be there now. You could come with me, open the door with that lock-picking set of yours."

"Sorry, I'm busy," he said, glancing around at his apartment. "Why don't you go over now and pick them yourself?"

"I don't have one of those sets."

"Just go. You know how to break and enter as well as anyone."

"I gotta get those boxes out of there. Can you help me?"

"Sorry," he said. "Not possible. I hurt my arm in the accident. I'm in the middle of something and can't leave. You're on your own. Besides, it's not my problem."

"Son of a *bitch*. Ron should have disposed of the ashes right away. Daryl should've never kept them in the first place."

"Too late now," he said, a smile on his face. *The damn loser.* "Besides, might I remind you that he was cleaning up your shit, not his."

"I know, I know... Still, if Daryl had buried the ashes instead of keeping them, we wouldn't be in this predicament now."

"He kept them because he wanted to make sure none of you guys betrayed him. He took care of the mess you and Ron made or you would have gone to prison for life."

"Your father kept them," Hammond replied, his voice angry. "So he could blackmail me and Ron all this fucking time. Why Ron didn't get rid of them I have no idea. Damn hoarder. Now, I have to go and get them before anyone looks inside."

He smiled to himself. *Yeah, but his hoarding worked out well for me.*

"You sound worried," he said with a smile. "Should have thought about that before you guys killed Janine."

"Go to hell," Hammond replied, his voice acid. He hung up.

He snorted and turned off his cell.

Loser.

Grown man shitting his pants over something he could easily fix by going over to the house and taking back his own property. Of course, police might be quite interested in what his property comprised – the ashes of two murdered girls from Paradise Hill, and some very outlawed pornography plus some trinkets and other incriminating evidence…

The rat bastard deserved it if he got nailed for them all.

Mixing Zoe's ashes in with Janine's was a stroke of genius on his part. If anyone went down for her murder, it wasn't going to be him. He'd love to see Hammond tagged with both murders. Hell, Hammond might even get tagged with Melissa's, if things worked out just right and they identified Zoe's charm bracelet.

Those boxes contained a lot of evidence…

He rubbed his head, his fingers running over his brush cut. He liked to keep his hair short, Marine-short. White-walls, they called them. He would have liked to have joined the Marines and have been a Marine Scout Sniper, but he couldn't pass the physical because of his damn flat feet.

He'd planned on going into law enforcement, getting on with the department in Yakima, but then he got caught and sent to jail for something so stupid, he could kick himself. There was really no way he could work in law enforcement after that. Couldn't even get a freaking security guard job.

Thanks, Hammond, you scumbag.

He'd taken the rap for the man when the stupid bastard went and got caught stealing a high-end car.

Don't let them take me. If I go down, I'll be put away for thirty years. I'll die in there. Don't let them take me...

So he'd taken the rap. It had put a real damper on his life as a budding serial killer.

He had to, because Hammond had something on him too. Something that could lead to his death. While Washington State didn't have the death penalty, just across the border in Idaho, they did.

No matter. They had something on each other.

Stalemate.

Blood wasn't thicker than water – at least not in the Hammond family.

He got up and went to the bathroom, staring at his face in the mirror over the sink. The bandage had some seepage and so he really should get it checked. The doc said if he was going to get an infection, he'd get it in the first three days. He figured he'd take a trip over to the clinic and get it checked. On the way, he'd pick up something to drink. He planned to spend the night in watching football.

Hammond could take care of his own mess. He'd be happy to watch it all go down in the daily newspaper, whatever happened.

THE NURSE at the clinic checked his wound. The expression on her face suggested the would wasn't healing properly.

"Looks like you got an infection brewing. I'm going to get the doctor to take a look and maybe put you on some antibiotics."

He nodded and waited for the doctor to give him the once-over. He'd already waited half an hour and wanted to get to the store soon so he could catch the game on cable. The doc finally came in and checked the stitches, said the nurse should clean it and put a fresh bandage on and then he'd give him a prescription for an antibiotic.

He got out of there as fast as he could, and drove to the 7-Eleven downtown to pick up a few snacks. He was across the street from the police station standing in line waiting to pay for his chips and salsa when he saw John Hammond's truck screech to a halt in front of the police station. His jaw dropped open completely when he saw Hammond get out of his truck and walk to the front entrance, a shotgun in hand.

What the…

Hammond had lost his mind.

CHAPTER TWENTY-NINE

Tess waited in the entry to the police station while Michael ran up the stairs to the second floor. While he was gone, Tess checked her messages and surfed Facebook on her cell, checking on her friends back in Seattle.

There was a message from Kate, her editor, asking how things were going, so Tess texted back.

Everything's fine – except that I was attacked by a man in a bala-clava in my motel room and maybe my father was friends with a serial killer but kept it secret all these years. Worse still, he might have been the killer and burned his victims, keeping their ashes in a jar in his attic...

She didn't send it. No need to get Kate all concerned about her.

Instead, she deleted that and sent a text about the Zoe Wallace case being reopened and the developments in the Melissa Foster case.

When Michael returned, they went out to the car and drove to the bar for supper. The place was busy when they arrived, filled with people looking to get an early start on the evening. They went into the dark interior and looked for a place to sit. Behind the antique bar with its polished chrome fixtures was a series of glass shelves on which bottles of liquor were displayed. There was a pool table and dart board in the back and several people were playing. Tess estimated there were about two dozen people in total. Country music was playing on the jukebox.

She smiled when the bartender placed a glass of draft on the bar top in front of her. She and Michael tapped glasses and each took a long pull of their beers.

"So, what's your theory of the case?" she asked, turning to Michael.

He rubbed his chin thoughtfully.

"Honestly?" he said and gave her a frustrated look. "I don't know. It seems like we have two cases. Janine was forty years ago. Lisa was next, followed by Zoe and then Melissa. Plus the five in neighboring counties. Hard to imagine the four are linked and involve the same killer but it is possible. We still don't know for sure that Janine is dead. We don't know that Lisa is dead. They could both have been taken and are alive somewhere, caught up in the sex trafficking trade. The other five girls are still missing."

She considered. "I don't they're all linked, but I don't know."

"What's your theory then?" Michael asked, smiling at her. "You studied criminology. You've covered crime in Washington State for a few years."

She shrugged. "We have two bodies and two missing girls. We know someone killed both Zoe and Melissa and it was probably the same person, right? Same age. Went missing in the same way – after dark when they should have been going home. We have the bracelet Zoe wore when she went missing, that turned up in Melissa's hand. Both were vulnerable girls from broken homes with parents who were stressed and maybe not able to keep as close a watch over them as they needed. It could be one killer, but why the twenty year gap in the disappearances? There were no girls missing in that twenty year period."

Michael shrugged and took out his cell. "Maybe the first was an accident but then the killer got a taste for it and the next girl was Lisa. After that, it was eight years to Zoe and ten years to Melissa, if we only count the girls from Paradise Hill. There are five others between Lisa and Melissa. Maybe our killer traveled outside the town for his victims. It's pretty rare but possible."

For the next hour, they talked about the cases in Washington State over the past four decades. It was great to have Michael as a friend. He could offer so much personal experience and professional insight into the cases, all of which she could use to flesh out her story for the *Sentinel*.

He was a real godsend in more than one way.

"Can I get you another round?" Nancy, their bartender, picked up their empty glasses and wiped down the bar top.

"Sure," Tess said, still thirsty.

When Nancy turned back to grab new glasses, Michael's cell chimed and he removed it from a pocket in his jacket.

"Crap," he said and dialed a number quickly.

"What is it?" Tess asked.

Michael shook his head and held up his finger.

"What happened?" he said. He listened to whomever was on the other line, rubbing his chin and jaw, which was covered in a few days' worth of stubble.

"Okay, I'll bring her over. Is everyone all right?"

He listened some more, and Tess got a sinking feeling in her gut.

Michael put away his cell and threw a few bills onto the bar top beside the tab.

"Forget the round. We have to go."

Nancy took the money, thanking Michael for the tip.

"What's happened?" Tess asked as they went outside.

Michael exhaled. "Our friend John Hammond just showed up at your father's house and shoved his way inside, determined to get the boxes."

"Oh, no," Tess said, imagining it in her mind's eye. "Were the Mastersons still there? Why didn't they call me?"

She pulled out her cell and saw there was a message.

GRANT: Had to call the police. John Hammond broke in and threatened us. We're still here with the police. The front door was broken. I'll wait for you.

"OH, HE LEFT A MESSAGE," she said and held out her phone for him to see. "I had it on vibrate and missed it."

"Let's go," he said, and led the way out of the bar. "I guess Grant tried to stop him but he pulled out a shotgun and chased them away. Grant called the police and they're at the house now. They went to Hammond's house and business but he's gone."

"Oh, God, he really freaked out." Tess followed Michael to the Jeep, which was parked down the street. "What was he looking for? The porn or the ashes?"

"Maybe both."

As they drove off, a chill went through Tess.

"What happens now that he realizes they're missing?"

"He knows it's all over but the crying."

"Do you think he's dangerous? Is he the man who attacked me?"

"I think he's our man," Michael said and shook his head.

"He seemed so nice."

"You can't tell by looking at these guys. If we could, we'd be able to find these creeps faster and prevent them from committing their crimes. Unfortunately, they look a lot like you and me."

THEY RACED to Tess's father's house and when they arrived, the Chief's vehicle was parked in the driveway, as well as a patrol car. The Masterson's truck was parked beside it.

They left the Jeep and went to the front door, which was open, the door broken off the hinge. Hammond must have been desperate to have done that.

Tess went through the doorway and into the living room, where the Mastersons sat talking to Chief Hammond and Officer Moore, who was taking their statement.

"There you are," Chief Hammond said and stood when Tess walked in. "We were just speaking with the Mastersons about what happened."

"Thank you, Chief," she replied and went to where Grant was sitting. "I'm so sorry this happened and I wasn't here."

"No problem," he said. "We're okay, but it was scary."

"Mr. Hammond pushed his way inside, threatened the Mastersons and went to the attic," Chief Hammond said. "That's when they called us. He came back down and was quite upset. Left without a word and no boxes. Whatever he was looking for, he didn't find it."

Michael turned to Tess. "I guess he knows we turned the contents over to police."

"Looks like it," she replied, biting her bottom lip. "Now what?"

They turned to Chief Hammond.

"We sent officers to the Hammond house and his place of business, but Mr. Hammond wasn't there."

It was at that moment that Chief Hammond got a call on his cell.

"Shit," he muttered after listening for a moment. "Okay. We'll be right there." He stood abruptly, turning to Michael. "There's an incident at the station." He pointed to the other police officer. "Let's go. Hammond shot Clint during an altercation at the station. He fled the scene on foot and he and Garth are barricaded in a house down the street. The emergency response team is on scene. Luckily, we just ran an exercise on dealing with an active shooter, and everyone's up on their business. We'll take information on this later."

Michael turned to Tess. "I'm going."

"Are you sure?" she asked softly, reaching out to touch his arm. "Isn't this the kind of thing you're supposed to avoid?"

"I have to go," he said and followed Chief Hammond and Moore out the doorway.

Tess stood at the window and watched the as the Chief got in his vehicle and Moore in his, then drive off. Michael followed them in his Jeep.

She turned back to the Mastersons. "You should go home now. I'm so sorry this happened to you."

Grant waved his hand dismissively. "Nothing you could have done. I'm glad we got out of this without a scratch, although your door needs to be put back on. If you need me to, I can get some lumber and rehang the door."

"Thanks," Tess said and ran her hand through her hair, trying to think of what she could do to help. "I have no clue how to hang a door. I'd appreciate the help."

Grant went to the door after grabbing his jacket. His wife, Elaine, followed. "I'll be back with some materials I need. Luckily, I have some tools in my trunk."

"I'll be here."

When they were gone, Tess sat on the sofa and tried to take it all in.

They'd obviously scared Hammond when they showed up asking about the contents of the storage unit. He'd been scared enough to go to her father's house and force his way in so he could find whatever it was he thought was in the boxes – the porn, the ashes, the scrapbook, or all three. Then he was upset enough to go to the police station and try to get them from inside.

What the hell would have come over the man? Why would he think he could go inside and just take evidence out of the station?

He was out of his mind.

CHAPTER THIRTY

Michael drove as fast as he could to keep up with Chief Hammond and the other officer, who raced through the streets of Paradise Hill with their lights flashing and sirens blaring.

Adrenaline surged through him as he screeched to a halt behind the chief, following the two men to the scene. The parking lot was currently surrounded by several police cars and a black Humvee that a charitable resident had donated to the station. Two of the officers had donned their SWAT gear and were in position, their rifles trained on a nearby house in which Hammond and his son were holed up.

"What have we got?" Hammond asked one of his officers, who was standing behind the open door of his sedan. "How's Clint?"

"He's at the ER. Shoulder wound. He'll be fine."

"Thank God," Hammond said, removing his hat and running a hand over his brush cut. "What happened?"

"Hammond barricaded the door and broke a window. There's a barrel pointing out the window," he said, pointing to one of the smaller windows at the side of the house. "Looks like the bathroom window. Small, shoulder-high."

"Any idea of what set him off?"

"Apparently," the officer said, "he called to ask about some boxes from Ron McClintock's and Clint said he wasn't allowed to discuss evidence in an ongoing case. That was enough to send Hammond off the deep end, I guess."

"Has anyone been in communication with him yet?"

The officer shook his head. "No. They wanted to wait for you, since he's your cousin."

"I'll give it a try. Do we have his cell number?"

The officer read off a phone number and Hammond called Hammond using the department's tactical communications system.

When Hammond answered, the Chief nodded and they began recording the conversation.

"John," Hammond said. "What's going on? What's happened?"

There was a pause. Finally, Hammond spoke.

"You know damn well what happened."

Hammond glanced at Michael, his eyebrows raised. He thumbed the mic.

"I think he knows about the jar of remains."

Michael nodded.

The Chief spike into the mic. "I don't have a clue what happened, John. Why don't you tell me?"

"I didn't mean to do it," Hammond said, a catch in his voice.

"Do what, John? What didn't you mean to do?"

Michael could hear the man crying. Finally, he sniffed and cleared his throat.

"You know damn well. It was an accident, I swear. She

was so drunk. I never meant to hurt her, but she drank too much. I thought she was fine because she got up after we were done and she was fine, I swear. Then she just stopped breathing but I didn't mean to kill her."

"Who is 'she,' John? Who do you mean? Do you mean Daryl Kincaid?" Chief Hammond turned to Michael and nodded knowingly. He put the receiver back up to his ear. "Who didn't you mean to kill?"

"You know who."

Hammond shook his head. "No, I don't. There are several missing girls from Paradise Hill. Tell me which one you mean."

"I didn't mean to do it," Hammond said, his voice now low, emotionless. "We were all scared. We panicked and Daryl said he'd take care of things."

"What did Daryl do?"

Chief Hammond turned to Michael, his thumb off the mic. "Daryl Kincaid. He wasn't in prison yet when Zoe went missing. Are they talking about Zoe? The ashes in that jar were Zoe's."

"Could be. We don't know who else is in there."

There was a pause and Michael heard Garth speak to his father.

"You sonofabitch," Garth said, his voice filled with acid. "What are you talking about?"

"Go," his father said. "Go back to the living room."

"I'm not going anywhere until you tell me what's going on."

There was a pause and then Hammond spoke once more, barely above a whisper.

"I didn't mean to kill her. I'm so sorry."

That was it.

The next thing they heard was shouting and then a loud bang.

"Jesus," Chief Hammond said, his body startling. "John!" he shouted into the receiver. "John, what just happened?"

He waited but there was no response. Then, they heard another bang.

"John – can you hear me?"

There was only silence.

"Go, go, go," Hammond yelled to the two SWAT officers, who gestured to two other police officers. The four went to the front door, weapons drawn, and pushed the door open with a battering ram. Then, they filed inside, crouched, one in the lead with his weapon pointed ahead, the others following, their hands on each other's shoulders, weapons at the ready.

Michael heard them calling out 'clear' after they'd checked each room. One SWAT officer finally came to the front door.

"They're both dead," he said, removing the black covering from his face. "You can come in."

"God Almighty," Chief Hammond muttered beside Michael. He took the sidewalk to the front door and disappeared inside.

Michael was tempted to go in as well, but then he thought better of it. He didn't need to see a dead John Hammond and his son.

Murder-suicide.

Had John killed Garth to prevent him from finding out the truth – that he was a killer, even if he claimed that the death had been accidental? It sounded like a poor excuse. Why would he even be in a position to accidentally kill Zoe?

Had he abducted her? Had Zoe been over at John's house to play with Serena, Garth's daughter?

Now, they'd never know the full story or which girl John meant – Zoe? Or Melissa? If Daryl Kincaid was involved, he must have been referring to Zoe for Daryl had been in prison for the past decade. It had to be Zoe.

Michael took out his cell and called Tess.

"What's going on?" she said, her voice breathless.

"John Hammond and his son Garth are both dead."

"What? Oh my God, Michael! What happened?"

Michael rubbed his temple. "He shot Garth and then himself."

"Holy..." Tess was silent for a moment. "Did they try to talk him down?"

"Yes, in fact. Hammond talked to him. Asked him why he was doing this, and Hammond said the Chief already knew. He confessed to killing 'her.' He said Daryl Kincaid 'took care of things,' but if so, that was over a decade ago because Kincaid's been in prison for almost ten years. He must mean Zoe."

"And whoever else was in the jar."

"He only said 'her,' in the singular. He didn't say 'them' so I'm not sure."

"That's strange. If Kincaid put Zoe in the jar, maybe he put someone else in as well? How else would another set of remains get into the jar? It had to be put there by someone with access to the storage unit – or my father's house."

"Your father and Kincaid were friends before he went to prison. Maybe Kincaid put them in. But they were in Hammond's storage unit. And in your father's house."

Tess sighed on the other end of the line. "I hope we get

results back from the DNA test soon. When is your guy going to have them?"

"Maybe tomorrow."

"God, what's going to happen now?"

Michael considered for a moment, watching as the police officers talked among themselves at the doorway. A car drove up and he turned to check out the driver.

It was Dr. Prosser. He got out of his car and came over to Michael, bringing his black bag with him.

"Hold on a sec," Michael said to Tess. "The coroner's here. I'll call you back."

After Tess said goodbye, Michael ended the call and turned to Dr. Prosser.

"How are you, sir?" he said and extended his hand.

"Too many deaths for a town so small," the older man replied, shaking Michael's hand. "I thought I'd have it easy but people keep dying or being murdered in Paradise Hill."

"I'll leave you to it," Michael said, and watched as the man walked up the steps to the front door and disappeared into the dark interior.

There was nothing else Michael could do, so he decided to go back to Tess's father's house. He'd talk to Tess and do some more sleuthing in the boxes. He felt like there was more to find. In particular, he was interested in whatever cabins Hammond and Kincaid had used in the past. The bodies had been burned, it had to be in some kind of fire, whether in a fire pit or in a burn barrel. There might still be remains that they could use to tie the murders to.

WHEN HE ARRIVED BACK at the house, Tess was watching

while Mr. Masterson fixed the door jamb so he could rehang the door.

"Hey," she said, her arms crossed, an expression of concern in her eyes. "What the hell is going on?"

"Dr. Prosser's doing his thing," Michael said as he came inside, squeezing past Masterson, who was screwing in the door hinges. "Do you know which cabins your dad used during the years? Which ones did you and Thad go to with him when you were kids?"

"My father had a favorite cabin," she said. "He always booked that one in particular, farthest from town. I saw some receipts in one of the boxes."

He followed her to the pile of boxes in the corner of the dining room that had belonged to her father.

"The police will probably want to take these into evidence, won't they?" she asked. "I don't know which boxes are my father's and which are Hammond's. I assumed they were all my father's."

"Have you already looked through them?"

"Most of them."

He shrugged. "Technically we should leave them since they'll be evidence, but I'm damn curious about the cabins."

Tess opened a few boxes and then pulled out a file folder. Inside were sheets of paper and while he watched, she fished through them, finally pulling out one in particular.

"There," she said and held out a receipt from Mountain View Cabins. It was for a cabin on Mountain View Road that bordered the lake outside Paradise Hill. "This is the one we used to rent. It was closest to the lake. Great fishing."

He took the receipt and called the number listed on the header. After several rings, a male voice answered.

"Gilroy Rentals," the man said.

"Hello," Michael said, rubbing his forehead, trying to come up with a cover story on the fly. "This is Special Agent Carter with the Seattle office of the FBI. I'd like to talk to you about cabin rentals – in particular, the cabin at the end of Mountain View Road. Could you meet us there and let us see it?"

"I know who you are," Gilroy said. "You're Michael Carter."

"I am," Michael replied.

"Is this official business?" Gilroy asked.

"Not yet, but it may be, depending on what we find."

There was silence for a moment, but then Gilroy responded. "Sure. I'll meet you there in fifteen."

"Thanks," Michael said and ended the call. He turned to Tess and handed the receipt back to her. "Feel like taking a drive out there?"

She put the receipt back into the file and replaced the lid. "Let's go."

CHAPTER THIRTY-ONE

While Tess spoke with the cleaner, asking him to lock the door when he left, Michael went out to the driveway and started the Jeep.

After Tess got in, he took the mountain road that led to the lake just outside of town. The road was rough, pock-marked with ruts and potholes, but his Jeep handled it well. The cabins on this road were more basic than those closer to the town, which were meant more for tourists who wanted the wilderness experience without the wilderness. The cabins further into the mountains were the kind real hunters and fishermen preferred.

He drove up to the cabin, parking beside a rusting Ford truck, which he assumed was Gilroy's.

Dan Gilroy was an older man about Chief Hammond's age. He wore a pair of denim overalls and a sheepskin jacket, and, on his head, a cap with the image of a snow-capped mountain and *Gilroy's Rentals* emblazoned in red.

They shook hands, and Michael walked around the property with Tess and Gilroy following.

"When was the last time this cabin was rented?" Michael asked.

"Not this summer," he said. "The roof." He pointed to the building. "It leaks and we haven't had the cash flow to fix it. The last time it was rented was in 2016. A couple of guys from Yakima."

"How often is the cabin cleaned?"

"When it's rented, it would be cleaned after every customer, of course," Gilroy said, frowning.

"What about the burn barrel? The fire pit?"

"We don't empty them unless they need to be emptied. That's left up to the cleaners."

The cabin had a huge stack of cordwood out back in a shelter against the wall facing the mountain. Surrounded completely by tall fir trees, the building was secluded, but there was a narrow gap between the trees that led to the lake. A small dock that was used as a boat launch, an old wooden boat, its paint peeled off due to exposure to the weather, was half sunken next to the dock. In the backyard was a fire pit and at the side of the property was a cement slab with an old rusting barrel.

Michael went to the burn barrel, removed the flat piece of metal that covered it, and checked inside. At the bottom was about a foot of charred material. He couldn't tell what it was, but often renters burned the remains of fish or any animals they may have caught, as well as the garbage that they didn't want to haul into town to the dump.

"Do you mind?" Michael said and pointed to the barrel. "I want to see what's inside."

"Sure," the owner said, shrugging. "As long as you clean it up."

Michael grabbed the bottom of the barrel and upended it. The barrel was old and rusted through in several spots, and it turned over easily. The charred material poured out and spread on the cement pad. He tapped the rim against the cement a few times to dislodge whatever material might have been in the bottom. Then he grabbed a stick from the ground and poked through the ashes.

Gilroy and Tess came closer and watched. He combed through the ashes until he found what looked like bone and separated it from the rest.

"Looky here," he said. Sure enough, he'd found what looked like a tooth. A molar of some kind. "Is that animal or human?" He glanced up at Gilroy.

"Were you *expecting* a human?" Gilroy asked in disbelief.

"You never know," Michael said and eyed Tess, whose eyebrows were raised.

"Where would the contents be deposited when the barrel was cleaned?"

Gilroy glanced around and then pointed to a pile of leaves and dirt a few feet away.

"Looks like here," he said and stubbed the mound with his foot. Under a thin layer of leaves and pine needles, they could see black ash.

"Do you mind if I dig in it?" Michael asked, glancing around the yard. "Is there a spade around or anything I could use?"

"Sure, if you want," Gilroy said and went to the shed. He had a metal ring attached to his belt with multiple keys on it, and selected one key to open the lock. Gilroy went inside and Michael followed him, eager to inspect the contents.

A selection of hoes and rakes, shovels and an old wheelbarrow. Several bags of quick-set concrete were laid out on the floor and several empty plastic tubs had been stacked inside each other.

"What are those used for?" Michael asked, pointing to the plastic barrel. It looked remarkably similar to the kind Melissa had been found inside.

"Don't know where they came from," Gilroy said and rubbed his chin thoughtfully. "I guess you could put ice in them and store fish or other game. Store rainwater, too."

They both turned and glanced at the rear of the cabin and sure enough, there was a downspout that emptied into a blue barrel. It had a wooden lid with a notch carved out so the downspout could fit right in.

Michael nodded.

"Cement?" he asked, eyeing Gilroy.

"I know what you're thinking," Gilroy said. "You're thinking the same thing I am. Little Melissa Foster was put in one like that and it was filled with cement. I read about it in the paper."

"That's exactly what I was thinking."

"You figure someone used this to do it?" Gilroy looked around, toeing the dirt in the shed. "This cabin hasn't been used all summer. Roof leaks. I haven't had the money to pay for repairs. Not in this economy."

"Does anyone else have keys?"

Gilroy shrugged. "The Hammonds owned these cabins back in the day. I took them over when John had some trouble and couldn't pay the taxes. I have no idea if he had any spare keys. I assumed he turned them over when he sold the place to me. We shook on it, and I trusted him."

"He did time for fraud," Michael said dryly.

Gilroy slipped his hands in his jacket pocket and rocked

forward on his feet. "I knew him since we were in high school."

Michael didn't respond, exasperated with the small-town mentality. Either people were prejudiced against someone because of old family feuds, or they were partial to them because of blood and familiarity. Evidence didn't seem to sway them one way or the other. Gilroy trusted Hammond and even a brush with the law didn't change that.

Michael took out his cell and called Agent Nash, the officer in charge of the Melissa Foster case.

"Yeah, you might want to come down and see this," he said when Nash answered. "I'm at the Gilroy cabin at the end of Mountain View Road. There's a shed here with large blue barrels and bags of quick-set cement."

"That sounds suspiciously like something I'd like to see. I'll be there in ten. Thanks for the heads-up. What are you doing there?"

"Just checking out a hunch."

"Seems like your hunch was right."

"It just might be."

Michael ended the call and turned to Gilroy. "Special Agent Nash from the Seattle office is coming by to look at these," he said and pointed into the shed. "Try to think of anyone who might have access to this shed. Especially this summer. Did you come by and check the cabin earlier in the summer?"

"I did," he said.

"Was that before or after Melissa went missing?"

Gilroy made a face and scratched his chin. "After. She went missing in April. I checked this place at the beginning of the season, so that would be May."

Michael nodded. "You weren't back after?"

"Nope. First week of May's when I check the cabins, make sure they're cleaned and stocked. Would have been around May fifth or so. That's when we noticed that there was a leak. Ruined the floor. Did a lot of damage and there was just no way I had the funds to fix it. Can't do it myself because of my back."

"You didn't notice anything different about the cabin? Nothing moved or changed?"

"Nothing, but I wasn't looking for anything neither."

Gilroy leaned back, one hand on his back like he was in pain.

"Bad back?"

"Yeah, I was in that accident with your dad," he said to Tess. "Knocked myself pretty bad. Haven't been the same since. It's why he stopped coming out here and fishing. Used to be his favorite place in summer and fall."

"He used to bring us out here years and years ago," Tess said, her voice wistful. "I have good memories of this place and the lake."

"He'd been coming here since he was a boy," Gilroy said. "I did as well. We used to party out at the lake when we were in high school together. Lotta babies conceived right here in these cabins during the summer, I'd say." He gave Michael a grin. "Ron was the only one of the three boys who didn't get a girl pregnant before he married her."

"Three boys?" Michael asked, curious about what Gilroy knew about Hammond and McClintock. They were both dead now and there would be no interviews conducted to suss out what either of them knew about Zoe's death, or Melissa's.

"Yeah, John Hammond, Ron McClintock, and Daryl Kincaid. They were as tight as could be all the way through school, but after high school, Daryl went a different path. He had a temper – sure was a wild one, sleeping with everybody's sisters. He's got a few bastards around town. Sorry," he said to Tess. "Excuse my language."

Tess waved at him. "I work the crime beat." She smiled.

"He and John were paying for hookers," Gilroy added. "Young ones. Debbie left John when she found out, and he lost touch with Garth for a while. Must have been terribly hard for him, losing his boy like that. Debbie had a real hard time managing."

Tess stood beside them, staring out at the sun setting over the lake, casting long shadows from the trees. Michael could guess what she was thinking – how hard had it been for her father to lose her and Thad?

Michael turned to Gilroy. "John went to the police station earlier this afternoon and shot up the entry, then holed up with Garth in a house beside the station."

The look on Gilroy's face was almost comic, it was so extreme.

"You're shitting me," Gilroy said.

"Unfortunately, no," Michael replied. "He spoke with Chief Hammond, then he shot Garth, killing him, and then he killed himself."

"He shot Garth?" Gilroy said, his face blanching. He looked completely confused. "Are you sure?"

"Unfortunately, yes."

Gilroy covered his eyes. When he pulled his hand away, he had tears in them. "He shot Garth?"

"Yes," Michael said and shook his head. "I'm really sorry. You were close?"

Gilroy squeezed his head. "John was my cousin." He

stood in silence for a moment and Michael exchanged a meaningful look with Tess.

"He shot Garth... Why would he shoot his own son?" Gilroy asked, dumbfounded.

"I'm guessing he didn't want him to know the truth."

"What truth?"

"He admitted he killed someone, accidentally. Might be Zoe."

Gilroy slapped his head with both hands, holding it like he was in pain. He turned around in a circle.

"Oh my God," he said. "Oh my dear God. Why? Why would he do that?"

"I'm sorry you had to find out this way. I didn't know you were a relative."

Gilroy shook his head. He took out his cell and called someone. "I have to go. Can I trust you to lock up when you leave? I gotta go and see John Senior. He'll be devastated."

"I'll make sure to close things up. I really appreciate your letting us see the place. The FBI will probably be taking it over as a potential crime scene. And I'm sorry about John and Garth."

Gilroy left without another word. Tess turned to Michael, a grimace on her face.

"That was pretty bad."

"I know," Michael replied, rubbing his forehead. "I honestly didn't know they were related or I would have tried to break it to him more gently."

"God, what is going on in this town?" Tess said with a heavy sigh. "Lisa, Zoe, and Melissa all go missing. Zoe's ashes turn up in my father's attic, Melissa's body turns up in one of Gilroy's cabins. Someone kept a scrapbook of stories about Janine and other crimes in the town. I was attacked. John

Hammond kills his son and then himself? Some quiet small town."

"Small towns are big enough to have a few really sick people in them," Michael said. "Whenever you get a thousand or more people, you can expect at least twenty with anti-social personality disorder. They're your regular criminals, gang members, unscrupulous religious leaders, abusive parents, rapists, you name it. Even a serial killer."

"Do you think John Hammond was a serial killer?"

"He confessed to killing someone," he said, remembering the sound of Hammond's panicked voice on the tactical phone. "He doesn't strike me as someone who could pull off three murders and keep under our radar, but with these guys, especially the organized type, you can't tell."

"Maybe when we look more closely at him, things will fall into place. "

"I hope so," Michael said. "The one thing that bothers me is, I've sat in on interviews with some child predators. They typically don't cry. They don't whine. They believe what they're doing is justified. They don't apologize. If Hammond is the killer, he broke with what I know about this kind of killer."

"Maybe he really didn't want his son to know."

"Maybe. Psychopaths can form relationships and even care about other people – to the extent that they provide the serial killer with cover or even a comfortable home environment. They usually want to take credit when they're caught. It's like some kind of ranking with them. John Hammond was afraid. He was terrified that anyone would find out he was a killer – especially his son." Michael shrugged. "I'm sure the FBI will spend some time going over Hammond's past and

SUSAN LUND

we'll find evidence that explains some of this. Links we never saw before."

He turned to Tess.

"After Nash gets here and takes a look around, how about we try once more and get a drink? I need one after that."

She nodded. "Sounds like a plan."

CHAPTER THIRTY-TWO

An hour later, after they turned the site over to Special Agent Nash, Michael and Tess went into town for something to eat. After they ate, Tess only wanted to go to Mrs. Carter's, have a hot bath and go to bed.

"Sorry to be a party pooper, but I'm exhausted," she said when Michael suggested they watch more The Walking Dead. "I think I'll go to bed and read."

"No need to explain," he said and gave her a smile. "It's been a pretty eventful week for you, to say the least."

"Has it only been a week?" Tess said, surprised at how fast the time had passed. So much had happened since she arrived back in Paradise Hills, it felt like much more time had gone by.

Tess had a bath and then got into her pajamas. Before she got into bed, she bent down and opened up one of the boxes she'd brought with her dad's journals stacked inside. She'd worked her way through the journal and had made it to Halloween 1978 - the year Janine went missing. The journal recounted his costume for the high school dance. He went as a greaser, a character from the popular book, The Outsiders. Then, more entries about Thanksgiving and spending it with his grandparents.

Then she found it – the date read January, 1978. Her father had just turned sixteen and was in his sophomore year of high school.

The entries started out full of ambition. It was a new year and he was going to write every night, like his English teacher suggested for all budding authors. The teacher, a Mr. Jones, told the students to find the stories in the everyday world. So, her father had attempted to do just that, writing about his day, but trying to make it into a story.

In the first dozen or so entries, most of the passages were observations about school and the various characters that populated his classes. Jocks, artist-types, preppies, hoods and nerds. He classified himself as somewhere between a jock and a nerd because of his desire to be a writer.

Tess snuggled into bed with her father's journal, flipping through entries about the latest football games, parties at the lake and how much work his math and physics classes were that year. She skipped forward, wondering how far the journal went and saw that it ended in April. After that, there were no entries.

She went back, trying to find the weekend Janine had died. But there was nothing except a short story.

The Girl From Paradise Hill
by
Ron McClintock.

HE'D WRITTEN the story in careful handwriting, beginning it
with a notice.

*THIS IS A WORK OF FICTION. Any resemblance to people currently
living or dead is purely accidental.*
   The three of them were in total shit.

*HE ALWAYS LIKED HER. They used to sit together and talk at the park
while she was watching her little brother. People talked about her, said
she was a slut, but he thought she was nice. Before she ran away, they
went to games together sometimes, and kissed behind the bleachers.*

   *He gave her a mood ring, and she asked if it meant they were going
steady. He said it was up to her. She laughed and said they were friends,
and it was a friendship ring. That made him embarrassed and a bit hurt
but he just shrugged it off, trying to be a man.*

   *Then, she had trouble at home and ran away. She stopped going to
school and he never saw her anymore except at parties where she always
drank a lot and she always threw up. Guys all said she was a wild one
and that if you got her drunk, she was up for a gangbang. That her
mother was a whore who worked at the hotel bar in Yakima and she was
a chip off the old block.*

   *The three guys were partying with a bunch of kids from school that
night at one of the cabins Jim's dad owned. She was there and she
smiled when she saw Rob. He hadn't seen her for a while but she came
right up to him.*

   "I still wear it," she said and showed Rob her hand.

   She was already drunk, and Rob could see that she was stumbling.

He was worried about her because Don had always liked her and Rob knew what he'd do if Don got his hands on her.

She left and after the guys had a few more beers, they left too and drove along the road back to town. It was after midnight and they found her walking alone, stumbling along the road. It was cold and the kids she left with kicked her out miles away from town after she puked in the car. She probably would have frozen to death but maybe she would have lived if three guys hadn't found her. That's what's so hard.

She might have lived.

They picked her up and she wanted to keep partying. She must have thought they had beer or weed. They went back to the cabin. She was really drunk, and she and Rob ended up in the bedroom. He thought she wanted it because she pulled him down onto the bed.

They had sex and it was all over so fast he didn't get to really enjoy it but she seemed to by the way she moaned.

"More beer," she said. But he said he didn't have any left.

She got mad and left the room, then went to Don.

"Give me a beer," she said and he said, "I will but you have to come with me in the bedroom."

She said, "Whatever." Don took his six-pack of beer and they went into the bedroom.

Rob and Jim drank a few beers and when Don came out, he pointed into the room.

"Your turn, Jim."

Jim took two beers and went into the bedroom with her.

Rob and Don drank a beer together and decided to crash at the cabin for the night. They smoked some more weed and passed out around three a.m.

In the morning, before the sun had even risen, Jim came out holding onto his pants which were undone.

"I don't think she's breathing."

Don got up and looked into the bedroom. "What the fuck did you do, Jim?" Don said.

"She drank too much. She must have puked when she passed out."

Rob and Don went into the room and there she was, naked and lying on her back, with her jeans pulled down around her ankles. Her eyes were closed and puke was coming out of her mouth and on the bed beside her head.

Rob knew they should have taken her to the ER but Don felt for a pulse and couldn't find one.

Jim freaked.

"We gotta take her to the hospital," Rob said, but Don said "She's dead, you idiot. Jim killed her. She was already so drunk and then he gave her more beer. She's underage. If the cops find out, he's going away for murder. All of us are. We all did her and she was underage."

"She was still alive!" Jim said. He started to cry.

"Now what do we do?" Rob said. He felt like crying too because he always liked her. She was nice to him and now she was dead.

"I'll take care of it," Don said. "You crybabies can leave if you want. Come back and get me later."

"What are you going to do?" Jim asked.

"I said I'm taking care of it, idiot. Go home, sissies."

So they did but Rob knew they shouldn't have let that psycho deal with it. Jim was still crying. Rob was really mad at him. He took Jim home and dropped him off. Old Man Harrison was watching, waiting for them. Rob saw him through the window. Jim went inside. If his dad knew what he'd just done he'd call the cops and have them throw him in jail he was such a hardass.

Rob went back to the cabin the next morning and no one was around. Don must have walked back into town.

Later, he checked on Don who was living at his dad's place. His dad was out of town so he was alone at the house.

"What did you do? Did you bury her?"

"I cut her body up and burned it in the burn barrel. Here she is," he said and held up a jar filled with ashes. "I took care of it, like I said I would."

"You fucking psycho. What are you going to do with that?"

"I'm going to keep it to make sure you keep your mouths shut. If you say anything to anyone about this, I'll give this to the police. We're all guilty. We gave her beer. We all had sex with her and she's under age. If one of us goes down, we all go down. We have to stick together on this."

"You should bury the ashes. That's evidence," I told him. "If any one finds it, we're toast."

He didn't want to. "I'm keeping these so neither of you can blame it on me. I don't trust you not to confess. If you try, all three of us will go down. Don't even think about turning yourselves in or we'll go down for statutory rape and murder. We'll go to jail and you know what happens there — you'll get ass raped and be some big fucker's girlfriend."

Then he threw Rob her mood ring — the ring Rob gave her. "Here," he said. I" thought you'd like to keep this for old times' sake."

Rob knew Don. He was crazy enough that if they did anything against him, he'd kill them.

Only a psycho would cut a girl up and burn her body.

The three of them were so completely screwed.

TESS COVERED HER MOUTH. Substitute Ron for Rob, Daryl for Don, John for Jim, and Hammond for Harrison and the story was a confession -- the truth of what happened to Janine one cold night in January, 1978.

Her father... All those years, he lived with the secret of Janine's death.

She got up and pulled a robe around her, then left her bedroom, the journal in her hand. In the living room,

Michael was alone on the sofa, drinking hot chocolate and watching television.

"You need to read this," she said and held the journal out for Michael. "Read the story I have open."

Michael took the journal and sat up straighter, his expression turning serious, his brow furrowed. He read the first page and then shifted his position before turning a page to read further.

Finally, he glanced up at her.

"Holy crap. This is what happened, right?"

"I think so."

Michael read some more.

"Your dad didn't kill her," he said. "She died accidentally from aspiration of her own vomit while intoxicated. They panicked and burned her body."

Tess covered her eyes, the truth finally sinking in. "My father helped cover it up all those years," Tess said. "He did have sex with her and she was underage."

"Did you read this?" Michael asked and handed the journal back. She read over the next few pages, which was some notes for the rest of the story, but were probably her father going over the murder again and again, trying to find the way out.

He always knew Don was a psycho. Don was always strange, growing up, catching frogs and sticking thumbtacks in their brains. Chasing cats, swinging them around in bags and laughing when they stumbled around after.

He never felt pain when he got in a fight and got hurt.

Should Rob go and confess anyway? Should he go and tell them he never hurt her?

She was only thirteen and he could get in trouble for statutory rape. They'd put him in jail. He didn't want to go to jail.

He didn't hurt her. If only they hadn't gone back to the cabin. If only they hadn't given her more beer. She'd still be alive. If only Don hadn't offered to take care of it.

They should have gone right to the ER with her. Maybe she'd still be alive.

What the hell did Don know, anyway?

Now they all looked guilty. It was an accident but how can they ever prove it?

How can they prove it was an accident?

They couldn't, especially after Don burned her body.

They were so screwed.

"Why would he cut up and burn the body?" she asked, staring at Michael. "How could he even think of cutting up a dead body and burning it instead of going to the ER? Maybe save her life? Only a psycho could do that."

"Even your dad called him a psycho."

"Most kids would go right to the police and turn themselves in. They didn't. They panicked and let Daryl take charge. He was the oldest. Daryl cut up and burned the body. Then he blackmailed them both with the ashes. All those years."

Tess sat on the sofa beside Michael with the journal in her hands and flipped through the pages. The event was a clear demarcation in her father's life. Before that night, he had tried to find the stories in his everyday life. He hoped it would help him become a writer – maybe write mystery or science fiction – and had received great marks for his creative writing in high school. After that night, he stopped writing about his dreams. He stopped writing about anything but the crime. His pages documented the missing persons case and what the police were doing, who they were interviewing, what Daryl was doing and saying.

He became obsessed with Janine's death and the aftermath. Then all the other crimes, maybe trying to understand it all.

"My poor father," she said, shaking her head, her emotions welling up. "He got caught up in a mess, and it changed everything," she said, flipping through the journal. "But he didn't kill her."

They were teenage boys. What did they know? Maybe if they'd gone to the police and confessed, they would have gotten off lightly. Her father had no criminal or juvenile record. He would have probably received probation or something light. Her grandfather was a good dad. He would have stood in court with her father and made sure things were put right.

Instead, they'd covered up the murder and by doing so, made it worse. Her father had been changed by it, never really getting over it, always being so quiet. Living with guilt all those years.

Tess wiped her cheeks. "I guess we should turn this over to Chief Hammond. He'll be able to close one case with it."

Michael nodded and took the journal from her. "Daryl's in jail now. He's the only one left who could be charged. But we still don't know how Zoe's ashes got into the jar. John must have done it. Or Daryl."

Tess sighed. The cleaners still had at least another few days of work left to finish up the sorting and de-junking. They were cleaning slowly as they went, one room at a time.

"Whatever the case, Chief Hammond will want to send a forensic team in."

"I'm so tired," Tess said and slumped beside him. "Honestly, I feel like I could sleep for a week."

Michael nodded and turned the journal over in his hand, examining the final entry.

"I'll give this to Hammond in the morning. I have a feeling he's going to want to go through your father's house with a fine-toothed comb to see if there's anything else in evidence that could help out other cases," he said and then closed the journal. "You go to bed."

"I will," Tess said. "Should I call the cleaners and tell them to hold off until you talk to Chief Hammond?"

"I think so."

Tess took out her cell and left a message with the Mastersons, telling them she'd pay for the work already done but needed them to stop for the time being. She ended the call and turned to Michael.

"I'm exhausted. I'll see you in the morning."

She stood up and Michael did as well. Then, he took her into his arms, holding her tightly. It felt good. She needed that.

She glanced up at him. "Thank you."

"For what?" he said softly.

"For being here. I don't know what I would have done without you."

He smiled and stroked her cheek softly. "Glad to be of service."

"Do you think John Hammond was my attacker?"

"Don't know," Michael said. "Why would he attack you?"

Tess shrugged. "Maybe he killed Zoe and is angry because I'm writing an investigative report about the murders in Paradise Hill and he wanted to scare me away."

"Maybe," Michael replied, but his expression said he

didn't believe it. "They'll search his house and business to look for evidence. We'll find evidence, if there is any to find."

He continued to hold her for another moment and then released her. She gave him a smile and went to her bedroom, closing the door behind her. Then, she crept back into bed and switched off the light on the bedside table but sleep was a long time coming.

CHAPTER THIRTY-THREE

The next morning, Michael sat across from Chief Hammond on the chair facing the desk while Hammond read the journal entry and the short story. Special Agent Nash joined them, but he was talking on his cell to someone back in Seattle. Chief Hammond flipped a page in the journal.

"Well isn't that a sonofabitch," he said softly, rubbing his forehead. "Who would have thought? He's my cousin. Known him all my life. I would never peg him for a killer."

"Janine's death was an accident."

"But he had Zoe's ashes. That suggests he killed her. Or maybe Garth killed her? Zoe knew Garth's daughter. Did John burn the body and hide the ashes in with Janine?"

"I'm not sure," Michael replied. "Until we know more, it's all just speculation. We need Ron's and John's houses to be gone through for evidence to link to Zoe's and maybe Melissa's disappearances and deaths."

Hammond took in a deep breath. "I can believe Janine's

death was accidental but I just can't believe John became a child killer. He had an alibi for Zoe."

Michael thought back to the case. A decade earlier, he had just finished his BA and was attending FBI training at Quantico. Her case was one of the first he'd read up on, because profilers at the Bureau's Behavioral Sciences Unit were trying to connect a number of missing girl cases across the state.

Like several other cases, Zoe had gone missing from the playground by her house, which was next to a forested area and a road that traveled deeper into the mountain valley behind Paradise Hill.

"What do you remember from the case?" he asked Hammond, who leaned back, pushing his glasses up onto his head, rubbing his eyes like he was tired.

"I remember we spent a lot of time searching the forests and abandoned buildings by the lake, but never found a single piece of evidence. She just disappeared."

"You liked Garth for it, based on what I read in the file."

"We did, but he and his father had an alibi. He was out of town with John, picking up a new truck. He had receipts for the hotel in Spokane and for the restaurant where they ate. They both went to the dealer the next morning and Garth drove the new truck back to Paradise Hill."

"No one else was promising as a suspect?"

Michael already knew but wanted to hear it from Hammond, who had been an officer when the disappearance took place.

"The usual suspects. Daryl Kincaid was one of the local creeps, but he had an alibi as well. Was with his friends in the bar all evening and late into morning."

"Any other suspects?"

"None that we could place at the playground at that time. Someone must have been watching her and snatched her up when she left, and it was dark enough not to be seen. Had to have a vehicle. Otherwise, someone would have seen her walking with an adult."

"Someone picked her up, killed her, and burned her remains. Put them in a jar already containing Janine's ashes, that somehow ended up in John Hammond's storage locker and then in Ron McClintock's attic. It had to be either John Hammond or his son but why did John use the singular? There's another body in that jar."

"Maybe he didn't know?" Hammond replied, his head tilted to one side. "Pretty strange for the ashes of two murdered girls to end up in the same jar without the two being connected."

Michael shrugged. "Thirty years between them. I can't believe someone would wait that long to kill another girl. More than likely there are others we just haven't connected yet. Like Lisa," Michael said. "And by my last count, at least five others in neighboring counties, not to mention others closer to Seattle and Tacoma. But he said *her*, not *them*."

"He was upset and may not have been articulate," Hammond countered. "Might not have wanted Garth to know there were more." Chief Hammond moved the file on his desk, closing the cover. "If we get those results back from the crime lab in Seattle, I'm thinking we can at least close two murders. It's pretty clear those ashes belong to Janine."

"I'll call to confirm," Michael said and took out his cell. He dialed the number of his contact in the lab.

Jameson answered on the fourth ring.

"Hey," Michael said, recognizing the man from his peculiar always-tired-sounding voice. "It's Michael Carter calling from Paradise Hill."

"Hey, Mike," Jameson said, sounding bored. "What's up? You doing okay?"

"I'm fine," Michael said. "I'm wondering if those results for the DNA match on the burnt remains came through yet."

"Let me check," Jameson said and there was a silence on the line. Michael heard a chair scrape against the floor and footsteps. About two minutes later, Jameson picked the receiver back up. "Okay, I got a preliminary result on that profile. There is a pretty good match consistent with the subject being a first- or second-degree relative to the reference sample."

"Fantastic. Is there any way you can you email that to me?"

"I'll send it ASAP."

"Thanks for your help," Michael said. "Above and beyond, man."

"Don't mention it. Take me out for a beer when you get back."

"I will."

They said goodbye and Michael put his cell away.

Nash had finished his call and was now standing beside Chief Hammond's desk, looking over the file.

"Looks like that was definitely Janine in the jar, based on comparison to her aunt's DNA profile," Michael said. "So now we have two murders thirty years apart. We have a journal entry thinly disguised as a short story that was written after Janine went missing that more or less accuses Ron McClintock, John Hammond and Daryl Kincaid of the accidental killing of Janine and Daryl Kincaid of disposing of the body. All three of them had sex with an underage girl. We have the ashes of Zoe mixed in with Janine. Someone killed Zoe and burned her body and then mixed the ashes. We have the charm bracelet found in Melissa's hand -- the charm bracelet that belonged to Zoe. It has to be either John Hammond himself, Garth Hammond or someone who had access to the jar. I think we should get a crew over to Ron McClintock's house and spend some time going through the contents of the attic where Hammond's possessions were stored. Also, we need to check out any storage units linked to the four men to see if anything's in there now. Could be more evidence."

Nash nodded. "I'll send a team there ASAP. The way it's looking, we might be able to pin them all on Hammond. He did confess to killing at least one girl. He knew we had the ashes and so he probably knew we had or would have ID'd them both."

"He said *her*, not *them*," Michael reiterated. "If he'd said *them*, I'd be a hundred percent in agreement with you, but he didn't. He said *her*. Who else might have had access to the storage unit or Ron McClintock's attic?"

"Just Garth Hammond," Hammond offered. "But anyone who had access to Ron McClintock's house."

Michael shrugged. "Could be a number of people."

"And Ron's dead, so," Hammond added with a shrug.

The email came through a couple of minutes later and Michael read it over before handing his cell to Nash.

Nash read it over quickly and raised his eyebrows. "There it is, Chief," he said, handing the cell to Hammond. "Your Janine Marshall case. Closed."

"Looks like it. Isn't that a sonofabitch?" Chief Hammond said again, taking the cell from Nash. "I'd always hoped she was still alive and went to Seattle to live." Hammond shook his head and turned to Michael. "You want to send me a copy for our files?"

"I'll send it right away."

"Well," Chief Hammond said, leaning back in his chair, his hands on the edge of the desk. "I have some relatives who are going to be very upset at these developments. I better go and see if I can mollify them. They're horrified that John killed Garth and they'll be even more horrified that he's been implicated in Janine's death."

Michael stood. "When will you hold a news conference?"

"First thing this afternoon after we get everything in place with the Feds. I'd appreciate if you both could meet with me beforehand so we can do some looking at the Zoe Wallace case so we can decide how to proceed. I'm happy to close both, but I'll let you Feds decide that, since you're here. Plus, we have Melissa. Her body was found at one of the cabins that Hammond used to own. Might be three cases we can wrap up in one."

"That would be nice, but I'm not so sure about that," Michael added. "Of the three men, I like Daryl Kincaid the most for Zoe, but he's been in the pen since after her death so there's no way we can link Melissa to him."

"Well, our potential killer is dead and he admitted to being responsible for Janine's death," Hammond said. "I'll have to talk to the Assistant DA about any charges arising from this," he said, holding up the journal," but frankly, the statute of limitations has already run out on any case related to Janine except murder. The only person left to nail is Kincaid. If they can't prove murder, any charges would be less than ten years, such as accessory after the fact, indignities to a body, what have you. It's all over but the paperwork to my way of thinking."

"Whoa," Michael said. "Not so fast. We have a lot of investigating to do before we can close any case." He turned to Nash for his take, but he shrugged.

"We got new cases up north. I'll be leaving as soon as I can to work them – but we'll talk later. Say, three o'clock? That'll give me time to do some email and phone calls."

"Okay, but I think Janine's family might want to see some kind of justice for her," Chief Hammond said.

"We'll do what the law allows," Nash said. "We'll talk this afternoon with the D.A. see what's possible."

"See you then," Michael said and left the office. He drove back to his mother's, wanting to let Tess know what the results were.

He should feel good about things. He had the remains of two missing girls in a jar and a verbal confession to the killing – albeit accidental – of one of them. He had a written record implicating John Hammond and the two other men in the accidental death of Janine Marshall, statutory rape, providing alcohol to a minor, and indignities to a body, but without the ability to interrogate the man, he had no chance to get a confession to Zoe's murder.

Although Janine's death had been accidental, Zoe's was pretty much one hundred percent not. Neither was Melissa's.

He drove off in his Jeep, going over the evidence in his head, itching to go over the cases again and refresh himself on who they had interviewed for the case five years earlier.

He realized that, even if his leave wasn't up for another couple of weeks, he was back to work.

WHEN HE GOT BACK to the house, his mother was gone. Tess was sitting at the kitchen island, a mug of coffee in her hand.

"Where's Mom?"

"Ellensburg," Tess said, smiling.

Michael knew right away what it was – Kirsten. She was in labor.

"Your sister thinks she's in labor and so she and your mom drove to Ellensburg to be with her at the hospital. She didn't want to bother you when you were at the police station working on the case."

"She should have called me," he said and frowned. "I told her to call me any time of the day or night. She's in Ellensburg? I'll go right away."

"She said not to worry. Your mom's with her. She'll call when she really goes into labor. You don't need to go yet."

Michael exhaled. "She'll be fast, though. It's her third."

"She'll call. She doesn't want you to go and then spend the entire night sleeping on the chair. Once she gets some more progress, she'll call. Relax."

"I came here to be with her when she goes into labor. I'm going. I'm sorry to leave you all alone. Will you be okay? You're not worried about staying alone?"

"Go be with your sister," Tess said with a smile. "Meet your new nephew. If John Hammond was my attacker, he's dead now. I'll be fine."

"Thanks," Michael said. "I'll have to call Chief Hammond. He's holding a press conference this afternoon to discuss the two cases and wanted me there. I'll have to let him know I won't be attending."

Tess nodded. "Give Kirsten a hug for me."

"I will."

Then Michael went to the closet and got a black duffel bag and a pillow out of the closet. He held them both up high. "My assistant doula bag and pillow." He gave Tess a smile, then left the house.

"Won't Phil be jealous?" Tess asked.

"He faints at the sight of blood so it's me or no one."

"Good luck."

ON THE ROAD TO ELLENSBURG, he tried not to speed, but it was damn hard.

Excitement built in him that Kirsten was in labor and would be producing his new nephew sometime in the next twenty-four hours.

It was a nice antidote to the nastiness of the past twenty-four.

CHAPTER THIRTY-FOUR

The next morning Tess showered and dressed, then went to the kitchen to watch the morning news. Mrs. Carter arrived home earlier and was making coffee.

"The latest news conference is going to start any moment," Mrs. Carter said, handing Tess a mug and holding out the carafe of coffee. "Kirsten's still in labor so I came home to take my pills, which I forgot in our rush when Kirsten went into labor. I'm going back, so I'm afraid you're on your own for the rest of the day."

"Michael's staying?"

"You bet he is. I guess being with Kirsten is some solace for him since he doesn't get to see his own boys as often as before."

Tess fixed her coffee and sat on the sofa, watching the local station, which showed a set of microphones in front of a podium with the Paradise Hill Police logo on the front. Behind it was a curtain. Someone popped their head into the frame and added one more microphone.

SUSAN LUND

She had just settled in when, from stage left, Chief Hammond entered, and beside him FBI Special Agent Nash from Seattle who was in charge of the case.

Hammond faced the cameras and tapped one of the microphones. Then he cleared his voice and began speaking.

"Ladies and gentlemen of the press, citizens of Paradise Hill, I want to take this opportunity to update everyone on the developments in the case. Once again, I want to thank Special Agent Nash and all the officers from the Paradise Hill Police Department and the Kittitas County Sheriff's Department who worked on these cases, in years past and more recently. Your hard work and dedication have made these developments in the case possible."

He went over the FBI's results, showing that the ashes which had come from John Hammond's storage unit and had been found in her father's attic contained the DNA from two missing girls – Janine Marshall and Zoe Wallace.

"We're pleased that, as of this morning, we can confidently say these two cases are closed, given the confession of John Hammond to the deaths and other evidence which corroborated that fact. The Melissa Ford case is still open, but we will continue to look for links between that murder and John Hammond, or until some other suspect becomes central. However, our preliminary review of the evidence suggests that the cases are connected."

Tess frowned, for he was making it sound as if they had already wrapped both cases up and were thinking of tying in Melissa's case as well.

Tess didn't know what to think.

The reporters asked a few perfunctory questions about the officer who had been shot, who was fine, and about the other cases, which were still outstanding.

320

He thanked everyone one more time and then the news conference ended. The FBI special agent seemed quite happy to shake Chief Hammond's hand and the two walked off camera.

That was it. Janine's and Zoe's cases had all but been closed, as far as the police and FBI were concerned and they were talking like Melissa's case would soon be as well. Tess wasn't convinced that Michael would agree, but he wasn't there to argue the case. He was in Ellensburg with his sister helping her through labor and delivery, and wasn't the agent in charge anyway.

Tess wondered what he'd do when he found out. She took out her cell and sent him a text.

TESS: Did you watch the news conference? Do you agree with Chief Hammond about closing the two cases?

MICHAEL: We're getting close to pushing at this point so no, I haven't been watching. I figured he wanted to close them both. I think it's too soon to be so confident, but it's not my case. I'll see what I can do when I go back to work. Until then, I have little say in any of this. Gotta go. Talk later.

TESS: Sorry to bother you. Give Kirsten my love.

MICHAEL: I will.

EARLY IN THE AFTERNOON, Michael sent a text, announcing the birth.

MICHAEL: Baby and mother both fine, but Kirsten staying in the delivery room overnight due to a "boggy uterus". Mom and I will be back soon.

Tess smiled and sent him a text in reply.

TESS: Aw, poor Kirsten. Give them both my love.
MICHAEL: I will.

When Michael and Mrs. Carter arrived, Tess was excited to hear the details and see the pictures.

"How are you?" she asked Mrs. Carter, who looked a bit haggard. "How's Kirsten and the baby."

"We're all fine. Michael's a rock. There was a bit of excitement when Kirsten was bleeding a bit too heavily, but they got it under control fast. She'll stay in Ellensburg for another twenty-four hours just to be safe."

"I'm so glad everything worked out." She watched Michael, who seemed just as tired.

"She was a trouper," he said and flopped down on the sofa. "Phil came in after all the excitement was over and the blood was cleaned up."

"Poor guy," Tess said. "Missing his own child's birth."

"Better he stay outside than come in and fall over in a dead faint."

On the television was the local news, muted. A reporter came on and there was a repeat of the news conference from earlier. Michael found the remote and turned up the volume. The three of them watched the repeat and when it was done, Michael muted it again and sat forward.

"I don't agree," he said, shaking his head. He glanced at Tess. "I don't think Hammond killed Zoe. I think maybe Kincaid did. I don't care that the ashes were mixed. Someone else killed her and put those ashes in. Unless I can see the clear line from Janine to Zoe and from Hammond to Zoe, I think it's premature to link the two and close them both with Hammond as the killer."

Tess nodded in agreement. "I feel the same way."

Michael sighed. "When I go back to work, I'll see what I can do, but in the meantime, I'm going to do some late-night reading to see what evidence exists that could connect them." He stood up. "Now I'm going to bed. I feel like I need to sleep for twenty-four hours. I'm going to drive back Ellensburg tonight before visiting hours are over and see Kirsten and little Louis. You want to come along?"

"Louis?" Kirsten said, glancing at Mrs. Carter. "That's so sweet. I'd love to."

Louis was the late Mr. Carter's first name. Michael gave Tess a smile before leaving the living room.

Tess turned to Mrs. Carter. "Are you going back tonight?"

She nodded. "We can all go together."

Tess smiled, eager to see her old friend's new son.

FOR THE REST of the afternoon, Tess sat and watched the news, reading over public documents that had been posted on The Missing website. She made notes on what had been made public, knowing that Michael would have access to FBI files. Now that her father had been buried and the contents of the house were under a sort of quarantine until the FBI forensic unit had done their search for evidence, she had nothing to do but research.

Later, before the sun set, Tess took a drive to the cemetery and decided to stop and visit her father's grave. She parked the car and walked down the narrow path between sections to find the freshly covered grave where her father was buried.

She stood at the foot of the grave and read over the temporary marker.

RONALD JAMES McCLINTOCK
b. 1962 – d. 2018
Gone but not forgotten.

SHE FELT like she finally understood her father a lot better than when she had driven up to Paradise Hill to bury him.

When she'd returned to Paradise Hill, she had thought of her father as distant and self-absorbed. All her life, after she and her mother and brother left town, she'd felt like her father had abandoned them. Now she had an entirely different view of him. He was a man with a dark secret that had been plaguing him ever since the event that had changed his life. He'd probably thought he could forget it, shoving it back into his memory and trying to live a normal life, but when Lisa went missing, it must have all seemed to come back again.

He felt ongoing guilt for his role in Janine's death. He felt blackmailed by Daryl Kincaid, and trapped into a conspiracy with the other two men to keep it secret. He'd become obsessed with Janine's case, following it in his scrapbook and then focusing on the other crimes in the small town.

It was a trauma that he carried around the rest of his life, ending up lonely and alone in a house filled with junk he couldn't throw out, ravaged by a cancer that ate away at him from the inside out.

It seemed like a metaphor for the secret he had harbored since that night in 1978 when the pretty girl with long brown hair died that cold November night, the girl whose ashes were a reminder of his role in the cover-up.

Had he known the ashes were up in the attic all those years? Did they haunt him every day? Was that when he'd started to hoard – because he couldn't bear to part with the ashes of the girl he'd been sweet on but who had died, whose death was never really mourned properly?

Tess didn't know, but as she stood with tears in her eyes and examined her father's grave, she felt sad for him. She wished she'd had the chance to get to know him better, wished he hadn't felt he had to die all alone without any family at his side. She wished she'd had the chance to say he'd been young and foolish and made a mistake but he was loved anyway, and that he had to forgive himself.

She heard someone come up behind her. Her instinct was to jerk around, in case it was the man who had attacked her, but it was only Michael.

"Oh, my God, you scared me," she said, covering her heart with her hand.

"Sorry, sorry," he said, holding his hands out toward her. "I forgot. I should have called out to you so you knew I was coming but I didn't want to disturb you."

He walked over to her side and glanced down at the headstone. Then he looked at her as she wiped tears off her cheek.

"Hey," he said, and slipped his arm around her shoulder, pulling her against him. "It's okay to feel sad. You lost your father. Even though you weren't close, he mattered in your life."

"I know," she said, and his tender words only made her tears flow harder. She smiled through her tears and buried her face in the crook of his shoulder, glad to feel his arms wrap around her. "He was so alone at the end."

They stood in an embrace for a moment. He didn't seem eager to end it and neither did Tess. Finally, she took in a deep breath and turned back to stare at the headstone, Michael's arms still around her like it was natura.

"He spent all those years feeling guilt over Janine's death and his role in the cover-up."

"It must have haunted him," Michael said, echoing her thoughts. "If he knew the ashes were there, he probably kept them because he didn't want to see them go to the dump."

"Probably."

He turned her around in his arms, meeting her eyes. "Like I said, I don't think your father was a serial killer or a pornographer, Tess. I think he just got mixed up in a bad situation, and spent the rest of his life regretting it. If anything, I like Daryl Kincaid -- or Garth for Zoe. Maybe Garth for Melissa. Until we see more evidence one way or the other, I think we have to hold out judgment."

Finally, Tess nodded and pulled away, forcing a smile. "So, what's next? When are you going back to work?"

He shrugged, and stared off in the distance for a moment. "I was planning on staying off work for at least six weeks, but I think once Kirsten's home and doing okay, I'm going back."

He turned to look her in the eyes. "I can still work on the cases in the meantime, even if they're rushing to close them both and from the looks of it, Melissa's case as well. Care to join forces with me? I need someone to help sort through everything – in an unofficial capacity, of course."

"I'm your man," Tess replied with a smile. "I know a few hundred avid amateur sleuths who love this kind of stuff and will be only too happy to help."

"Good," Michael said and reached out to squeeze her arm. "I don't know why Chief Hammond and Nash are so eager to close the cases, but I'm not liking it and I'm not letting it go so easily. It'll have to be done on the side of my desk, though. I think our next focus will be Melissa and any links with Hammond, Garth or John."

"Sounds exciting," Tess said, eager to help Michael and understand how his mind worked when on a case. "I'm sure my editor will be only too happy for me to take this on for a separate piece."

"Fantastic," Michael said. "Let's pick up Mom and go see baby Louis."

And so they did.

CHAPTER THIRTY-FIVE

H e watched them from the forest, the two of them standing by Ron's grave.

How sweet... They seemed to be getting closer and were clearly either romantically involved or close to being so.

From watching the news conference, he figured that the police were eager to wrap up the two cases they had – Janine and Zoe. That was great. If they searched around in Ron McClintock's trash-heap of a house, they might find a way to link to Melissa as well that would nail Hammond to the case. They would already have realized that the bracelet Melissa wore belonged to Zoe and the only way she could have been holding it was if Zoe's killer put it there.

If everything worked out the way he wanted, Hammond would take the rap for all three.

John Hammond killing Garth and then himself was icing on the cake. Now, all eyes were focused on John and Garth – not elsewhere. There was evidence that could tie them to all three girls from Paradise Hill.

Just the way he liked it.

When Michael and Tess left the forest and drove off, he walked back to his bike and took it along the back roads to the garage, where he parked it and went back to work, trying to fix one of the trucks in the garage. He should have felt sorry for Hammond, both John and Garth, but he didn't.

John was a loser who had panicked and done the wrong thing back in '78. Kincaid had made it worse. They should have gone right to the police and turned themselves in. They would have probably got reduced sentences.

"Eugene," one of the guys from work called out. "I tried to find you earlier. Your dad called and wanted you to come over for supper tonight."

"Thanks," Eugene called. "I was out back searching for a part I needed for the truck."

Eugene thought about his adopted father – Chief Hammond. Hammond had adopted him when he was only five, rescuing him from the meth and crack house he lived in with his mother, Hammond's kid sister Heather after she died.

He was Daryl Kincaid's bastard.

Eugene had taken Hammond's name instead of Kincaid's – that rat bastard.

It provided the perfect cover – the Chief's son. Not only did no one suspect him of anything, he had access to Chief Hammond's mind for the father and son often talked about cases. Hammond revealed things to Eugene that he shouldn't have, encouraging him in his passion for law enforcement even though Eugene would never be able to join any police force.

He finished installing the part and got into his truck, pulling out of the parking lot.

What he had planned for the night?

First, he'd have supper with the old man and learn all the juicy details about the cases so he could plot his next move.

Then, he'd do whatever the hell he felt like.

Little Miss Redhead Tess McClintock was still in town, and he still had an itch to pay her a personal visit, but the next time he did, he'd make sure Carter was nowhere in sight to rescue her.

As he drove off down Paradise Hill's main street and the last rays of sunlight spiked through the tall pines, that thought made him smile.

END OF BOOK ONE

IF YOU ENJOYED THIS BOOK, please help out the author and consider leaving a review — reviews help out authors and get the word out about books you enjoyed. Thank you!

BOOK TWO: THE GIRL WHO CRIED TOO MUCH, will be released October 22, 2018!

You can preorder now:

The Girl Who Cried Too Much

JOIN SUSAN LUND'S newsletter to get updates and sneak previews of the second instalment of the McClintock-Carter series of crime thrillers.

ABOUT THE AUTHOR

Susan Lund is an emerging author of crime thrillers and romantic suspense. She lives in a forest near the ocean with her family of humans and animals.

Join her newsletter to get updates and sneak previews of the second instalment of the McClintock-Carter series of crime thrillers.

http://eepurl.com/dAfi6j

Made in the USA
Middletown, DE
13 January 2021

31472625R00208